Dead Man's Token

Dead Man's Token

Book Five of the Latter Annals of Lystra

Robin Hardy

Westford Press

Dead Man's Token: Book Five of the Latter Annals of Lystra
Christian fantasy/series

2nd edition
ISBN: 978-1496098726

Copyright © 2007, 2011, 2014 Robin Hardy.

Portions of this book may be reproduced according to the fair use doctrine as stated in § 107 of the U.S. Copyright Law; otherwise, please contact the publisher for written permission.

Westford Press
mail@westfordpress.com

The verse in Chapter 4 is Psalm 48:14 from the King James Version of the Bible.

Cover image © Nejron Photo

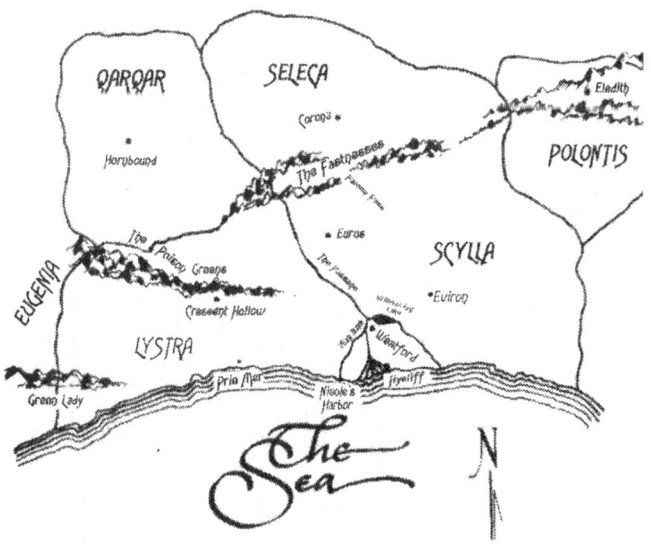

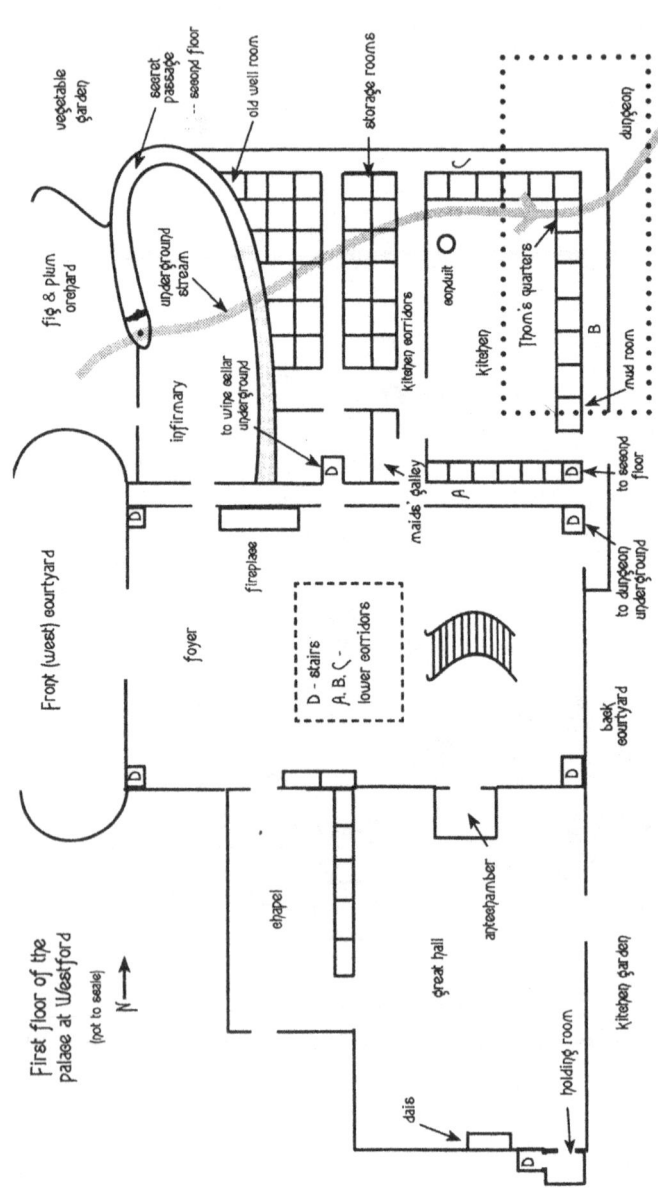

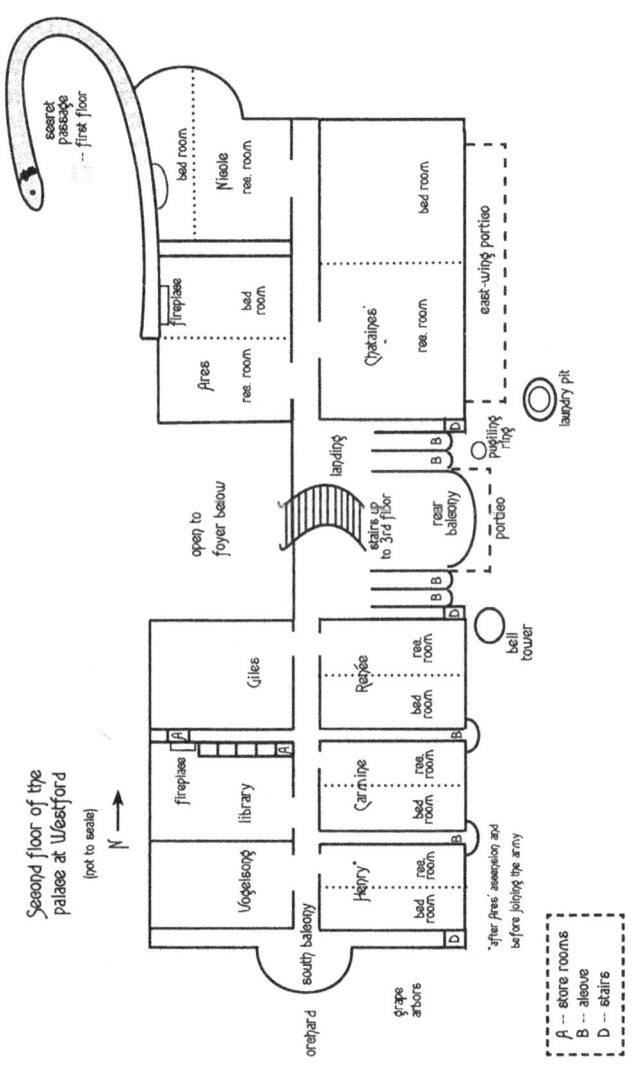

1

Ares whispered, "I feel my weakness. I feel my strength slipping away by the day."

The priest shifted sympathetically. "You are not as young as you once were, my child."

No, he was not. Ares did not know his age, but he was 42 this year. It had been eight years since he had gained the throne of Lystra, the heritage of his great-great-grandfather, Roman, that had been stripped away by treachery and murder. It had been eight years and a few months since he had taken the beautiful peasant girl, Nicole, as wife. She was now Surchataine beside him, and mother of his twin daughters.

Ares shook his head heavily. "It is more than that. It is the weight of the burden. I feel . . . inadequate to carry the weight. That, in part, is why I began coming to confession some weeks ago."

In his disquiet, Ares did not notice that the priest's compassionate smile had taken on the barest tinge of satisfaction. Almost gloating, he studied the Surchatain's lined face, cleft by the deep, ugly scar. The brown hair was sprinkled with gray, especially at the temples, and the hand that stroked the weary brow trembled slightly.

"I am forced to see, again, that I cannot rely on my own strength. Flesh will fail me. Only the hand of God can sustain me," Ares said, grappling with this most unrelenting truth in its latest incarnation.

The priest quoted, "'As for man, his days are like grass, for the wind passes over it, and it is gone, and its place knows it no more.'" Ares raised his face to regard him, and the priest returned a gaze of kind concern.

A sentry appeared at the chapel door, saluting. "Pardon, Surchatain. You had asked to be informed of the apportionment council's decisions. They are ready to report to you."

Breathing something between a groan and a sigh, Ares stood. The priest stood to bow very low, and Ares regarded him again. As he exited the chapel with the sentry, Ares paused yet a third time to glance back at the cassocked figure.

"Surchatain?" the sentry queried.

"I had not spoken of passing away," Ares muttered.

"Sir?" the sentry asked.

"Nothing." Ares turned to trot up the broad, curving stairway. On his way up, he glanced aside at the banner of the lion and the cross that Nicole had commissioned, patterned after that of Roman, and it suddenly dawned on him that there was a promise attached to that banner.

Ares had not regained the throne by his own strength or cunning—he had simply struggled through one crisis after another as best he could, and the province fell into his lap. Nor had he defended Westford, or kept peace in Lystra, by his own ability. He had taken pains to do what lay within his power, but it was the Lord who wove Ares' efforts into an effective campaign. Ares knew this. Why was he doubting now? With a self-deprecatory snort at his own faithlessness, he turned his thoughts reluctantly toward percentages and census figures.

The moment the Surchatain and sentry were safely on the staircase, the priest gestured to a servant. "Tell him the time is ripe. Go!" With a bow, the servant hurried off.

Dead Man's Token

For the next several hours, Ares sat in the council chambers on the third floor with his nobles and administrators reviewing their recommendations for revised taxes on the largest estates in Lystra, as well as the settlement of boundary or property disputes.

This onerous task came around once every three years, like a recurring plague. The apportionment council meetings had grown especially cumbersome since the province had doubled in size shortly after Ares had become Surchatain. As much as he would love to delegate final approval of apportionments to Counselor Carmine or Counselor Vogelsong, the nobility clamored for the Surchatain's personal attention. And setting taxes for the next three years required the wisdom of Solomon, for while the lords hated paying, they hated more having their estates devalued in front of their peers. So the hedging and hair-splitting were almost enough to force any sane man to leap through the nearest leaded-glass window.

"Which brings us to the estate of Lord Davignon," Carmine said crisply, turning a leaf in a large ledger while the Steward, Giles, shifted importantly toward the lord in question, who straightened. "You've done admirably over the last three years, sir. Your sheep have quadrupled in number, and your investment in the Qarqarian copper mines has returned a stunning hundred-and-fifty percent return. Is that correct, Steward?" Squinting at the ledger, Carmine leaned over to Giles.

"Actually, Counselor, the figure is one hundred-fifty-five percent." Giles ticked off a row of computations with his quill pen, peering with satisfaction through his new gold-framed reading glasses. While Carmine and Giles dressed in competitive finery, Carmine's ego forbade the use of reading glasses even as Giles' ego demanded it. Younger and handsomer than Ares, Carmine did not wish to clutter his fine features with an old person's seeing aid. Giles, bald atop a fringe of wild brown hair, welcomed gold accessories anywhere on his person.

"Ah. Then that places your annual tax at five hundred seventy-five royals, Lord Davignon—quite a jump from your last apportionment, I fear, but—one must bear the burden of wealth, eh?" Carmine asked as one aristocrat to another.

"True." The lord raised his brows in refined resignation. Ares smiled wryly at Carmine's ability to wrest heavy taxes from the nobles without a murmur of complaint in return.

"Surchatain?" Carmine turned to Ares, who tiredly nodded his assent for the twenty-eighth time.

With a flourish of Carmine's pen, the deed was done. "Very good. We turn now to the dispute between—"

A trumpet alarm sounded and the council members sat up in startlement. The door to the room burst open, and a sentry gasped, "Surchatain—"

That is all he managed to say before he was thrust aside by Commander Thom. His boyish look of years past was all but obliterated by the hardness in the blue eyes, the close-cropped hair, and the short, stiff beard. He entered calmly, saluting. "Surchatain, pardon the intrusion. A contender for the throne has arrived to challenge you."

Ares blinked in disbelief. "What?"

Thom answered dryly, "He comes claiming that the Law of Roman permits his challenge on the grounds of your . . . weakness."

At that last word, steel began to form in Ares' bones, starting at his feet, causing him to stand deliberately. "And who is my challenger?" he asked softly.

"Athian, son of Lord Backvold," Thom said.

The whole council turned to stare at Backvold, who went pale to the point of translucence. Ares said, "According to the Law, my deposal hinges on the vote of the council. Does this council agree with Athian?"

A vigorous round of denials answered him. Ares looked at

Backvold. "Does your son know that he forfeits his life with this action, as well as all of your property?"

"I beg your indulgence to—let me go reason with him, Surchatain," Backvold gasped, and Ares nodded.

As Lord Backvold flew from the room, Counselor Carmine stood to grasp Ares' elbow. "A word with you and your Commander, Surchatain." No other administrator could get away with grabbing the Surchatain by the arm like that, but as it was Carmine, Ares permitted himself to be herded outside into the corridor with Thom. When Giles hurried to the door to join them, Carmine shut it in his face.

"Ares." The Surchatain's old friend turned to him in dead earnest. "We all know that the Law does not require you to face this challenger. But I believe Thom will concur when I say that you must, given that it is a nobleman's son." Ares glanced at Thom, who nodded firmly. Then Ares looked back at Carmine as he continued, "If you rely on the Law alone to shield you, the rumor will take root and spread that you *are* weak. Then challengers will multiply like flies. Dispose of this threat personally, and the rumor is put to rest."

"Should I kill him?" Ares asked. The Law prescribed death for attempted usurpation, but Ares abhorred bloodshed.

"If he dies, it should be by your hand. Not the executioner," Thom said.

"Very well. I will meet him." Ares gestured to the sentry, who approached. "Summon the challenger to the pugiling field. I will be down shortly." The sentry ran off, and Ares commenced an unhurried walk down the corridor with his Counselor on one side and Commander on the other. Ares' manner seemed to indicate he welcomed any interruption of the apportionment meeting, even one so extreme.

"I remember Athian. I met him not long ago. I don't want to kill him; he's just a youth," Ares complained. "Who has put him up to this? Backvold?"

He looked to Carmine for an answer. The Counselor

shrugged. "Who knows? It could be Athian's own wild-headed notion. Schemes germinate, grow and die overnight. It does seem rather bold—I don't recall a challenger since Lute, and he presumed to come only because he thought he had the throne in lock. I wonder what this Athian thinks he knows?"

"He specifically mentioned my weakness," Ares murmured. "Carmine . . . how long has the priest been in service at the palace?"

"Goodness! Forever and ever. From the beginning of time," Carmine elaborated.

"No. Old Father Fasoro died. The new priest is Haward. He's been in service for perhaps three months," Thom said.

"I knew that. Why had I forgotten that?" Carmine muttered, alarmed. He did not wish Ares to know that he had been negligent in attending services.

"Why do you ask, Surchatain?" Thom said.

"Who recommended him?" Ares asked. They rounded a corner and turned down the back steps toward the grounds. Out a window, Ares glimpsed a large crowd gathering. *Perhaps the servants think they will get the day off if I am killed*, he ruminated.

"I don't know who recommended the new priest." Thom's brows drew down, and his lips tightened under his beard.

Carmine paused. "Father Haward? I thought he was in the service of Lady Auer."

"Lord Backvold's sister," Ares said dismally.

"You offended her deeply when you removed her from the dinner guest list," Carmine noted.

Ares sighed, "That was our dear Chataine Renée's doing. She didn't like Lady Auer's dress." In a murmur, he added, "And for a dispute about tailors, I have to kill a boy."

They emerged onto the grounds, warm in the June sun, and Ares spotted his challenger standing defiantly in the center of the roped-off pugiling ring. Yes, it was Athian, but no longer the boy that Ares thought he remembered. Athian was a large, muscular young man, probably outweighing him by ten pounds. Athian's father, having evidently failed in his efforts to dissuade him, was nowhere to be seen.

As Ares removed his black brocade shortcoat, he told Thom and Carmine, "If he kills me, see that Nicole ascends the throne according to the Law."

"I will not allow him to kill you, Surchatain," Thom said while Carmine concurred, "Nonsense."

Rubbing dirt into his hands, Ares glanced up at the young contender. "Then . . . when I take him down, see that he is pronounced dead quickly, and taken to the infirmary."

Both subordinates frowned in disapproval and Carmine objected, "That is quite risky, Ares."

"It may render the whole proceedings useless," Thom pointed out. "Just kill him and be done with it."

"No, save his life if you can . . . for his father's sake," Ares uttered, bending to slip through the ropes.

Word had raced through the palace like a rabid dog that the Surchatain was meeting a challenger in hand-to-hand combat. Nicole was disbelieving until she hurried out to the rear balcony and spotted Ares preparing himself on the grounds below.

Faint, she sagged against a pillar. "Dear God . . . my Lord Jesus . . . strengthen and protect him . . . shield him with your love," she whispered. Then she seized a passing maid. "Find Bonnie and Sophie—they should be in their quarters—make sure they do not come out and see this!"

"Yes, Lady!"

The maid hurried away, and Nicole looked down again at the pugiling ring, surrounded by a tight crowd of soldiers, servants, and courtiers.

The maid found seven-year-old Bonnie with Renée, giggling over a new batch of makeup. It was undoubtedly Bonnie the maid saw, who aspired to emulate Renée in every detail of dress and mannerism, while her identical twin would have worn pants, were she allowed. Mistakenly believing both children to be in the company of their "aunt," the maid bowed out without disturbing them.

But the other seven-year-old, Sophie, was not with her sister. She had been in the kitchen corridor when the startling challenge had been aired in the great hall. From there, she had only to run outside, elude her guardian, shimmy up a post, and climb onto the east portico roof to command a clear view of the pugiling ring. The sentry who had been assigned to ward her today located her in time to station himself beneath her before the contest began.

Never seeing him, her eyes intently followed her adored father as he climbed through the ropes into the ring to face his opponent.

"Athian, what are you doing?" Ares asked quietly.

The young man shouted in reply, "You're spent and tired, old man! It's time for fresh blood to rule! Lystra needs strength!" He seemed to be making his case to the crowd, who watched in curious silence, neither booing nor cheering him.

"Athian—don't. I respect your father. I don't want to hurt him," Ares said. "Or you."

"Choose a judge, old man!" Athian said with a laugh.

Ares gestured. "Thom."

The Commander, who had been at ringside beside the Counselor, stepped in between the combatants. "Do you accept me as judge of this match, Athian?"

"As long as you agree not to call it until one of us is dead," Athian said with a toss of his curly head.

"Summon Doctor Savary," Thom instructed a soldier, adding to Athian, "He shall issue the final judgment." Then the Commander advised Ares, "As the challenged party, you shall choose weapons, Surchatain."

Ares evaluated his young challenger. A nobleman's son would certainly have been trained with the long sword, mace, and bow. But he was not in the army, which, in addition to these weapons, trained with poles, as so many of the mercenaries they met in battle used spears or javelins. "I choose pugiling sticks," Ares said.

"Those sticks with pads?" Athian asked in disbelief.

"Without the pads. Get us pugiling sticks with the pads removed," Ares instructed Thom, who nodded hesitantly even as he gestured to his soldiers. Neither Ares nor Athian wore any protective gear, and neither requested it, for whatever one was equipped with, the other was allowed as well.

The weapons were brought—six-foot oaken poles with dull ends. Athian hefted his experimentally. "'Twill be a slow and painful death, but I can kill you with this," he allowed.

Some of the more bloodthirsty in the crowd began voicing their encouragement to the pair. Nicole clutched the balcony pillar and Carmine's mind was racing to find a point of order on which to object. Thom was whispering instructions to his Seconds in Command, Rhode and Oswald. Of all the spectators, Sophie was the most composed—even detached. She had not the slightest fear for her father. He was the Surchatain.

"Are you ready?" Thom asked tensely. The two combatants faced each other about four feet apart. Athian crouched, gripping his pole lengthwise across his body. But Ares held his pole vertically by his left side, one end stuck in the ground. As a matter of fact, the way he was holding it—his left hand clutching it at shoulder level and his right gripping it waist-high—gave the impression that he was resting his weight on it, like a crutch. Athian jeered at him, and the crowd became more vocal.

Thom's eyes flicked to Oswald and Rhode, standing just outside the ropes at the very edge of the ring, ready for whatever might be required of them. "Begin!" Thom stepped back, slashing a hand in the signal to start.

Both combatants sprang at once. Athian swung the end of

his stick toward Ares' face, but in such close quarters, had not adequately reckoned how much he would have to draw the long pole back in order to jab effectively with the end.

Ares, meanwhile, used his stick as a fulcrum to jump almost horizontal, knocking Athian's pole away and kicking him solidly in the throat. The young man fell with a thud, his stick dropping atop him. Ares swung around on the pole and landed on his feet. It all happened in the blink of an eye.

Thom threw himself over the young man. "He's dead!" he shouted. As howls of disbelief were raised from the crowd, Thom gestured to Carmine. Ares yanked his pole from the ground and held it ready.

"Finish him! Thrust him through!" someone shouted in disgust, but Ares ignored him.

Entering the ring hastily, Carmine also made a show of examining the body. "He is dead! Let the doctor through!" he ordered, his hand sweeping the crowd.

Thom was kneeling on the young man's left hand, holding his right, to immobilize them. "Be still! You're dead!" Thom hissed at him. In his agony, Athian quieted.

The crowd parted reluctantly for Doctor Savary, grim-faced, to make his way into the ring. Bending over the supine form while Carmine spoke in his ear, he concurred loudly, "The man is dead!" To Thom, he whispered, "Get your men to carry him quickly to the infirmary. Keep the people back!"

Thom had only to motion at his Seconds for them to rush into the ring and gently lift the young man. "Carry him face up while I hold his head," the doctor hissed at Oswald, who complied.

Meanwhile, Captain Yonge, carrying out the Commander's orders, had directed all soldiers in the area, including Sophie's guardian, to clear a path through the crowd so that no one got close enough to see the body. With the doctor on their heels, Oswald and Rhode carried Athian quickly across the grounds to the palace infirmary.

Still in the ring, Ares began twirling the pugiling stick expertly, as Nicole had seen him do countless times in practice, before Renée would dump a bucket of wash water on him. "Next!" he shouted.

The crowd stilled, refocusing their attention from the departing challenger to the Surchatain. "I am accepting challengers today because the apportionment council is meeting. We need new revenues. After you challenge me and you die, your estate goes to the palace treasury! Who is my next challenger?" he invited loudly, hoisting the stick.

The crowd was silent, with eyes downcast. There might have been a ripple of shame for their too-eager embrace of a challenge to their Surchatain. "No one?" Ares shouted, and no one replied. "Then you are dismissed." Tossing the stick to a soldier, he bent to climb through the ropes, and the crowd docilely dispersed—although the servants, embroiled in excited discussions about the match, took their time returning to their chores. Nicole, on the balcony, closed her eyes to breathe a grateful prayer. Sophie climbed down from the portico roof with thoughtful coolness.

Redonning his coat, Ares gestured to Thom and Carmine to accompany him while he entered the palace and turned down the side corridor toward the infirmary. Ares winced, placing a hand on a strained muscle in his back as he instructed a sentry, "Have Counselor Vogelsong prepare an order of banishment for Lady Auer." Then he told Thom, "You will deliver it to her today," and Thom nodded.

The three entered the infirmary and looked to a small side room where Lord Backvold could be seen beyond the partly closed door. Doctor Savary beckoned them into the room and shut the door after them. The five of them completely filled the room as they stood over the pallet on which a sixth man lay. Lord Backvold fell on his knees before Ares, who glanced at him before looking to the ashen, sweating man on the pallet.

"Will he live?" Ares asked the doctor.

"Possibly, but he must not be moved yet. His throat is crushed, and any movement obstructs his air," Doctor Savary replied.

Ares addressed the father, "Stand up, Lord Backvold." With bowed head and hands folded abjectly, Backvold stood. "I choose to believe that you had no knowledge of your son's treachery," Ares told him, "but I believe your sister, the Lady Auer, did. I am banishing her and conferring her estate to your keeping. Your son, whether he lives or dies, must also be removed from Lystra. You may keep him here until he recuperates enough to be moved, but if his presence is discovered and my victory called into question, he will be put to death. Do you understand?"

"Yes, Surchatain. God bless you," Backvold whispered.

"That is my hope," Ares murmured. He, Thom, and Carmine left the infirmary.

As Thom departed to clear the grounds and see that Lady Auer's order of banishment was executed, Carmine remained with Ares. The Counselor placed slender fingers contemplatively on his puckered lips, then noted, "Lord Backvold is highly regarded among the nobles of Crescent Hollow, some of whom were less than thrilled when you annexed Calle Valley. I should say that henceforth he will be one of your staunchest allies in the area. Well done, Surchatain."

Ares nodded vaguely. "I have one other minor matter to attend before we resume the apportionment hearings."

"We will await you." Carmine bowed before turning to the staircase. Ares went to the chapel alone.

When he emerged through the back door several minutes later, he calmly wiped his hands before instructing a sentry, "Summon Counselor Vogelsong to the door of the council meeting room. And take care of that." He jerked his head toward the open door of the chapel.

The sentry saluted, looking into the room, then gestured

to a fellow guard. By the time Ares had mounted two flights of stairs to reach the door of the council room himself, Vogelsong was coming down the corridor to meet him.

Bowing, the young counselor glanced nervously at the meeting in progress. Having been given liberty from this function in order to see to other business, he was anxious that this privilege not be rescinded. "I have just sent Lady Auer's order of banishment down to the Commander. Is there another matter, Surchatain?"

"Yes. Counselor, we need a new priest. I wish you to interview candidates which Sister Agnes will recommend, and select one. He must be discreet and loyal and wise and learned in the Holy Canon."

"Certainly, Surchatain. What . . . happened to Father Haward?" Vogelsong asked.

"I believe he is being carried out," Ares replied, turning into the council chambers. Vogelsong gulped and began to sputter compliance, but the chamber door closed.

Moments after Vogelsong had departed, Nicole entered the corridor and paused before that door. She keenly wanted to blaze through it and throw herself on her husband, crying, *"How could you? How could you entertain a challenger in combat?"* For once, she wanted to throw a fit worthy of Renée. The sentry beside the door stood at attention, ready to open it at her command.

But she couldn't do it. She was never comfortable drawing stares in the way that was second nature to beautiful, self-assured Renée. Nicole would just have to wait until Ares was ready to explain it to her. But—she couldn't wait. She *had to know* why he would place his rulership and his life at the mercy of this unknown upstart. Who was this Athian, anyway? She had never heard of him. What made him think he was entitled to the throne? And what would happen when word got out that Lystra was up for grabs to the first challenger who could defeat an aging warrior in combat?

With a sharp exhalation, as though she had been struck in the stomach, Nicole sank back against the wall. Ares was getting older, and she could not bear to think of it.

Footsteps approached; she looked up at Henry coming down the corridor. Chatain Henry, now 15, was taller than she was—a sturdy, sunburnt Green recruit, proud of the fact that his former guardian, Ares, showed no favoritism in placing him in the army and allowing him to toil away at all the disagreeable duties lavished on the Greens. That Henry did his share promptly and without complaint was earning him reserved respect, even among those who remembered that he was the grandson of the usurper who had killed Ares' grandfather to take the throne.

"Is he in there?" Henry asked, nodding toward the closed door.

"Yes," Nicole said, lifting herself from the wall. Ten years older than Henry, she had still-youthful skin, clear green eyes, and thick chestnut hair that flowed down her back behind her cap.

First-time visitors to the court had to be warned that the lady who wore relatively modest, simple gowns, no makeup, and conducted herself quietly was the Surchataine, rather than the dazzling, opulently dressed blonde who commanded all eyes wherever she went. Those visitors who made the mistake of addressing Renée as Surchataine earned special attention from her, which was intoxicating until they discovered that this was the one social gaffe that Ares found unforgivable. He had been known to refuse audiences to such ill-informed and unmannerly guests. Part of the problem was that Nicole never could get used to being called *Surchataine*, preferring her old title of *Lady*. The tone Ares used in saying that word made her cling to it.

"Did you see it?" Henry whispered eagerly, throwing himself back against the wall beside her. "Did you see him dispatch Athian? Wasn't it great? Hoose and I are going to get him to teach us that move. Everyone agrees that Athian never saw it coming."

Nicole's heart rose in slight encouragement. "Everyone? What are the soldiers saying?"

Henry blinked at her. "About what?"

"About Ares!" she said, exasperated.

He looked blank. "I . . . haven't heard much. What do you mean?"

"What will happen with the next challenger? Or the next?" she asked, aggrieved.

"Ares will kill them, just like he did Athian," Henry said reproachfully. "What are you worried about? When Ares is old and bent, he will just beat them to death with his cane!"

Nicole exhaled a laugh, and Henry returned his attention to the closed door. Despite his eagerness, he knew better than to interrupt the meeting. Ares had a method of breaking in unruly Greens that provoked terror among them: he placed them under Merle (the head laundress) for a fortnight, to carry out her every command, regardless how inane. Following two weeks' domestication under her unceasing, rapierlike tongue, the recruits were grateful to return to grueling physical labor under their commanding officers.

After a few moments of silence, Nicole asked, "How is Melva coming along in her studies?"

Melva, 19, was the Chataine of Qarqar who remained at Westford until such time that Ares deemed her fit to assume rulership of her province. Henry and Melva were being tutored together in the Law of Roman, which was prerequisite to any courtly position in Lystra (or Qarqar, in Ares' thinking). But Melva, having come under Renée's spell, showed much less interest in the Law than in dancing, dresses, and jewelry.

Henry shrugged. "She keeps failing her preliminary tests, and Ares keeps asking Doudney about her progress, so he has started chewing his hair."

"What? Who?" she asked.

"Doudney. The new tutor," Henry explained.

"Another one?" she asked

"They never last very long," Henry allowed. "It's . . . frustrating. Why won't Ares go ahead and let me be examined for certification? I've been ready for a long time. I've even memorized tax rates," he vented. Steward Giles was notorious for tripping up examinants with questions about obscure numbers.

"I'm sure I don't know, Henry," she murmured, when she was fairly sure that Ares postponed Henry's certification hearing because he thought him too young. As for Nicole, she was still the only woman at the court of Westford to have been certified in the Law.

"He's not thinking I'll fall in love with Melva by having to take classes with her, is he?" Henry asked.

Nicole glanced at the sentry, who, as trained, behaved like a block of stone that could hear nothing but commands. She asked Henry carefully, "Why would you think that?"

"I know he wants Melva to marry someone he's sure will be loyal to him. Doesn't everything point to me as the most promising candidate?" he asked, confidant of his own attractiveness and political worth. Deliberating the wisest response, Nicole had yet to answer when Henry threw himself on her other side in restless eagerness. "What can I do to make Sophie like me?" he asked, making a transparent leap to the next logical point (in his mind).

"Oh, Henry. You will have to give her time. She does not have eyes for anyone but her father. Even I have trouble getting her attention," Nicole said, smiling.

The door to the council room suddenly opened, and Ares filled the doorway. He glanced from Nicole to Henry, then his eyes rested on his wife again as he exited. Giles squeezed out behind him, thrilled to finally have his ear and determined to hold it as he expounded on some pressing point regarding the computation of interest due on back taxes.

But the Steward was no match for Henry. Like his half-sister, Renée, he knew something about seizing the floor. "Ares! Hoose and a bunch of the others are waiting by the pugiling ring. We want you to show us how to do that move you used on Athian!" The volume of his voice drowned out Giles entirely.

Ares smiled slightly, watching his wife's reaction. "I am not the best one to teach you that, Henry—I executed it so poorly that I almost fell on my backside coming down. You should learn it from the one who taught it to me."

"Who is that?" Henry asked in wonder.

"Purdy," Ares answered.

"Purdy?" Henry repeated in disbelief. "The—the goatherd you brought back from Prie Mer?"

"The same," Ares said, glancing again at Nicole.

"But—he's not even a soldier—"

"No, but at times he had to defend his flocks from thieves, and so became very skilled at using his staff. I thought some of his tactics might prove effective with spears or javelins," Ares said.

Two years ago, after returning from Hornbound, Ares had given Purdy another aid in tending the vast flocks of sheep and goats at Westford: the short, stout canine, Puck. He disappeared from beside Ares' feet one morning to be found efficiently rounding up a wandering flock; ever after, he had belonged to Purdy.

Henry mulled over Ares' suggestion while Giles watched for an opening like a cougar waiting to pounce. "Purdy. All right, I'll summon him," Henry decided, moving away.

Giles stepped forward but Ares said in a low, threatening tone, "Henry." The boy looked back in alarm, and Ares reminded him, "Greens do not summon anyone, but they wait until they are dismissed and then they salute."

"Yes, Surchatain." Henry straightened, saluting crisply. The image of the laundress' sneer filled his heart with dread.

"You may go," Ares said, to Henry's great relief.

Giles, with the floor once again, took a long breath in preparation for pressing his point to a victorious conclusion—but again, he failed to reckon with the power of the modest lady with sultry green eyes. She looked at her husband and he said, "Excuse me, Giles," as he extended his arm to her. She took it, and they departed down the stairs toward the Surchatain's quarters.

Carmine paused by Giles' elbow while he stood staring forlornly at the escaping opportunity. Patting his shoulder, Carmine murmured, "It's much better to catch him after he leaves her, you know. Then he's always smiling." Reflecting on that, Giles brightened.

The Surchatain's quarters consisted of a spacious pair of rooms. The outer room, or the receiving room, was where Ares conducted business, received visitors, and wrote correspondence. All the maps and records that he or his officers required were housed in this room, although Giles, Carmine, Thom and Vogelsong kept their own records pertaining to their responsibilities. Ares had removed to the fourth-floor treasury most of the luxuries with which his predecessor had filled this room; the only decorative element that remained was the original, frayed, rat-gnawed banner of his ancestor, Roman, cleaned and repaired as much as possible for its age. Ares felt a great affinity for that weathered bit of history.

The inner room, the bedchamber, was where he and Nicole slept together. In deference to her, this large room was more comfortably appointed. It contained a garderobe equipped with running water from the rooftop cistern, as well as a sunken tub. A great fireplace, six feet tall, five feet wide, and four feet deep, was built into the wall next to the garderobe—although in summer, only small fires were lit at night.

When Ares and Nicole walked into this dim, windowless

chamber, he turned to her, pensively awaiting whatever rebuke might be brewing under that lovely exterior. He knew that if she had not witnessed the match, she must have heard about it. With his attention secured, she parted her lips and whispered, "Well done, my lord," even as tears welled up in her eyes.

Letting out his breath, he gathered her up to him, kissing the tears that tracked down her face. Choosing not to waste time on explanations or apologies, he felt the back of her dress for the buttons that easily came away from their holdings. At times like this, he was appreciative for her simplicity of attire. As he laid her on the firm bed, she whispered, "How much time do you have?"

"I will make time, Lady," he muttered, bending to shuck off his dress blacks.

"Oh, Ares—I've missed you so," she breathed, running her hands over his taut abdomen. He did not allow his age to be an excuse for softening of his body—every day he could still be found on the grounds drilling the men. He had a special touch imparting the basics of soldiering to the very newest Green recruits. They held him in awe, and the allure of having the Surchatain's personal attention insured that the Green Regiment was always filled to capacity.

Given rare privacy now, he briefly regarded his young wife sprawled in the sheets before throwing himself atop her. There was one delicious moment of skin against skin—then a knocking was heard at the outer door. Nicole groaned in dismay and Ares clenched his teeth.

He shoved himself up from the bed. Passing into the receiving room, he grabbed a scarlet robe which he threw on before opening the door into the corridor.

Standing outside was the tutor, Doudney, twisting his fingers nervously in his thin hair. At any other time he might have fainted upon seeing the Surchatain dressed so, for no one ever saw him in anything other than his dress blacks, excepting the few times he went into battle.

"I trust this is urgent, Tutor," Ares breathed, with a black glance at the sentry who had given him access.

"Not urgent, Surchatain, I'm sure, only—knowing how my lord insists on regular class times for the Chataines, I beg my lord to instruct Chataine Sophie to come to the library for her lessons. Her sister is waiting," Doudney said, blinking rapidly.

Ares paused. "Of course. Where is Sophie?"

"She is not with my lord and lady . . . ?" Doudney asked, trailing off weakly.

"No," Ares said, his heart rate escalating.

"Well then—we—"

"You can't find her?" Ares asked tensely. Given Bonnie and Sophie's relationship to the most powerful man in Lystra, the girls were always under discreet guard.

The tutor began blathering helplessly. Ares cut him off with, "I will be out at once." To the sentry, he instructed, "*Everyone* is to turn out to search for her," then he shut the door.

2

Throwing off the robe, Ares returned to the bedchamber where he had left his clothes, and Nicole sat up. "Sophie is missing," he said calmly, and she climbed down from the mattress.

By the time he had dressed and emerged from his chambers to rejoin the tutor, Thom and another soldier were coming down the corridor toward him. As they drew up and saluted, Ares regarded the glazed, tense expression of the young man with Thom. "You were warding Sophie today?" Ares asked him.

"Yes, Surchatain," he said.

"Surchatain, this is Hevlik. He is one of my best," Thom said defensively.

Ares raised his chin in acknowledgment. "What happened?"

As he was beginning to reply, Nicole, dressed, came out to join them. The paleness of her face did not make his story easier to tell. He paused to bow to her, then said, "Surchatain and Lady, I was with the Chataine outside the kitchen when the challenge to my lord came. Directly she ran outside and climbed up on the portico roof so she could see." Nicole exhaled and he blinked, aware that this was something Sophie was not allowed to do.

Hevlik continued, "I stood under the portico to see what I might while keeping watch on her. When the match had ended, Captain Yonge came 'round ordering all soldiers to fall in line to control the crowd. He pointed right at me and where I should go—I shouted up at the Chataine to stay put while I carried out my Captain's orders. It was but a moment later that the Seconds passed with the body, and I returned to the passageway to find the Chataine gone. I have been looking for her ever since."

"Did you ask if anyone had seen her?" Ares asked.

"Yes, Surchatain. One of the maids had seen her heading toward the vegetable garden. I searched it thoroughly—twice. She was not there," Hevlik asserted. "Although . . ." he trailed off as if reconsidering what he had almost said.

"Yes?" Ares lowered his brows at him.

"I . . . thought I had spotted her footprints in the garden, but they could not have been hers, because . . . they . . . led straight into the wall," he admitted with an embarrassed shrug at the absurdity.

Nicole gasped; Thom asked Ares, "Wasn't there a secret passage that led out to the garden? But—it was sealed up."

"We shall see," Ares said in a gravelly voice. "Send lanterns and arms to the vegetable garden," he instructed the sentry. To the dazed tutor, Ares said, "Thank you for alerting me. You may see that Bonnie proceeds with her lessons." Then he, Nicole, Thom and Hevlik went down the corridor toward the staircase with restrained haste.

"A secret passage, Commander?" Hevlik whispered in dismay. "I did not know about this."

Thom shook his head. "It was before your time, Hevlik."

Arriving downstairs, they passed through various lower corridors before opening the creaking iron gate leading into the vegetable garden. There were numerous gardens in the palace environs; the largest, dubbed "the kitchen garden" years ago when it might have been the only one, was actually off the great hall and contained the rose garden within its borders. The vegetable garden at the northwest corner of the palace was, in fact, much closer to the kitchen. "Show me the footprints you saw," Ares instructed Hevlik.

As Hevlik pointed, they all looked down, and Thom muttered, "Goats." Scanning the ground all around, he observed, "Purdy's goats got into the garden again, and hordes of maids were required to get them out. That's all I see." They could also hear the bleating of strays that Puck had yet to round up.

Looking up, Ares strode to a portion of the palace wall and scrutinized it, running a hand over the roughly plastered exterior. "Wasn't the entrance about here?" he mused.

"I thought it was farther down," Thom said, looking down the wall.

"The ivy on the corner has grown since then," Nicole said. "But I remember the way the shadow of the branches fell over the door when Chiacos came out. . . ." Chiacos, the Polonti guide who had brought Melva to Westford, had been trapped in the passage for several days before Melva had revealed his whereabouts to Ares. After serving as guide and scout for Ares, he had disappeared years ago.

"Are those the prints you saw?" Thom asked Hevlik, pointing to a mishmash on the ground. Hevlik looked around, hesitant to answer.

Nicole pensively touched the wall beside the vine and pieces of loose plaster fell into her hand, revealing the crack of the door. "Ares, it has been opened!" she cried.

"Yes, Commander," Hevlik replied.

Ares moved to her side to peel off chips of plastering with his fingertips. Then he strained to get a firm enough grip on the edge to pry the heavy door open. As sweat trickled down the side of his face, he muttered, "She could not have opened this by herself." Finally, he heaved it open as two sentries entered the garden behind him with swords, axes, and lanterns.

Nicole took a lantern and held it into the dark, cool passage-way. Ares moved her hand with the lantern down to cast the light on the ground. The floor of the passage, being one with the foundation of the palace, was stone, but a thick layer of dirt and wood humus covered it. Observing the array of footprints in this mixture, Ares said, "She has been in here . . . and not alone."

Hevlik crouched to study the prints. "Someone opened it from within, and let her in."

"A man," Thom said, surveying the ground. Ares stared at the second set of larger prints beside those of the little girl. They were made by square-toed boots with a prominent hobnail in the right heel. Then he took one of the swords and hefted it purposefully.

Nicole lifted the lantern into the musty, curving passage to their right, toward the front of the palace. "They went down this way."

Ares reached for the lantern she held. "Lady—"

She surrendered the lantern, but said quietly, "No, Ares. I will not wait here."

He inhaled, then nodded and gestured to the sentries. "Fall in behind us."

With Nicole close beside him, Ares held the lantern out so that its soft yellow glow illumined the large footprints next to the little ones. Careful not to mar the prints, the trackers followed them down the passage. The air was heavy and cool, as in a tomb that had not been opened for many years. The confines of the tunnel, being only four feet wide at this point, forced Nicole to follow him by a pace or two, but her eyes were fixed ahead, searching for signs in the dim circle of light. Behind her and Ares came Thom, Hevlik, and the three sentries, also armed.

The first fifty feet were covered quickly, for the passage

curved gently with no opening on either hand. Then there loomed in front of them an abrupt dead end of rock and earth. The tunnel had caved in here long ago, as Ares knew.

Nicole's breathing became strained; Ares swung the lantern to look closely at one wall, then the other. Behind him, Thom was scanning the ground by the light of the second lantern. "Here, Surchatain," he said, his voice echoing off the dead stone.

Ares looked down at the footprints heading into the wall, then raised the lantern to reveal the minute outline of another door. Handing off the sword, he put his shoulder to one side of the door; when that would not give, he heaved on the other side, and the stone groaned open. At this point, he vaguely remembered that most of the passageway doors were hung on a pivot in the middle, so that either side of the door could be opened in or out.

They stepped out into the fig and plum orchard, separated by a wall from the vegetable garden. After the spectacle of Athian's challenge, servants were just now returning to the task of harvesting the ripest of the breba, or overwintering crop of figs. The afternoon sun gilded the spreading fig leaves that were not in shadow. The plum trees had lost their white blossoms to the burgeoning fruit, but they would not ripen for some weeks yet. In the farthest corner of the orchard was where the beekeeper kept his hives, as the honeybees were essential for the plum trees to set fruit.

"I never knew about this second door. It was not sealed," Ares said tightly. While Nicole anxiously scanned the orchard, Thom and Hevlik were searching the ground. Ares gave the lantern to one sentry, telling him, "Have the Second Oswald send searchers throughout the passage. He charted it the first time for me, and I want to know if any of the other doors along it have been opened."

"Surchatain!" The guard replied, saluting, and sprinted away.

"What do you see?" Ares asked Thom.

He paused, studying the soft earth. "They came out here, and went straight out for ten paces, but . . . too many others have crossed their path. . . ."

"Has anyone seen Sophie?" Nicole shouted. Startled, the servants halted their work and bowed. Since no one was about to admit slacking off elsewhere, no one answered. So she repeated, "Did anyone see Chataine Sophie here?"

A manservant who had entered the orchard only moments ago said, "Pardon, Lady, but I do believe I saw her just now in the foyer with the Chatain." Despite his reserved wording, he was confident of whom he saw. Although the girls were identical, no one had confused one for the other since they were toddlers with some power of choice over clothes and companions.

"She was with Henry?" Nicole asked in surprise.

"Yes, Lady," he bowed.

She and Ares stared at each other, then turned so abruptly in the same direction that they ran into each other. He held her shoulders and she gripped his elbows momentarily before they reoriented themselves to briskly reenter the palace by means of the door that led into the lower corridor running past the infirmary. From here they entered the front foyer, followed by the rest of the search party. Hearing the children's voices, they all looked up to see Henry and Sophie arguing halfway up the staircase.

"Henry! Sophie!" Ares said, his deep voice ringing off the stone. Since he rarely raised his voice, almost everyone in the crowded foyer stopped to stare. The two children turned, and with parting gibes at each other, descended to meet the variously angry and indignant adults.

Ares collected himself to say, "Sophie, your mother and I wish to speak to you and Henry—here. Come aside into the chapel, if you will." He extended a hand to the chapel off the foyer. While Thom, Hevlik, and the sentries resigned themselves to wait outside, Ares and Nicole ushered the two renegades into the chapel. Before the door closed behind them, Sophie glimpsed Hevlik's reproachful gaze and guessed what this was about.

In the quietness of the deserted chapel, Ares looked down on his daughter. It was not her long chestnut hair, heart-shaped face, or large green eyes that made his heart constrict whenever he looked at her—it was her unwavering, rapt devotion. Ares sometimes forgot that Bonnie and Sophie were identical because they looked so different to him. Bonnie reserved her adoration for Renée. But Sophie so desperately wanted to please her father and knew his expectations so well, that what few times he had to correct her were excruciating for them both.

Today, however, she looked unperturbed, for she had a ready explanation. "Papa, I know I'm supposed to stay with my guardian, but he was called away to duty, and since I know I'm not supposed to climb on things, I knew I should get down from the roof. So I went to the vegetable garden to play. I can always play there if I don't get in anyone's way," she dutifully recited.

Ares turned his scar toward Henry. "Why did you take her into the secret passage?"

Henry blinked. "What? What secret passage?"

"The passage that opened into the vegetable garden, that I had sealed up after Chiacos was trapped in it," Ares said with a shade of impatience.

Henry had known about it at one time, but as he tended to wipe out anything associated with his father Cedric, it was not surprising that this memory died, too. At his continued protestations of ignorance, Ares' questioning took on a sharper tone. Nicole finally broke in to ask Henry, "What were you arguing about on the stairway?"

"I found her in the orchard when I knew it was time for her lessons with Bonnie. So I made her come in, and I was taking her up to the library," Henry said defensively. Belatedly, Ares glanced down at Henry's boots. While they were as big as a man's, they were not square-toed at all, but the round toe that most of the young men preferred nowadays. The footprints in the passage were not Henry's.

"Where? Where in the orchard did you find her?" Nicole asked Henry, with a glance at her daughter.

"Near the outer wall, by the fig trees," Henry said, then explained, "I was looking for Purdy."

Nicole looked at Sophie's downcast face. "Is this true, dear?"

Sophie didn't answer. So Ares knelt to be eye level with her and asked softly, "Sophie, who took you into the passage in the wall?"

"Nobody. It opened by itself," she murmured.

Ares looked up at Nicole, who returned a tense gaze. She was alarmed that anything—or anyone—could compel Sophie to lie to her father. "Lady, will you and Henry excuse us for a moment?" he said.

Nicole curtsied and Henry saluted, but on the way out, he was a trifle loud in asking her, "Why is Ares blaming me for what Sophie did?"

"He's not, Henry," she said mildly as he opened the chapel doors. "We just misunderstood what happened. We are very grateful that you found her." When Henry closed the doors behind them, Thom and Hevlik stood at attention, waiting for her word.

Nicole gave Henry permission to resume his search for Purdy, then explained the situation thus far to the others. Hevlik asked the Commander, "Your instructions, sir?" His set face indicated he was expecting punishment.

Thom paused. "Await the Chataine and finish your shift," he said with a glance toward the closed chapel doors. Hevlik saluted, and Thom bowed to Nicole. "Please excuse me, Lady—I left Magnus' messenger cooling his heels." Surchatain

Magnus was the ruler of neighboring Scylla, with whom Lystra enjoyed a longstanding, if delicate, truce.

She nodded, but before Thom departed, he added, "I will issue a general instruction that, henceforth, guardians are not to leave their charges even when a superior officer summons. That should satisfy the Surchatain." He did not add aloud, *and possibly avert repercussions from today.*

"Commander," Hevlik acknowledged in relief, and Nicole smiled.

In the chapel, Ares sat on a bench and opened his arms. "Come." Sophie hardly required the invitation to scramble up on his knees. With neither plastering nor chandeliers, this small hall was still one of the brightest rooms in the palace, for it had a large window set high in its angled roof, facing south.

Sophie was too young to know how this window had come about—that workers on the rooftop had inadvertently discovered rotten shingles by dropping a heavy pouch of iron nails through them, narrowly missing the priest below. The resultant shaft of sunlight streaming down from above compelled the impetuous confession of so many sins that Ares desired to preserve it—hence the uncolored, unadorned glass. Still, the shadows created by the leading spoke to the superstitious and the guilty alike, and the confessions continued.

Encompassed by light, Ares held his daughter quietly for a moment, enabling her to get comfortable in his lap. Then he said, "Sophie, you know you must not lie to me."

"Oh, I know, Papa," she said, clearly horrified at the idea.

"Well, then . . . we were very worried when you got away from your guardian. He must be punished for that, you know, when it was really your fault."

"I'm sorry," she murmured, remorseful.

"And then, we found that a secret passage that had been sealed up before you were born had been opened again. We found your footprints with those of a man. Sophie . . . we must know who took you into the passage," Ares said.

She looked troubled. "There was no one, Papa. It just opened, and I went in. I was curious because no one else was around."

He studied her, but it was useless to argue the point. Whatever had actually happened in the garden, she believed what she was telling him. It was possible, he reflected, for someone dressed in dark clothes to open the passage and stand back so that she could not see him. Ares would have to return to the passage and look closely at the footprints to determine whether the intruder had walked alongside her or behind her—even then, Ares might not be able to tell. So he progressed to the next question. "Then what happened?"

"Well, the door closed behind me, so I had to go somewhere. I felt my way along until I came to a big pile of rocks—I was going to try to climb over them when another door opened. I ran out into the fig orchard and . . . was trying to find out if the tunnel went out past the wall," she said tentatively, and Ares detected a trace of prevarication.

"It must have been very dark and scary in the tunnel," he observed.

"A little bit," she admitted.

"Did you hear anything?" he asked.

"I don't *think* so," she said, and he could not tell what she meant by that. He did remember Doudney's telling him that Sophie had an extraordinarily active imagination—that she seemed to have gotten Bonnie's share as well as her own.

Leaving that as well, he asked, "So then, after you went out into the fig orchard, did the door stand open?"

"No. It shut quick right behind me," she said uneasily.

Ares weighed the evidence. It was clear that someone had been in the passage. The question was, was that someone there for the purpose of luring her away? Or did she happen upon the door opening when someone was trying to make a stealthy exit? "I see," he murmured.

He stood with her in his arms. "Well, I must give you back up to Doudney. He was most distressed by your absence."

Sophie leaned into his neck, sighing, "Latin is *hard*, Papa."

"If it weren't hard, it wouldn't be worth learning. Someday you will be glad to know it," he said, not for the first time.

"Because many of the old books are in Latin, and the Ruler must know how to read the old books." She repeated the rationale that inspired her the most.

"The Ruler must know," he agreed, opening the chapel doors. Outside, he set her on her feet and told her guardian, "The Chataine is ready to return to her lessons." Hevlik saluted and nodded to her, but she insisted on bestowing a kiss on her father's scarred cheek before turning to the stairway. That, in itself, was the infallible distinguishment between the twins. Ares could tell them apart blindfolded when they kissed him goodnight: Bonnie always kissed his clean cheek; Sophie always kissed his scar.

"Where is Thom?" Ares asked, watching his daughter and her guardian ascend the stairs.

Nicole replied, "With Magnus' messenger, I believe. But what did she say, Ares?"

"She insists that the door opened of its own and closed again when she was inside. She saw no one. But when she reached the cave-in, the door to the fig orchard opened. I believe she was looking for something at the orchard wall, but she would not say what," he replied.

"Was she telling the truth?" Nicole asked.

"I believe so," he said. "She believed what she told me, but I do not think she told me everything on her mind."

At that point, the Commander's Second, Oswald, approached and saluted. Ares was no small man, but Oswald was a head taller yet. The big man's curling red hair and beard were tinged with grey, though he was at least ten years younger than the Surchatain. Nicole always kept an anxious eye on Oswald's general health, as he had spent three years in the portal, where time stood still. Ares and Nicole had entered the portal, too—only later learning that it was supposedly cursed.

When Ares nodded, Oswald said, "Surchatain, we have finished combing the secret passage. All chains and locks that I had placed on the doors are still there. They have not been disturbed. But on the ground floor, the door that I had sealed up has been broken open. A second door leading into the fig orchard—which I did not know existed—has been opened. The door that I thought led to the kitchen actually opens on the kitchen storerooms, only there's so much piled on the wall against it, there's no going through there. And a good portion of the rocks and dirt from the cave-in has been cleaned out."

"What?" Ares rasped. Some heads swung in their direction, so he lowered his voice. "Someone is trying to clear the passage to its end?"

"It appears so, Surchatain," Oswald admitted.

"And it leads out beyond the wall?" Nicole asked.

"I was told that it did at one time, though it would require yet another curve. I do not know how long ago it caved in," Ares said tentatively. "Oswald . . . are there tracks in the upper passages on the second floor? Has anyone been spying through the peepholes?"

"No, Surchatain, we saw no evidence of that. All was thick with dust. Nothing had been disturbed before we entered," Oswald replied.

"You saw evidence of entry only on the ground floor," Ares repeated.

"Yes, Surchatain. Only in the passage that runs through the palace wall facing the garden and orchard."

Ares looked off, thinking. After a moment, Oswald asked, "Shall we seal it up again, sir?"

Ares shook his head. "If we do, then we cannot find out who is trying to use it. Post a guard at the entrance to the garden starting tonight. It will have to be someone who can stay awake through the night without any light at all. Inform the Commander of this."

"Surchatain. Lady." Oswald saluted to him, bowed to her, and left to carry out his orders.

Ares took Nicole's hand and kissed it. "She is safe, at any rate," he murmured.

"For now," she said.

With resignation, Sophie took her seat beside her sister in the second-floor library. They sat at a long table cluttered with books and tablets. Bonnie looked over, smirking with superiority. "I've already finished for the day, so Aunt Renée is taking me to get fitted for a new dress from Lord Preus," she whispered. Bonnie already had twice the number of dresses as Sophie, forcing Ares to put a cap on Renée's buying privileges on behalf of Bonnie.

"How can you think about dresses when someone is trying to kill Papa?" Sophie hissed.

"What?" Bonnie squeaked.

Doudney interrupted, "Chataine Bonnie, I fear that you must repeat your Latin exercises for the day. They are not as your father directed." That is, they were not right. The tutor nervously placed a wax tablet before her, and Bonnie's face screwed up in its perpetual pout.

With a shade more confidence, Doudney placed a like tablet in front of her sister. "Thank you for joining us, Chataine Sophie. We are in the present tense of second conjugation verbs. Now, Chataines, write on your tablets after me, if you please: *videre*, to see. *Video*, I see. *Vides*, you see. *Videt*, he or she sees. . . ."

With a disgusted sigh, Bonnie picked up her engraved ivory stylus and trailed it listlessly through the wax. Sophie, lip bit in concentration, copied the words that the tutor wrote on the board before them, but her mind was heavy with graver thoughts.

After Ares had taken leave of his wife, he sat at a large table in the receiving room of the Surchatain's chambers to try to address some of the more urgent communications that silently awaited his attention. The moment he had gotten settled in front of an imposing pile of correspondence, the sentry knocked at the outer door. "Enter," Ares said, halfheartedly wondering if there remained any mortal action he could complete without interruption. Dying, perhaps.

Straight-backed, the sentry stepped inside and said, "Lord Backvold requests your ear, Surchatain."

Ares nodded, and the sentry stepped aside for the lord to enter and bow. "I must thank you again, Surchatain, for your kindness to me in sparing—" he cut short and looked at the sentry in alarm.

"Speak freely. He will repeat nothing," Ares said. A glance at the sentry was sufficient warning that the cost for betraying this confidence would be his life.

"Thank you, Surchatain. Again, I must thank you for sparing my son," Backvold said, perspiring.

"He is better, then?" Ares asked, with a glance at the topmost letter on his pile.

"He is alive. But I strongly desire to remove him to a safe place for mending," Backvold said.

"Do so," Ares instructed.

"I would, but doing so without being seen is more difficult, Surchatain. Therefore, I have come to request the use of the secret passage for removing him from the palace," the lord said.

Ares quickly looked up. "The passage that opens into the vegetable garden? How do you know about that?"

As Backvold was stammering a reply, Ares realized that the question was pointless. Numerous servants had seen the search party enter the tunnel through the garden and exit into the fig and plum orchard. That is not to mention how many others saw Oswald and his men traipsing in and out. "Never mind," Ares sighed. "But no—the passage is not safe for you to use. However, tell Doctor Savary I give leave for him to arrange a guard to transport your son in secret."

Lord Backvold bowed deeply. "Bless you, Surchatain. God bless your house."

"Amen. You may go," Ares dismissed him.

The lord left in the company of the sentry, and Ares returned to the topmost letter. It was from Klar of Eugenia regarding the trade tariffs into Lystra and questioning the necessity thereof. Ares' first impulse was to delegate the answering of it to Giles, then he reconsidered. That could lead to war, as the tariffs were Giles' idea, and he would defend them to the death, no doubt.

Ares was formulating a reply himself when the outer door burst open to accommodate Renée's standard grand entrance. He glanced at the flustered sentry behind her, but there would be no punishment for him. There was no guard on earth who could keep Renée out of someplace she desired to go.

"Ares, what are you doing?" she cried, tossing her luxuriant blond hair that cascaded from a tiara. She had stopped calling him "Papa" when his daughters began calling him "Papa" because it looked ridiculous for a now-27-year-old woman to be addressing him in the same terms as young children did.

"I am trying to raise enough revenue to keep you and Bonnie in dresses," he said dryly. "What is it, Chataine?" he asked, only to look back down at the letter.

"Ares—you—" she began, uncharacteristically flustered, and he looked up, reaching for the quill and ink. "You have put Bonnie on a most unreasonable budget," she said, affronted.

Ares smiled at having so accurately divined her concern before she uttered it. "Not I," he disavowed. "That was the

Surchataine's doing. Bonnie has too many dresses already; she will not share them with Sophie, and it is patently unfair to buy more for one than for the other," he said as he pulled out a fresh sheet of parchment, dipped his quill, and began flowery greetings to Klar.

"But Sophie's not interested in dresses! Heaven knows I've tried to teach her," Renée said, exasperated. Ares looked up thoughtfully, but declined to comment. On paper, he expressed deep regrets for the tariffs. "Ares, this is for the future good of Lystra," she argued, beginning to pace in her swirling, ornate dress. His eyes flicked up in interest. "At least *one* of your daughters should be tutored in the courtly arts for presentation to eligible Chatains!"

Ares considered that Nicole, having grown up as a pauper on the coast, had a twelve-day-crash course in courtly manners before being presented to the court at Westford—and wound up becoming Surchataine. When he thought back to dancing with her that first evening of her arrival, and feeling her hand on his neck, his fingers loosened on the quill and his face took on a softness that incited Renée to pounce. "You see that I'm right, don't you? Oh, Ares, let us get her at least one new dress for the June festival!"

This festival was an innovation wrought by Ares, Carmine, Giles, and the merchant guilds of Westford. Wishing to draw the moneyed nobles from the spring fair in Crescent Hollow without competing with it, they concocted a seven-day extravaganza of booths and entertainments to be held just south of Westford during the third week of June.

Last year had been the inaugural event, which was such a resounding success that the merchants laid immediate plans for its expansion the following year. This required using the field where Ares' boys, his army of Green recruits, had been slaughtered by the invading Qarqarians eight years ago. The crosses that marked their many graves had long since crumbled, but to Ares the ground was sacred, and he could not bear to think of holding entertainments over their bones. To the dismay of the merchants, the expansion was denied. The guilds appealed, but Ares was steadfast.

Nicole had broken the stalemate, as usual, by coming to Ares with a compromise. Let a large plaque be erected in the middle of the festival, she said, which told the story of the Greens' heroic stand on that very spot to save Westford. Then everyone attending—thousands of people—would read of it and remember their sacrifice. Ares agreed to this, and plans were resumed for the festival, now two weeks away.

While halfheartedly considering Renée's present dilemma, Ares wrote to Klar with wounded indignation about a few unscrupulous merchants from Eugenia who crossed the border to undercut Lystran merchants with cheap copies of their best wares. Finishing that sentence, he told Renée, "I will compromise with you on this," and she listened suspiciously. "If you will surrender one of your dresses to the treasury, I will allow you to buy one for Bonnie." He redipped his quill.

Her tinted lips parted in distress. "But—Ares—one of my dresses costs twice what a dress for Bonnie costs!"

"Excellent. Then you can buy two dresses: one for Bonnie and one for Sophie. And if they share, then they will each have two new dresses," Ares said, while expressing resigned regret to Klar that, as long as a few Eugenian merchants sought to sell counterfeit goods in Lystra, they would be subject to the tariffs. But should they produce *novelties* for sale—

Renée sighed, "Very well. I'll do it."

"Very good. When Giles brings me an estimate of the value of the dress you surrender, then I will apportion you that amount to buy the girls dresses," Ares said as he reached for the blotting paper and sealing wax.

"Not Giles! Carmine! Have Carmine make the appraisal," Renée insisted in a panic. The difference between the two men's estimates could be as much as six or seven royals.

Ares glanced up warily, knowing how Renée could still manipulate her ex-husband, Carmine. "Have them both appraise it, and I will split the difference between the two." He pressed his signet ring into the hot wax, sealing the letter with the Surchatain's authority.

"Very well," she said sullenly. Ares folded up the letter, sealing it again at its edge, then called in the sentry to hand it to him with instructions that it be delivered to Klar.

That done, Ares had the following twenty seconds to give his full attention to the next letter. It was from Lord Lieterstad, requesting protection for his merchants on a risky but potentially wildly profitable trading venture into Seleca, which was unfortunately still a haven for slave traders. Lystra's reward for her cooperation would be fully half of his profits. Ares was pivoting in his chair to the honeycomb behind him to look for the map of routes into Seleca when Renée purred, "What marriage offers have I received lately, Ares?"

"Umm," he exhaled noncommittally, turning back to the table to leaf through piles of papers until he found those originating from the Steward. It was Giles' responsibility to receive or procure at least one fresh marriage proposal a month from someone suitable for Renée—doing so salved her pride enough to save the treasury hundreds of royals per month. But since Renée had no intention of leaving Westford to marry anyone, she inevitably turned them down. As this fact was widely known, legitimate proposals were getting harder and harder to come by. Therefore, unknown to Ares, Giles had resorted to making them up.

Ares picked up an engraved scroll. "Well, this is from Lord Fancsali of Scylla. I understand that he was so helpful to Magnus in repelling the slave trade back into Seleca that Magnus awarded him a large estate just outside of Eviron—less than a day's ride from Westford. I heard that he's done quite well logging on his estate," Ares mused. All this was true, except that Lord Fancsali would have been most surprised to hear that he had proposed marriage to the Chataine Renée of Westford. Giles just assumed he would never hear of it.

"What does he look like?" Renée asked. "How old is he?"

"Frankly, Chataine, I have no idea. Only that he is quite wealthy," Ares said, selecting the map he required from the honeycomb and unrolling it.

"Well, I will think on it," Renée said loftily.

"Go do that, Chataine," Ares suggested, eyes on the map.

As she left his receiving room to do that, neither of them —nor Giles—knew that Lord Fancsali was, at that moment, making his own plans to attend the June festival in two weeks.

B

Given the circumstances, dinner at Westford that evening was rather lighthearted. Outwardly, there was no reason it should not be—the great hall was filled with flowers and greenery from the palace gardens; the wine was served in generous bowls; the food was the pride of the southern Continent.

There were seventy persons at the long table this evening. Ares, at the head, could see every face beneath hundreds of candles suspended in chandeliers fitted with silver awnings that reflected the light downward. Nicole was seated beside Ares on his right; to her right, around the corner of the table, were Bonnie, Renée, Thom and his wife Deirdre, Doctor Savary, the Second Rhode and his wife Soucie, then Captain Crager. Along the other side of the table, at Ares' left hand, sat Sophie, Carmine, Giles and his wife Genevieve, Vogelsong, Melva, then the Second Oswald.

Henry had accepted his status as a Green, which meant that he ate in the mess with the other Greens. Ares' former page, Ben, also ate at mess. After Ares had retrieved Henry from slavery in Hornbound, Henry and Ben had conflicted so violently as to which would serve Ares that he was forced to remove Ben as his page. In compensation, Ares had appointed him to the Gold Regiment, a step up from the Green. Moreover, Ares had asked Thom to give Ben any plumb assignments that might be reasonably given a Gold. As a result of his courageous service, Ben was now in the Red, the second-highest regiment, next to the Blue.

Lord Faguy was seldom at table anymore, his shipping business in Prie Mer having burgeoned to the point that it required his constant attention. That is what he said, anyway, but others privately noted that he would have let the business run itself had Renée accepted his marriage proposal after the death of his mother. But she did not, so. . . .

The other places at the dinner table were occupied by the administrators, officers, nobles, and courtiers who had managed to find favor with both Ares and Renée. There were more than one courtier like Lady Auer who, after inadvertently offending Renée, found themselves excluded from the table.

Many of those began wondering aloud why the Surchatain continued to accommodate the grandchildren of a murderer and usurper to such an extraordinary degree. But though Ares offered no explanations, he had his reasons. First, he never forgot his oath of protection to Henry, which he considered to extend to Renée. Second, he never forgot that Renée was the one who had brought his dove, Nicole, to the palace, supplying him with a wife, and ultimately, the throne and heirs.

In addition, Renée had consistently proven her worth in un-expected ways which more than offset the cost of her upkeep. And those disgruntled courtiers discovered that, if they were patient, their dinner privileges were quietly restored once Renée had moved on to address more recent offenses.

Lady Vivian, Renée's mother, had been moved farther down the table to forestall further bickering between mother and daughter, which Ares found intolerable. In the process,

Vivian had discovered a suitor in Lord Notham, who had contrived to procure a seat at the lower end despite his daughter Rhea's ability to offend almost everyone she came across.

The rest of the table waited with bated breath to see what would happen when Renée should discover the budding love affair. In that event, the odds strongly favored Renée's moving Lady Vivian and Lord Notham back toward the front, so as to be able to toy with the happy couple.

Tonight, pea and onion soup, fried mushrooms, beef tongue in aspic, and croustades filled with calves' liver were set before the diners on pewter dishes. (Renée constantly lamented the fact that the gold dishes were not used except for special company, considering herself special enough for their use.) Bonnie screwed up her face at the grown-up dinner fare, then leaned over to whisper, "Mama, what is for dessert?"

"Orange fool, dear," Nicole murmured, lifting the soup bowl to sip noiselessly. Bonnie, brightening at the thought of the sweet orange custard seasoned with cinnamon and nutmeg, set about eating just enough liver to earn custard.

Watching her, Sophie gleaned that whatever was to come was worth choking down what sat before them now, and likewise picked up her child-sized fork. The girls were not required to sit at dinner with the adults in the great hall, but if they did, they had to eat what was served without complaining, else they would forfeit dessert. Or worse—they would be banished to the kitchen to eat with the other children.

Renée tossed her head as a precursor to speaking, thus aborting several other ongoing conversations. "Lord Fancsali of Scylla has sent me a marriage proposal," she announced.

"Another?" Carmine asked with an amused twinkle.

"What will you do, Aunt Renée?" Bonnie asked with mixed alarm and fascination.

Regarding her young protégé, Renée decided that a new

course in how to handle suitors was called for. "I may have to invite this one to Westford," she mused. "Giles, what does he look like?"

Genevieve elbowed her husband, who had been inattentive to this conversation. "Pardon?" He looked around, straightening his new tasseled hat.

"What does Lord Fancsali look like? Is he dashing at all?" Renée repeated.

Pleased to be asked by the Chataine to render an opinion on the dashingness of another—and entirely forgetting the forged proposal—Giles swiftly decided to propound in the lord's favor, as that seemed the surest way of holding the floor: "Fancsali of Eviron? Ah, there's a one! Not yet forty, I hear, and courageous to a fault. Single-handedly, with a handful of men, he drove a slaver's band of sixty into Falcon Pass and held them there with naught but rocks and arrows till Magnus could come drive them into the Fastnesses at the point of a spear! Rides like Apollo, like a bridegroom racing toward—" and with a sick lurch of the stomach, Giles remembered the forgery. He sat with open mouth and bulging eyes.

"It sounds as though an invitation to this Fancsali is overdue," Ares said mildly.

"I agree," Renée bubbled. Lifting a white hand, she ordered a sentry, "Summon Tanny."

This was done. Tanny, small and rather bent now, did not deliver messages anymore, but schooled a regiment of hardy carriers in this crucial employment. When he arrived and bowed to the head of the table, Renée commanded, "Tanny, you're to invite Lord Fancsali of Eviron to Westford for the June festival."

Before he could reply, Giles sprang from his seat. "Excuse me, Surchatain—Chataine—we must write out a proper invitation. Please allow me a moment's absence to attend this. I will return straightway—" Fleeing the table, he paused to utter to Tanny, "Send your messenger to my quarters." Tanny bowed again and Ares dismissed them both.

As Giles flew out, he almost collided with an incoming sentry, who adroitly sidestepped him to bend to Ares' ear and whisper, "The guard you required is on duty in the secret passage." Ares nodded and gestured for him to repeat his message to Thom, seated next to Renée. It was irritating to Ares not to be able to confer with his Commander at dinner anymore, but such were the concessions one made to seating etiquette.

In his chambers, Giles went straight to his enameled writing desk and seized a small parchment. This he rolled up blank, sealed it, and fastened it with a nice gold ribbon. When Tanny's messenger arrived at his door, Giles thrust the roll into his hand. "Take this and be gone for two days. But under no circumstances—I order you—under no condition should it reach Fancsali! Just—toss it in Willowring Lake and come back." The messenger looked dumbfounded, but Giles shooed him away. The Steward then composed himself with a stiff shot of ale from his personal store, then returned to the table to report that the messenger had been duly dispatched.

The messenger, however, having been trained by Tanny, knew the penalties for failure to deliver. He also knew the penalties for disobeying a direct order. So he took the scroll to his superior and reported everything the Steward had said.

Tanny listened gravely, then nodded. "Do as he says: take your horse and be gone for two days. I will dispose of this for you." The messenger saluted and departed empty-handed. Tanny knew what must be done with the message, but he dare not interrupt dinner to do it. So he went to the garden off the great hall and stood in the shadows, watching for the diners to leave the table.

Following dessert, the musicians were brought in to play for those who wished to dance. At that time, the officers who were not at table were called in, for dancing was an essential social form at Westford that everyone at court was expected to master. Henry, a superb dancer, was summoned to provide practice for Melva, Bonnie and Sophie. Renée danced almost exclusively with Carmine, as he was the best dancer at court—even better than Ares, who too grudgingly learned new dances.

As the musicians put bows to their vieles, Ares saw Thom waiting to confer with him, but Nicole laid a hand on his shoulder—so Thom must wait. Ares kissed that hand before leading her out onto the floor. Nicole closed her eyes as he slid his arm around her waist, and at the proper measure, swung her into a series of turns. This was Nicole's favorite dance, and had always been. Ares simply led her to the music. She did not have to think about intricate steps; she did not have to think at all; she only had to follow his lead. It was pure joy.

Holding her, looking down at her half-closed eyes and parted lips, Ares guided her to the doors standing open into the garden. As the music died away, he led her deeper into the shadows, past the globed lights on the path, until they were enclosed in the darkness. "I think I shall have to kidnap you to have you again, Lady," he whispered, seeking out her lips.

She stretched up to embrace his kiss. "Here? In the garden?" she murmured, and he could feel her willingness.

"Who would look for us here?" he chuckled, loosening her bodice. Then a soft cough was heard behind them.

Nicole gasped, clutching the front of her dress, and Ares spun. Tanny stepped close enough to be seen in the faint candlelight. "A thousand pardons, Surchatain. Allow me to slip by you, sir." In moving to the garden, they had pinned him in his spot of concealment.

"What were you doing there, Tanny?" Ares asked. If Tanny was out of place, there was a good reason for it.

Before he could answer, Sophie came to the doorway leading into the bright hall. "Papa? Mama?" she called, peering into the darkness. It was vain to hope that their exit had gone unnoticed.

"Here, darling. We'll be out in a moment," Nicole called, refastening her bodice. To Ares she murmured, "Yes, who would look for us here?"

He put his lips to her ear to whisper, "Put the girls to bed, then wait for me. Don't go to sleep." Sighing, she reached up and he kissed her hungrily. "Wait for me," he insisted.

After Nicole had left with Sophie, Ares turned to Tanny. "What did you need?"

"A word, Surchatain. If we may move to the light, sir," Tanny said, gesturing to one of the globed candles illumining the garden walk. When they had moved within its range, Tanny placed the small scroll in his hand and repeated everything the messenger had told him.

Ares stared down at the scroll, then glanced over his shoulder at the laughter and noise coming from the great hall. "Come with me," he directed, and Tanny did.

Because Ares rewarded loyalty with information and access, he took Tanny with him when he entered the hall and made eye contact with Thom. Casually, Thom followed them out of the hall to the broad, curving staircase. They went up to the Surchatain's receiving room and shut the door. Ares sat heavily at the large table while he fingered the scroll. "Giles told the messenger to destroy the invitation to Fancsali?" he asked.

"Yes, Surchatain," Tanny confirmed. Thom's eyebrows shot up in surprise.

"But to give the impression that it had been delivered," Ares continued.

"This is correct," Tanny said.

Ares turned the scroll over in his hands, then removed the ribbon, broke the seal, and unrolled it. He blinked. "It's blank."

Thom leaned forward to see. "A secret message?"

Ares swiveled to hold the parchment over the flame of the candle on the writing table. "No. It's really blank. I fail to understand why Giles would contrive to send a blank invitation to Fancsali."

"It would seem that the Steward does not wish Lord Fancsali to come," Tanny said quietly.

At the same time Thom was inquiring, "Should I summon Giles?"

"Yes. Wait—what did you say?" Ares asked Tanny, who repeated himself. Ares stared at him. "Why? After Giles made such a glowing speech about Fancsali at dinner, to suddenly decide that—" his eye landed on the marriage proposal from Fancsali lying open on the table.

"Let Giles explain this to you," Thom said impatiently.

"I should, but . . . whenever I correct him about anything, he gets so flustered that he can't manage accounts for days, and I need him at his best for the festival," Ares muttered, picking up the proposal. "This is Giles' handwriting."

"What is?" Thom asked, and Ares showed him the proposal. Tanny began quietly laughing.

"Yes, Tanny?" Ares asked.

The old messenger straightened and bowed. "Forgive me, Surchatain. I was recalling reports from my messengers that the Steward has been driven to soliciting proposals to the Chataine from various nobles around the area. For their convenience, he sometimes has the offers written out beforehand."

Ares scrutinized the proposal from Fancsali with its signature. "This is all of one hand—Giles'. And what is this seal? That looks like a lily. What is Fancsali's emblem?"

"A bear," Thom replied, frowning.

Ares sat back. "So Giles sent this in Fancsali's name!"

"So Giles can hardly issue an invitation to Fancsali in response to it," Thom said wryly. "What shall you do?"

"Nothing," Ares snorted. "Giles took care of it himself. I will have to meet Lord Fancsali another time. Thank you, Tanny. Good night. Oh, and Tanny, be sure to inform

Counselor Carmine of this little charade." Still smiling, Tanny bowed and withdrew. Ares tossed the blank scroll onto his supply of parchment for later use.

After Nicole had rushed through the girls' bedtime story and the maids had changed out the chamber pots, Sophie and Bonnie cuddled in the big feather bed. As every night, Bonnie wore her hair wrapped in bits of cloth to make it curl. Sophie, as usual, wore her hair pulled back, out of her face.

Once, about a year ago, weary of long hair, Sophie had taken a kitchen knife to her tresses, lopping a ten-inch chunk off the left side of her head before a horrified maid had stopped her. Sophie was unrepentant, and remonstrations had no effect—until they were seated at dinner. At that time, her father had glanced at her sadly and said, "I wish you would not mar yourself, Sophie." She never did it again.

When Henry had been their age, this sleeping room was his. The adjoining room, however, had been used for his father's mistresses. Following Ares' ascension, Henry had been moved to the south wing while the Surchatain's wing underwent extensive renovations. Then when the twins were born, the whole northeast corner of the second floor became their domain. And when Henry became a Green, he slept in the barracks with the other Greens.

Tonight, the girls made but a small impression in the center of the great bed. Bonnie whispered, "They're all gone. Can you tell me now?"

Sophie sat up, her little face somber in the dying firelight. (Evenings in June could still be cool, so one large, slow-burning log was usually burnt in bedroom fireplaces overnight.) "It was a ghost," she whispered. "A black ghost of death. I chased it out of the secret passage and it floated over the fig orchard wall. I was going after it when Henry stopped me and made me go back in," she said, disgusted.

"How do you know it was a ghost?" Bonnie shuddered.

"It was *all black*. It had *no face*," Sophie hissed. "And it left a dead man's token, just like Doudney said."

"Did you tell Papa about it?"

"Bonnie, you know he doesn't believe in ghosts. I can't just *tell* him about it—I have to *prove* it to him," Sophie said.

"How do you know it's trying to kill Papa? It may just be lost," Bonnie said wistfully.

"No. It was evil. I could feel it. I heard it rattle its fetters, and when it floated out into the orchard, it wouldn't stop when I shouted," Sophie said. "And I heard Counselor Carmine talking about the death threats Papa has been getting, and there was the challenge today, so I knew this was a ghost someone had called up to kill Papa."

Bonnie snorted impatiently. "Oh, you just got that from those ghost stories. That's why Papa told Doudney to stop reading them to us. Ghosts can't kill people! Besides, if Papa's in danger, why don't you tell him?"

"You don't understand," Sophie said, pouting. And Bonnie could not understand as long as Sophie held back the whole truth from her, which was: Sophie did not really believe that her Papa was in any danger from this ghost, or anyone. Hadn't she seen him kill the challenger just this afternoon? But this was something different, and exciting—a mystery that Sophie could explore all on her own.

She wanted Bonnie to help her, but if Bonnie refused to play along, then she would never see how pleased and surprised Papa would be when she got to the bottom of it all. Sophie envisioned herself leading Papa, Mama, and Counselor Carmine into a hidden room of the passage (just past that pile of rocks, she was sure) where the potions were mixed to summon the black ghost from its deathbed. Who was behind it? Giles, she thought. She never liked him. He was always trying to tell her what to do.

Plopping back down beside her sister, Sophie admitted, "Well, maybe it's not trying to hurt Papa. But wouldn't it be fun to find out what it really is?"

"Yes," Bonnie agreed.

"Then you'll help me?" Sophie asked, excited.

"Of course, silly. What do we do?"

"Tomorrow, we'll go to the secret passage again and wait for it!" Sophie said with resolve.

"Very well. Now let's go to sleep," Bonnie yawned. But Sophie lay awake for a long time, plotting their next move.

Immediately after Tanny had left the Surchatain's receiving room, Nicole entered, having succeeding in getting the girls to bed with less than an hour's story tonight. She nodded to Thom as he bowed to her, and only glanced at her husband on her way back to their bedchamber.

But that glance was pregnant with promise, so Ares rose immediately from the table. "Well, Thom—"

"Only one thing I wanted to apprise you of, quickly," Thom said. "Well, two things."

"Yes?" Ares said, with an almost desperate glance toward the bedchamber.

"First, the order of banishment was delivered to Lady Auer this afternoon. She has three days to settle her affairs and leave Lystra," Thom said.

"Good," Ares said, eyes on the bedchamber door.

"Also, I felt uneasy in my mind with one sentry in the secret passage. I assigned another to accompany him. Two should always be on watch, if possible," Thom said.

"Very well. Goodnight, Thom."

"Surchatain." Thom saluted, trying not to smile.

When Ares entered the bedchamber, the low glow of the fireplace ashes illumined Nicole waiting for him in bed. She was wearing her undergarments, loosened, but what caught his attention was her magnificent mane of chestnut hair, which she had just now taken down. She shook her head, and the glossy curls tumbled over her chest and shoulders. Ares shrugged off his shortcoat in one motion; as he was unbuttoning his shirt, a loud knock on the receiving-room door made him cringe. Nicole flopped back with a hopeless groan.

Still imagining that he could salvage the evening, Ares paced through the receiving room and opened the door. When he saw Giles standing determinedly in the corridor outside with his arms full of ledgers, his hopes were effectually crushed. And sure enough, by the time he got to bed hours later, he did not even attempt to wake her. So he just lay down at her back and gathered her close to him.

In the dead hour before dawn, Ares and Nicole were still entwined in the deepness of sleep. His left arm was tight around her ribcage; his face was buried in her neck, smothered with her hair. She, on her back, rested her right hand across his arm, while her left leg lay under his. If she felt any discomfort from his weight, it did not disturb her sleep. Neither of them heard the repeated, insistent knockings on the outer door of the receiving room.

When there was no reply, the visitor did an unprecedented thing: he entered the receiving room and knocked directly on the door of the bedchamber. Finally hearing, Ares sprang up, but Nicole merely rolled over.

The bedroom fire had completely died down, but Ares saw the glimmerings of light under the door in the receiving room. After pulling on lightweight cotton breeches that he kept by the bed, he pensively opened the door.

Thom stood outside in the receiving room with a sentry who carried a lantern. It was unclear whether the Commander had even been to bed that night. Ares shut the door to the bedchamber behind him, dread dropping in his stomach at Thom's hard face. "What is it?"

"I just now sent a pair to relieve the guards in the secret passage," Thom said. "They found one missing, and the other dead."

4

Ares stared at Thom without speaking for a moment. Then he asked, "How was he killed?"

Thom gave a short, bitter shake of his head. "I don't know. That he is dead is certain, but I saw no wounds. Doctor Savary is looking at him now."

"And is there no sign of what became of the second?" Ares asked.

"We are looking," Thom replied tersely.

Ares hung his head, closing his eyes. "Who was it?" he asked in a low voice.

Thom paused. "Riever is the man killed. Geurts is missing." Ares nodded. He did not know either of them, which meant they were new, and probably young. Thom added, "Surchatain, I recommend that, whatever we find, as soon as it is light, we seal up the passage again, this time with concretus —and post guards on the outside."

Ares nodded. "But search the passage thoroughly before it is sealed." With its irregular walls and nooks, it was possible for someone to hide in its shadows while it was being sealed— as had happened to Chiacos years before.

"Surchatain." Thom saluted and turned out again with the

sentry. They took their lantern, throwing the receiving room back into darkness as they closed the door.

Ares stood in the middle of the room, then turned toward the window, barely visible by the glints of far lights on the panes of glass. As was his custom, he opened this window and sat at it to pray. It was earlier than usual; sunrise was nowhere in evidence, but the need was too pressing to wait.

It had been years since he had lost a guard to intruders in his own city. Ares hated enough losing men in battle, but when they were killed in peace, it especially galled him. And in the palace—!

When he remembered that Sophie had been momentarily at this enemy's mercy, he broke into a cold sweat. But God in His kindness had not allowed harm to come to her, even shielding her from the realization of her peril.

"Lord God, highest lord of heaven and earth," Ares began in a whisper. "Surchatain Jesus, ruler of every province in every realm . . . help me know what to do. Send me insight, and wisdom, and defense, for I am weak and blind. I cannot see the purpose of this villainy. I cannot see the source of it. I cannot see how to answer it. Bring renown to your name in this, for I am nothing. . . ." He sat listening for voiceless encouragement, sifting through the chaff of drifting thoughts for the kernel of instruction that they might obscure.

He sat there a long time in halting prayer, feeling his way through the labyrinth of possibilities. The intruder must have been familiar enough with the palace at one time to know of a secret tunnel that had been sealed up eight years ago. It must be someone who would not arouse suspicion to be seen frequently in the vegetable garden. He had not attempted to use the upper levels, either to gain access to the Surchatain's quarters or for spying through the peepholes, but had been clearing away the obstruction to the outer wall. It would seem, therefore, that what he wanted was a secret access to the palace from outside—or vice versa.

Ares thought about Backvold's requesting use of the passage to transport his son, and wondered if the request was an attempt to cover his previous forays into the passage. But Backvold must know that such forays would become known. And the nobleman was too transparently shaken by his son's actions—Ares recognized a parent in distress.

He continued to think and pray, then when just enough grey light came upon the windowsill to see, Ares picked up his most recent little book, in which he copied down Scriptures and quotations that struck a chord in him. This he flipped open for appropriate words to meditate on, and the first thing he saw was: "For this God is our God for ever and ever: he will be our guide even unto death."

Ever since being in the portal, Ares had been haunted by the mystery of time. What was "for ever and ever"? What was eternity? For that matter, what was death, but a portal into timelessness? Like every other creature on earth, Ares would cross this portal some day—perhaps soon—and it was greatly strengthening to know that a compassionate, guiding hand would be on him that day.

With a moment's more reflection, however, he suddenly decided that there was another, more immediate facet to this verse: there was the promise that God would guide him to the cause of Riever's death.

Ares rose from the window seat and returned to the bedchamber to quietly sponge bathe, shave and dress while Nicole lay sleeping. He needed no light to do any of this, because his dress blacks were always put back in the same place after laundering, and he shaved by feel. So half an hour later he emerged ready for the day, and Nicole had never stirred.

He opened the receiving room door to the sentry standing in the corridor outside. "The kitchen mistress—what is her name?"

"Veola, Surchatain," the sentry replied, saluting.

"Veola. Summon her."

"Sir!" He moved off at a run, and moments later another sentry came to take his place.

Ares paced the receiving room, watching the orange glimmers of sunrise on the other horizon stretch over the far fields. Knowing that the kitchen servants began their day in the middle of the night, he would not have long to wait for the kitchen mistress—and moments later the knock on his door signaled Veola's arrival.

A very large woman, dignified, in command of her realm, she entered the Surchatain's receiving room with more curiosity than apprehension. Georges, the dinner master, set the day's menu in consultation with Nicole or Giles; Ares had never commented on the food other than to send occasional congratulatory gifts to the kitchen staff after they had particularly outdone themselves.

This morning, Veola curtsied, as well as such a large woman could. "My lord summons?"

"Yes, Veola. You may have seen some of the comings and goings recently around the outdoor passage I had sealed up some eight years ago. One door opens into the vegetable garden and another exits into the fig and plum orchard. I would like to know if you or any of your people have seen a stranger in the vicinity of the garden, a man who does not belong there."

"Many, Surchatain," she acknowledged with a tilt of her head.

"Many . . . ?" Ares gaped.

Veola explained, "The June festival, my lord. The Steward granted us permission to hire extra workers for harvesting and drying, making compotes and wreaths and such, so suddenly everyone 'round about Westford needing a silver piece or two has come tramping into the garden clamoring for work. As soon as the gates open, they flood in, and I fear I'll need soldiers today to clear away the lot of 'em. We've done hiring all the help we'll need."

Ares sagged in dismay. "Fine. Do that." He gestured at the sentry. "See that Mistress Veola has all the manpower she needs to keep trespassers out of the garden. And I want the names and villages of those hired for festival work."

"Surchatain." The sentry saluted and departed with Mistress Veola. Ares resumed pacing, contemplating this rude blow. Even if all of the villagers seeking work were innocent of this mischief, their presence would obscure the real culprit. Besides, the intruder had already achieved entrance and—here Ares stopped in midstride—how could he be sure that it wasn't someone already attached to the palace?

The knocking at the door made him jump, so that his voice had a catch in it when he called, "Enter!"

Another sentry opened the door. "Surchatain, the Commander requests your presence in the infirmary."

Ares exhaled, "I am coming."

Some minutes after he had gone, Nicole barely woke. The room was quite dark with no window, and the fire had burned down to grey ashes. But in her state of half-consciousness, she felt that someone was in the room. "Ares?" she murmured, lifting her head. But no one answered, so she lay down again and went back to sleep.

Meanwhile, Ares was descending the stairs with the sentry. The two of them turned off the staircase into the bustling foyer, already crowded with the business of the day, and Ares' eyes swept the occupants with vague unease. A traitor within the palace could do a vast lot of harm.

With the sentry at his elbow, Ares turned down the lower corridor leading to the infirmary. In the large receiving room, a few people, ill or injured, were waiting to see Doctor Savary or one of his assistants. Ares stepped into this room to be immediately beckoned to a small side room by the doctor himself.

Here, Thom was standing over the body of a young soldier laid out on a table. Ares looked down on him in distress as the doctor closed the door behind him. "Is this Riever?" Ares asked.

"Yes, Surchatain," Thom answered.

"How was he killed?" Ares asked Doctor Savary, who had come up beside him.

The doctor was young, but knowledgeable and deliberate. "I do not know, Surchatain. I have examined him carefully and found no marks on the body. It could be poison, but there was nothing found that could have been used to administer it, unless the assassin took it with him. But again, I find no bruises or marks of a struggle."

Ares was regarding the young casualty, who for all the world looked to be merely asleep, when the door banged open and what seemed like a horde of soldiers bustled in. In fact, it was only three—they carried a fourth who was moaning and catching his breath. "Geurts!" Thom exclaimed. "The other guard at the passage—"

"Lay him here," the doctor ordered, pointing to a second table against the wall.

As they did so, gently, Ares asked, "Where did you find him?"

"Just outside the wall, Surchatain—on the other side of the fig orchard," one said between breaths as they stepped back from the table.

Doctor Savary bent over the moaning patient to loosen his coat and examine him. Ares and Thom watched the doctor in tense silence while the three carriers dropped respectfully behind them.

After gently touching Geurts in the area of his bare chest and stomach, the Doctor turned to the Surchatain and Commander. "He appears to have several broken ribs, but I cannot tell how deeply he is hurt."

Ares nodded, leaning over the man. "Geurts, can you hear me?"

"Yes, Surchatain," he gasped.

"Very good. Can you tell me what happened?" Ares asked.

"As much I know. I was in the garden near the door, Riever just inside the passage with the door open a crack. It was—I don't know how long ago, but it was pitch black. I—heard him cry out, so I ran in. Riever was down—I felt something rushing to the end of the passage, so I—I—"

Geurts was momentarily overcome by the pain, so the doctor lifted his head to give him a draft of wine. Geurts drank, choked, and groaned. "It rushed out the door to the fig orchard, and I followed, though I could barely see ahead of me. Then it flew over the wall. I was climbing the wall after it when it doubled back and hit me straight in the chest," he said with a cough. "And I saw it no more."

"You did well, Geurts. The doctor will see to your injuries," Ares said, then jerked his head to Thom on his way out. Pausing, Ares pointed at the spokesman of the group who had brought Geurts in. "You—what is your name?"

"Kleven, sir." He saluted.

"You come with us." They started out, then Ares stopped so suddenly that the others almost ran into him. "What happened to Athian?" he asked Thom.

"His father took him last night," Thom quietly replied.

This news was additionally disquieting. Turning back to Doctor Savary, Ares asked him, "Did you see Backvold last night?"

The doctor looked up from his newest patient. "Yes, Surchatain. He brought a shroud and wrapped up his son as if he were dead, then made a show of carrying him out in a casket."

"How late was that?" Ares asked.

"It was before the gates closed for the evening, Surchatain. He wanted a large crowd to witness the body being removed," the doctor replied.

"Was Athian dead?" Ares asked.

"Not at the time he was taken out. I do not know how he fared after being moved," Savary said, intent on further examination of Geurts' injuries.

Ares paused to mutter to Thom, "I want to know whether Athian lives and if he has been removed from the province." Thom relayed the order to another, then he and Kleven followed Ares outside to the vegetable garden. Glancing over the numerous servants hauling in baskets of produce, Ares went to the door of the passage.

It stood open, two guards standing on the outside. They saluted as Ares and Thom approached, then stepped aside for the three to enter the passage with a lantern. Ares knelt and studied the disturbances in the dirt for a long time. "I see where Riever fell and Geurts entered," he said, pointing.

Then he stood and began walking slowly along the edge of the passage toward the front of the palace, holding the lantern close to the ground. "Then here are the footprints of our intruder, and these are Geurts' chasing him." Thom and Kleven followed, nodding. Ares returned to the doorway, saying, "But for all that, I do not see where our intruder entered. Thom—do you? Kleven?"

"No, Surchatain," Kleven replied, and Thom shook his head.

Ares looked more disturbed by the moment, but again leaving that for now, they went on down the passage to the second door, that to the fig and plum orchard. This door Thom propped open, as it would swing closed otherwise. They followed the trail of prints a few feet, then looked up at the hubbub of servants buzzing all over the orchard. The trail was buried under crisscrossing tracks from here on out. Ares turned to Kleven. "Can you show me from inside the orchard where you found Geurts?"

"I think so, Surchatain. This way. Commander," Kleven said, pointing. He led them on a straight path away from the passage door, past the spreading fig bushes to the ten-foot-tall stone wall. Finding toeholds between stone and mortar, Kleven scaled the wall as Geurts would have done in pursuit of the intruder. Walking atop the wall, which was about two feet thick, Kleven looked around and pointed. "There it is. That's where he was."

"Good." Ares then scaled the wall, with Thom following, and looked around. A stand of ancient oaks grew about thirty feet from the wall; beyond them was the road and beyond that, fields of summer wheat. Descending on the outside of the wall, Ares was careful to drop free of the tracks he wished to study.

Meanwhile, Thom stayed atop the wall. Ares took his time over the markings. "Yes—this is where Geurts fell. Who found him? You?" Ares asked Kleven, who replied in the affirmative. "And you called for help? And the other two ran from this direction to assist you?" Ares went on, all to Kleven's nodding.

Breathing out in exasperation, Ares scanned the ground in all directions. "Yes, I see all that! It's perfectly clear. What I do not see are any tracks from our intruder!"

"Surchatain." Thom knelt thoughtfully on the wall, and Ares looked up at him. "Did you think it strange that Geurts kept calling him 'it'? And . . . he said 'it flew' over the wall."

When Ares did not reply, Thom began to repeat himself, but Ares pointed over Thom's head, saying, "That's why."

Thom steadied himself on the wall to look up; Kleven craned his neck. And they saw that another ten feet above the top of the wall were the branches from the nearest oak tree thirty feet away. "That branch just above you is broken," Ares pointed out to Thom.

Thom protested, "But—he could not have jumped—"

"He had a rope," Ares said, scanning the branches. "He had a rope already tied in place. He swung out over the wall by means of the rope, then when Geurts followed, he swung back and struck him in the chest."

"Then Geurts would have fallen back to the inside of the wall," Thom argued.

"Not if he was already over the wall, or if he hit him a glancing blow. Had he kicked him full in the chest, Geurts would be dead as well," Ares said. Thom began to say something else, but Ares walked over to the trunk of the great oak and bent to study the ground around it.

"There," he said suddenly. "There are his tracks. He dropped from this tree and went—" Urgently, Ares began trotting with his eyes on the ground; Kleven was right behind him and Thom scaled down the wall to join them.

Ares broke through the stand of trees, following the tracks —then halted at the side of the road, already congested with traffic going to or from the palace. Instinctively, the three looked first one way, then the other, as if they might yet spot him. "Well, he used a rope. That's how he left no footprints, clever devil," Kleven mused.

"How he left no—" A strange look came over Ares' face, and he made a choking sound deep in his throat. He wheeled toward the nearest gate, as climbing this wall from the outside was nigh impossible. Thom and Kleven followed at a like pace.

Ares tore through the gate and ran back to the vegetable garden. The guards at the passage door were considerably startled when he grabbed a lantern and plunged into the dark tunnel with Kleven and Thom still on his heels.

Inside the passage, Ares knelt to study the prints again. Sure enough, he saw what he had missed the first time—they were square-toed boots, all right, but the telltale hobnail in the right heel was missing. Either the intruder had worn different boots last night, or there was a second man.

Jaw set, Ares lifted the lantern to look over his head at the ceiling. Its height varied as one progressed from the lower level to the upper—here, it was about ten feet. But even so, with just the lantern light, they could see the holes in the flooring beams of the room above. The trail of holes ran the length of the tunnel as far as they could see.

"What—?" muttered Kleven.

"He walked on the ceiling," Thom whispered in awe. "What do you suppose he used?"

"Some kind of adjustable chock, and rope," Ares said, face upraised. "This way, he left no sign of his presence, until Sophie saw him come out."

"Surchatain . . . did he—could he have deliberately made his exit during your match with Athian? When he thought everyone would be in the yard watching it?" Thom asked.

Ares turned to him pensively in the yellow lantern light, but Kleven, eyes still on the ceiling, had a further question that rattled Ares to his bones: "How far did he go?"

Heart hammering, Ares raised the lantern to stumble after the trail of holes up the steeply sloping passage to the second floor. He stopped at the door leading into the Surchataine's suite—no one slept here, at present. Nicole used the receiving room for personal matters and the bedchamber for storage. Bonnie and Sophie played occasionally in the Surchataine's receiving room but slept in Henry's old suite, which was not attached to the secret passage. But to satisfy himself, Ares rattled the rusty chains that secured this door closed, and they did not budge. The peephole to this bedchamber had been covered when the walls of this room were plastered several years ago.

Ares breathed out in some relief, but—the trail of holes led on, so he continued up the passage to where it terminated at the Surchatain's bedchamber. Here, his blood froze to see the disturbance in the dirt on the floor, which indicated that the intruder had dropped from the ceiling. Thom breathed: "The peephole has been dug out."

Handing the lantern to Kleven, Ares grabbed the rusty chains that secured the doorway, and they fell off in his hands. He pulled urgently on the handle while Thom put his shoulder to the other edge of the door, so that it opened readily into the great fireplace.

Blinking, Ares stepped into the warm ashes of the fireplace in his own sleeping chamber. Taking the lantern from Kleven again, he looked down at the ashes that had been scattered out onto the floor. Then he lifted the lantern toward the bed, and saw it mussed and empty. Nicole was gone.

5

Ares' breathing deepened to a rasp as he stepped toward the bed, left in disarray. Entering behind him, Thom ran to the door of the receiving room and threw it open, admitting some light from the window. He looked back to Ares with a brief shake of the head. That room was also empty. Before Ares could choke on the wrath and fear that welled up in him, something returned from his time of prayer this morning: there was a strengthening, a calmness that settled around him, freeing his mind to think. So he did. He looked around the bedchamber, thinking.

Every morning, Nicole followed the same routine: she would have her own prayer time, then eat a light breakfast in bed, after which Ursula, her maid, would help her dress and remind her of any appointments or obligations she had that day. Then Ursula would make the bed, straighten the room, and take laundry downstairs.

Today, there was no breakfast on the bedside table, eaten or not. There was no indication that Ursula had been here at all. But Ares walked around the bed deliberately, looking. Unless the night was very cold, Nicole slept in her undergarments, and then left them in the basket for Ursula to take downstairs after she was dressed. This basket held only Ares' dirty clothes.

He dropped on his knees to look under the bed, but found nothing. He opened the large standing wardrobe and saw nothing amiss, except—there was no sign that Nicole had dressed. And her scarlet robe, which matched his, still hung in the wardrobe. Ares closed it, then went back to the bed.

For the first time, he saw next to his own prints the tracks of the intruder on the rug leading from the fireplace to the bed. On these prints, the hobnail stood out starkly. Beside the bed, the footprints were smudged and overlapping—there had been a struggle. Then, with the ash worn off his feet, the prints of the intruder faded before they could tell Ares where he had gone.

Inhaling, Ares looked down the once-secret passage. It dead-ended just a few feet past this exit. Since the door from the passage to the Surchataine's quarters was still chained shut, that exit was not an option. Had the intruder taken Nicole out through the passage, the only exits that lay open to him were those downstairs, heavily guarded since early this morning. So he had to have taken her out through the palace. And how could he possibly do that?

Ares went out through the receiving room and opened the door. The sentry turned and almost jumped in surprise. "How long have you been there?" Ares asked him.

"Since—you yourself left this room, Surchatain!" he exclaimed.

"Every moment?" Ares asked.

The guard cringed. "I left only momentarily, to deliver messages."

Time enough to get her out, Ares thought bleakly. "Has anyone else come or gone?"

"No, sir."

"Summon the Surchataine's maid, Ursula," Ares instructed. The sentry nodded, setting off at a run, but looking back as if to see whether the Surchatain might disappear and reappear somewhere else.

Ares turned to Thom at his elbow. "Shut the gates. Search every room in the palace, beginning with this wing."

Thom gave these instructions to the approaching sentry, who sprinted away. But Kleven was still looking confused. "Pardon, Surchatain, but if the intruder decked Geurts jumping over the wall, then how—or when—could he come back to the tunnel and walk the ceiling up here to snatch the Lady Nicole?"

Ares looked at him. "You are assuming that there is only one," he said. "And that he left the palace at all."

At the same time that a sentry returned with Ursula in tow, the Second Rhode appeared leading a unit of men. The soldiers fanned out smartly to every doorway as Rhode saluted. "The gates have been closed, Surchatain, Commander. I have dispatched a unit to each wing of each floor. We should have all four floors searched within the hour."

Ares nodded vaguely, aware of a troubling inconsistency. Something was missing. He was overlooking something. . . . Shaking off the feeling, he turned to Ursula, who was standing in the receiving room. "Have you seen the Surchataine today?"

"No, Surchatain," she said, pouting. "She hasn't rung for me all morning, which is mighty strange." The embroidered cord that hung behind the bed ran through the floor to a bell in the maid's galley below. "You see, I wait right downstairs till she rings, which is usually about eight of the bells. . . ." As she continued to expound on the Lady Nicole's morning habits, and how she had not called upon her faithful maid to perform any of her normal duties this morning, Ares' face went slack. Staring at the wall behind her, he now knew what he had overlooked.

"She is not in the palace," he whispered. "He has taken her out."

"What?" Thom demanded. "Surchatain—how?"

Ares nodded toward the wall behind Ursula, where Roman's original five-by-six-foot banner hung—only it was gone. With his eyes fastened on the bare wall, he told Thom, "Question the guards and servants. See if any recall seeing a banner being taken out of the palace this morning. It would have been rolled up, carried or dragged. . . ."

Ursula, dismissed, flew down the stairs to report far and wide the stunning news that the Surchataine had been kidnapped out of her sleeping chamber.

By this time, Sophie and Bonnie had made their way out to the vegetable garden. But finding such a hubbub around the entrance to the secret passage, they quickly realized there was no exploring it. "What now?" Bonnie asked.

Sophie looked grave. "It got away over the orchard wall toward the trees. Don't ghosts hide among trees during the day, since they go up in smoke in the sunlight?"

"I don't know," Bonnie said, growing disinterested.

"Let's go ask Doudney," Sophie decided.

"Oh, no! He'll keep us and make us study!" Bonnie moaned.

"Look, I told you this might be dangerous. Are you going to help me?" Sophie demanded.

"You go ask Doudney, and I'll go ask Aunt Renée," Bonnie said.

"What does she know about ghosts?" Sophie asked derisively.

"She told me that her mother, Lady Vivian, is haunted by the ghost of her mother-in-law," Bonnie whispered.

"Really? All right, then—you go ask her, and I will talk to Doudney, and we'll meet up back in our room before lessons." The girls raced back to the stairway.

Minutes later, it was reported to Ares that, yes, a servant had been seen carrying out a large banner, rolled up, over his shoulder. When? Oh, perhaps half an hour ago—maybe longer. What did he look like? Well, he was tall—or rather short—and had brown hair—or black, depending on the witness. Ares dismissed them all. Then, searchers brought to him a black, hooded coat that had been tossed into a storage room. No one in the palace wore anything like it.

While the gates were shut and the searchers were combing the palace, Ares called for a canvass of persons on the palace grounds, including the standing army in the barracks, mess, and practice fields. Anyone whose identity and role in the palace could not be ascertained was to be brought to him. Anyone who was unaccountably missing was to be reported to him. Searchers were to seek out and set guards over Bonnie, Sophie, Carmine, Giles, Vogelsong, Renée, Melva and Henry. Additionally, he sent searchers out of the gates looking for a man carrying a banner, or witnesses who could point the way he might have gone. Then Ares sat in his receiving room with the hooded coat.

Over the next hour, the reports drifted back in to him. First, the sentries reported that Bonnie, Sophie, Melva and Henry were secured in the library with their tutor. Renée was in her quarters with a guard at the door, as were Carmine and Giles in their respective quarters. Vogelsong took longer to locate because, in preparation for the construction of a second library on the palace's fourth floor (which held only the treasury and nursery at present) he had been poring over ancient records that had been relegated to a distant downstairs storage room.

When Thom finally came to tell Ares that no unauthorized person had been located on the grounds, Ares nodded hazily, still holding the black coat. "Then open the gates. He is not here, and neither is she."

"He could have an accomplice remaining behind," Thom admitted. "But I don't see how we may discover *who*. . . ."

"We will not discover that until we catch our thief," Ares murmured. "Thom . . . have Lord Preus sent up."

"Surchatain." Thom saluted and left to see to the order, though he began to worry about Ares' mental state, in that he should be asking for Renée's dressmaker.

Meanwhile, the list of hirelings for the festival was brought to Ares. He sat to scan the sixty-five names and villages, then shook his head. What was he expecting to find? That the culprit would use his real name, underline it, and annotate it with his intentions? Laying the list aside, Ares took up the black coat that the searchers had found and sat at the window to study it minutely in the strong noontime light.

He turned the coat over in his hands, noting every detail. He picked one black hair about four inches long from the coat's shoulder, and then a second, similar hair from the upper back, and laid them over his palm to look at them in the light. He found a dead flea under one arm of the coat and nits along the collar. He continued going over the coat inch by inch, picking off eight wheat beards from both sleeves and the back of the coat. He smelled the coat, inside and out, and his eyes narrowed thoughtfully.

By this time, Lord Preus was shown into the receiving room. As he bowed, Ares, still sitting at the window, extended the coat to him. "Please tell me everything you can discern about this coat—where it was made, where it might be sold, who might buy it or wear it."

Sniffing, Preus took the coat to look down on it through his spectacles. "The first thing I can tell you, Surchatain, is that whoever owns it does not care about cleanliness!" he said, holding it distastefully at arm's length.

"I noticed that," Ares said.

Preus sighed, running a hand along the fabric. "An inferior wool, probably northern sheep—definitely northern."

"Northern Continental?" Ares asked.

"No, Surchatain, northern Lystran—bred between the Poison Greens and the Fastnesses," Preus answered. "It is coarse wool, poorly carded, unevenly woven, badly dyed. Its only merit is that it is cheap," he said with curled lip.

"I see. What about the cut?" asked Ares.

Preus held up the knee-length coat by the shoulders. "This is a popular style for outdoorsmen who work in the cold for long hours, and need to keep their arms free. The generous hood allows for hats and scarves underneath, you see. The arms are also longer than is standard, to help protect the hands from the cold. But the vent up the back from the hem to the seat allows for riding. This particular cut is favored by mercenaries clear from Dansington to Eurus."

A light went on in Ares' eyes. Who would wear a black cold-weather riding coat in June but someone who wished not to be seen in the dark? "Thank you, Lord Preus. You have been most helpful."

The master tailor bowed. "I would give everything I possessed, Surchatain, for the lady to be restored whole to you."

"Thank you, Lord Preus. You are dismissed," Ares said quietly.

After the tailor had gone, Ares summoned Thom again and told him, "We are looking for a Polonti mercenary who came back and forth through the wheat fields, scaling the wall by means of the overhanging oak branch. He—or his companions—have taken Nicole to the inn in Dansington. You may be able to catch them with fast horses before they arrive. They will have discarded the banner by now, so you must look for other means by which they will hide a—person."

Thom stared at him, then said levelly, "I will send my fastest riders at once, Surchatain." He exited so quickly that he inadvertently slammed the door in his wake. Ares continued to sit at the window, looking out over the fields. He called in the sentry to give an order that the oak branches overhanging the orchard wall be cut back to the trunk. And, he said, "Tell Oswald that I want every door in the passage sealed up again —this time with concrete. It will not be opened again."

Several minutes later, Thom returned to report, "Surchatain, I have sent a unit of fifty riders under Crager and Derrick with instructions to search just as you commanded. But . . . if you would, please tell me how you knew so—specifically that we are looking for a Polonti mercenary on his way to Dansington."

Ares nodded to the black coat on the floor at his feet. "You know that the Polonti are all of a type, with brown skin and straight, black hair."

"Yes," Thom nodded. It was unnecessary for him to point out that Ares' ancestor, Roman, was half-Polonti.

"I found hairs on the coat that could only be Polonti. And Lord Preus told me that the style of the coat is favored by mercenaries from Dansington to Eurus. That is a rather desolate area, you know, with few houses. But the inn in Dansington—which is a favored meeting place for mercenaries—uses poorly dried peat for fuel that smells rank. The odor clings yet to this coat," Ares said.

"I see," Thom breathed. "Then our chances of recovering the lady have risen greatly. I will await the return of the search party. Do you have any other commands?"

"Only a request . . . that you would pray for her," Ares whispered.

Saluting with less than his usual snap, Thom left. Ares remained at the window, looking out over the fields.

Shortly thereafter, a sentry knocked at the door. Ares turned his head languidly, willing the sudden constricting of his gut to ease. "Enter."

Doctor Savary stepped inside, a pensive look on his face. "Surchatain, pardon. I now believe I know how Riever was killed. I cannot believe I missed it earlier."

Ares sat up. "Yes?"

"I was going through his clothes when I found this. It had fallen down inside his shirt." The doctor held out a small square of cloth, somewhat stiff. Ares took it, frowning, then noted the noxiously sweet odor emanating from it. The doctor explained, "I believe that this cloth was drenched in a potion called bozah that puts a man to sleep when held over his face. I've never had occasion to study the raw stuff—it is illegal almost anywhere on the Continent, you know, and what is left here has dried, and so lost much of its potency—but I have heard accounts of its use—"

"—that when too much of it is used, the sleep can result in death," Ares said, nodding. "And since determining the right amount seems tricky, it is banned in almost every treaty. Only mercenaries risk using it. Even slave traders don't," Ares said. Handing back the cloth, he added, "Thank you, doctor. Keep me advised."

Savary bowed and departed. Ares sat for a moment, then leaned over and picked up the coat from the floor. He put his nose to the sleeves, particularly the cuffs, and detected faint traces of the same sweet odor. Dropping the coat, he went back to the bedchamber, leaving the door open wide to admit the light. Then he began shaking out the bedsheets, the pillows, and the covering. A small square of cotton cloth fell out. Ares picked it up and turned it over in his hands, but it was not necessary to hold it to his nose in order to detect the bozah.

Ares left the bed coverings in a jumbled heap and returned to the window seat in the receiving room. Some minutes later, another sentry knocked. "Enter," Ares said.

The sentry stepped just inside the door. "Surchatain, your daughters request an audience."

"Send them in."

The words were hardly out before Bonnie and Sophie came rushing to their father with tear-streaked faces. They threw themselves on him at the window, Bonnie crying, "Papa, what has happened to Mama?" while Sophie wept, "I thought it was just a ghost."

Without seeming to hear either, Ares held them, one on

each arm, as he had done since they were infants. "Quiet, Chataines," he said in mild reproof. They sniffled to relative silence, and he said, "She has been taken, but I have sent men to bring her back."

"Papa, who would take Mama?" Sophie asked brokenly.

"I do not know," he said.

"*Why* would they take her, Papa?" Bonnie demanded, her indignant self rising to the occasion.

Distress crossed his face, but Sophie asked, "Why did you not go bring her back yourself, Papa?"

His face cleared, and he explained, "Because others ride faster than I do, dear one. And if she is not where I think she is, then I may need to send someone elsewhere, quickly. The Ruler must learn to use his men as extensions of himself, because he cannot be everywhere at once. Do you understand?"

"Yes, Papa," Sophie murmured.

They quieted down on his arms, eyes closed. But when another knock came on the door a few minutes later, they sprang up. Ares gave permission to enter, and Henry stepped in, saluting. He tried to stand straight and soldierly, but his grey eyes were rimmed in red. "I just came to . . ." he barely opened his mouth, and Bonnie burst into tears again. Fighting back tears himself, he insisted, "You found me and brought me back. You will find the lady."

"Yes, Henry. We will," Ares said.

"May I . . . wait with you?" he asked.

"Here, Henry. You can sit over here by me," Sophie said, patting the window seat beside her as she sat on her father's leg. She may have been feeling a little penitent for her hard words to Henry when he had found her at the wall and made her come back in. Henry availed himself of her invitation, and sat beside them.

It was not long afterwards that another knock signaled the appearance of Renée and Melva. Renée tried to be nonchalant and breezy, but Melva was more transparently anxious. She was small and slight for nineteen, and in her present state, gave the impression of a little woodland creature that had been caught and caged. Ares gave them permission to wait with him as well.

Georges, the dinner master, was the next to seek entrance, requesting to know what the Surchatain would like to do about the seating at dinner. Ares looked out the window again in the late afternoon. "There will be no dinner tonight," he said.

"Surchatain?" Georges said, shocked.

"Dinner is canceled. Serve the household what the kitchen has prepared, but we will not gather for dinner without my wife," Ares said, gazing over the far fields.

"Yes, Surchatain. Would—my lord and his family care to dine here?" Georges asked in slight confusion.

"Yes, Georges! Bring us a nice picnic dinner," Renée said, always willing to make the best of someone else's bad situation.

Georges bowed and left badly shaken. In his twenty-two years of service, through assassinations, wars, plagues, and invasions, dinner at Westford had never before been canceled.

Oswald was the next to appear at the door, traces of drying concretus clinging to his work breeches. "Surchatain," he saluted, with a look of steel in his eyes, "the passage shall not be breached again as long as the palace walls stand."

"Thank you, Second." Ares smiled wanly.

"Requesting permission to ride after the search party, Surchatain," Oswald said stiffly.

"You're not fast enough to get there in time to do them any good, Oswald," Ares said.

"Sir—respectfully—you entrusted her to my care when you sent her away from Magnus and Tancred. You took me with you to get her out of that tower in Eurus. You must let me ride after them now! I cannot sit here and do nothing!" he exploded.

"Then go," Ares said quietly. Henry bounded up from his seat, but Ares just looked at him and uttered, "No." Henry slumped back down to the window seat.

Caught off guard at the unexpected leave, Oswald managed to salute before treading out. The solid, stone-reinforced floor shivered a bit under his step. Sophie buried her face in her father's black shortcoat.

"If anyone were to find her, it would be him," Renée observed. "He's the stubbornest man I think I've ever known. Do you know, once last week he wouldn't let me out after dark to make an emergency visit to Aron the jeweler?"

Oswald had stood up to Renée? Everyone looked at her in wonder, then at the door in renewed hope.

Not long after, another visitor desired entrance—one who made everyone in the room fall silent, all breathing suspended. Ares left the window seat for the first time in hours just to meet him halfway across the room. For this man, Lieutenant Moeck, was one of the riders sent to Dansington. He was one whom Ares knew. And he carried into the room a large banner, rolled up tightly. "Surchatain," he saluted. "We found this thrown off into the trees about a third of the way to Dansington."

Ares carefully unrolled the banner of his great-great-grandfather, Roman, that had been hanging in this room until this morning. In so doing, he lifted off it one long, chestnut-colored strand of hair. "Thank you, Lieutenant Moeck. You are dismissed."

6

All those in the room watched while Ares calmly rehung the banner in its place on the wall. "She—they carried her out in that?" Henry asked, stricken.

Ares cleared his throat. "Yes," he said, his back to them.

Bonnie fell onto Renée in a weeping fit. She held the girl gingerly, patting her on the back while keeping her wet face at bay, whispering, "The silk, dearest. Take care for the silk."

"Papa, what does that mean?" Sophie asked in agony.

He turned from the wall. "That we are getting close."

"How?" she cried.

"They took her on that road, Sophie. I wasn't even sure they had taken her that way," he said.

"But, Papa . . . you had to know. You're the Surchatain. You know everything," she insisted.

"Sophie, if I knew everything, they never would have been able to take her in the first place," he pointed out.

The abrupt realization of her father's fallibility crushed her. "But . . . but. . . ."

"Did I know everything, I would have no need to pray to God," he went on.

This she grasped. "Have you prayed for her, Papa?"

"All day," he said, reseating himself to take her on his lap and look out the window again. "Since the moment I knew she was gone."

"When your men find her, how long would it take them to bring her back?" Melva asked timidly.

"If they find her. . . . It depends on where. It is a day's ride to Dansington, so if she has been taken that far, the soonest our scouts could return with her would be tomorrow sometime," he said.

"Ooh, this is the worst waiting ever!" Bonnie exclaimed. "It's worse than waiting for the festival! Do you know that Aunt Renée is buying both of us new dresses for the festival?" Bonnie asked her sister excitedly.

Sophie screwed up her face in derision. "Who cares?"

"Wouldn't you like to be pretty, for a change?" Bonnie pleaded.

"I'm just as pretty as you!" Sophie shot back.

"Chataines! Enough," Ares said irritably, and Sophie laid her head on his chest again. The six of them continued to wait under the burden of heavy, creeping minutes.

Presently, Georges and his staff brought up their dinner of shirred eggs, baked smelts, lentil and short-rib stew, and steamed fig pudding for dessert. In order to accommodate the diners in a meeting room, the servants set up makeshift tables.

Ares directed that those waiting with him be served, but when Georges offered to set up his dinner before him on the windowseat, the Surchatain declined, looking out to the sunset spread over the horizon. On the other side of the palace, on the other side of the world, morning would come again.

In the midst of non-dinner, another visitor requested entrance. Carmine came in and bowed, then stood almost awkwardly among the servants who bustled around him. "Surchatain, I . . . heard that you were dining alone with family tonight, and I. . . ." For possibly the second time ever, Carmine's faculty for prepared speech failed him.

"Of course you may eat with us, dear Carmine," Renée said. Throwing a hand toward a servant, she ordered, "Set the Counselor a place here with Bonnie and myself." The servant, Georges, Carmine, and everyone except Renée and Bonnie looked at Ares. He smiled slightly, nodding, and Carmine was seated with the family.

Henry and Sophie were at a small table next to Ares on the window seat. When she saw the empty space in front of her father, she demanded, "Papa, where is your dinner?"

The others then noticed that, in fact, he did not have a plate. He said, "I will eat when your mother can join me."

Sophie and Henry simultaneously pushed away their plates. The others were studying the savory dishes in front of them with concerned indecision when Ares said, "The rest of you must eat. I will need you strong and alert." Since no one here would think of defying Ares on important matters, they certainly were not going to defy him over dinner.

They ate as the sun set and the servants brought in extra tapers to light the room all around. Renée grew restless, as there was obviously to be no dancing, and her suggestion to play games was met with strained silence.

Bonnie and Sophie were tired and cranky with the waiting and the apprehension. Leaving Renée, Bonnie wandered over to her father and climbed up on his lap. Sophie jealously scooted closer to his side. Yawning, Bonnie said, "Papa, we need a story. Mama always tells us a story at bedtime. Tell us a story."

Ares looked confounded. "I . . . don't know any stories, Bonnie."

"I will tell you a story," Melva offered. Everyone looked at her in surprise, especially Renée, who had forgotten that she was there.

"All right, if it's a good one," Bonnie said cautiously.

"What makes a good story?" Henry asked curiously.

"One with no boys!" Bonnie snapped.

"You will have to decide whether it is good or not. This story is about a girl who grew up in a village at the foot of the Fastnesses. Her mother died when she was just about your age, so her father began to take her with him on his travels, for he was a minstrel, and he went to all the great houses and royal courts singing and playing his lyre.

"Our little girl—I will call her Ella—loved going on these trips with her father, for she got to see many new things and interesting people. She learned how to read, which was a great accomplishment for someone of her station. She learned all about the countryside they traveled through, and she learned all about how the fine families lived. Ella wanted to be like them, so one night she prayed to God to let her live in a great house with a royal family," Melva told them.

"Then one day a terrible thing happened. As Ella and her father were traveling to the next town, they were set upon by a band of slavers. Ella's father was killed trying to protect her, and the slavers bound her hand and foot, put her in a cart, and took her to Corona to sell her in the slave market. It was a horrible, scary, dirty, noisy place, and Ella was very frightened. She cried and she cried. The slavers put her up on a large platform where people began bidding to buy her," Melva said. Bonnie showed signs of uneasiness, but Sophie listened intently. Ares was debating whether to interrupt, but decided to wait to see how explicit this story would get.

Melva continued, "A man in fine clothes bought her, and loaded her on a wagon with four or five other slaves he had bought—because now that is what she was. They joined a caravan and traveled to a distant province. Here they went up to the top of a great mountain standing all by itself, and the slaves were taken out to work. Ella discovered that she would be personal maid to the Chataine of the province, who was just a baby.

"So Ella began her duties. She fed the baby from a bottle, bathed her, changed her clothes, and watched over her just like a nursemaid. As the baby grew older, Ella taught her everything that she had learned herself about courtly life: how to dress, how to speak, how to read, and how to comport herself at table. Ella and the Chataine became very good friends," Melva said.

"Then one day, when the Chataine was about twelve years old, her father heard that the Surchatain of a nearby province had lost his wife, and was looking for another. So the Chataine's father made arrangements to send his daughter, in the company of Ella, to interview with the neighboring Surchatain to be his wife.

"But the night before they were to leave, Ella discovered that there was a plot afoot to kill the Chataine and her father, and take over the throne. So Ella left in secret with the Chataine and a Polonti guide. They escaped the soldiers who were supposed to protect them—but were really paid to kill them—and made the dangerous, three-day journey to visit the Surchatain who wanted a wife." There was not another sound in the room while everyone listened to Melva's story.

"The three of them were chased by wolves and slavers the whole way down, but because of Ella's courage and the skill of the Polonti guide, they arrived safely. But then they discovered that the Chatain of another province—I will call him Angus—wanted to kidnap the Chataine and marry her in order to gain control of her province. So Ella, to protect her charge, changed places with her. Ella posed as the Chataine so that when Angus invaded the city and stormed the palace to kidnap her, he believed Ella to be the Chataine he was looking for. She went with him willingly so that he would call off his attack and take his soldiers out of the city.

"When Angus and Ella arrived at his capital city, she resolved to tell him the truth about who she was, and take whatever punishment he should mete out to her. But then they were attacked by his younger brother, who had mustered soldiers to challenge Angus for the throne. There was a terrible battle, with many deaths, before Angus chased his brother into hiding. But Ella had been so brave and loyal to him through it all that Angus fell in love with her. So when she told him the truth—that she was a slave, not a Chataine—he said, 'I do not care, because now you are Surchataine.' So Ella and Angus were married, and had a son, and ruled their province in peace and prosperity," Melva finished.

"That's a good story," Bonnie sighed, and Sophie agreed. Smiling slightly, Ares watched Melva. The story was not entirely fictitious: it was about Melva's maid, Druella, and how she and Chiacos brought Melva herself to the palace at Westford when the former Surchatain Cedric (Henry and Renée's father) was looking for a new wife. Angus was in fact Magnus, who did indeed attack Westford to take Druella, whom he believed to be the Chataine of Qarqar. Magnus and Druella now ruled Scylla, and had a son who was a few months older than the twins. Ares had not heard that Magnus' younger brother, Tancred, had challenged Magnus' rule, but that was to be expected.

Renée would have recognized the story had she been paying attention, but she lost interest the moment it became apparent that the heroine was a slave. However, Henry and Carmine were watching Melva with knowing eyes.

"What happened to the real Chataine?" Carmine asked. "Did she ever get to rule her own province?"

"She doesn't want to," Melva said, looking aside.

Carmine glanced at Ares, who tilted his head quizzically, but Bonnie and Sophie were now very sleepy, having been fed dinner and a story. So, leaving Melva's enigmatic statement hanging unquestioned, Ares called in the sentry and nodded toward his daughters: "The Chataines are ready to retire to their chambers for the evening. Escort them and summon their maids."

They came directly awake. "No, Papa! We want to stay with you!" cried Sophie.

"What if we get snatched, too?" cried Bonnie.

"Papa, we want to know when Mama comes home," Sophie pleaded.

"I'll be afraid, watching for the wall to move all night. And you said it was a ghost!" Bonnie swung a small fist at her sister.

"Chataines!" Ares bridled his irritation, remembering they were only little girls. So he patiently explained, "The secret passage never ran by your chambers. Even if it did, it has been sealed with concretus. There are guards at your door and more guards at the head of the corridor. And, I promise that I will come wake you when your mother comes home." But this time, he had caught the mention of a ghost, and realized that Sophie had seen more than she admitted. But now was not the time to pursue that point.

"Allow me to escort them to their chambers," Carmine said, rising. "I thank you for the privilege of sharing your intimate dinner, Surchatain. And I thank you for the story, Chataine Melva. I shall be interested to hear more about the Chataine." He bowed.

The girls kissed their father and went with Carmine across the corridor. He deposited them in their quarters before their maids arrived, so Sophie turned to her sister with determination and said, "We are going to help Papa find out who has taken Mama."

"How can we?" Bonnie asked crossly, for she was tired.

"I don't know. But if a slave girl can grow up to be Surchataine, we should be able to help Papa," Sophie said stubbornly.

"All right. Tomorrow," Bonnie yawned, then sighed, "I hope she comes home soon."

"Why? You said you wished Aunt Renée was your mother," Sophie said spitefully.

Bonnie looked at her with wide, wounded eyes, then burst into tears. Sophie threw her arms around her in remorse. "I'm sorry, Bonnie. I didn't mean it. We'll help Papa find her tomorrow." Bonnie sniffled and nodded, then the maids came in.

Back in Ares' receiving room, Renée stood in a swirl of silk and damask. "We shall be retiring, as well. Come, Melva." Renée was much too proud to ask for an escort to walk the dark, shadowy stone corridors, but she did not want to walk them alone.

As they left, she muttered to Melva, "Darling, such a charming story. But you really should work up something a little more believable." Melva smiled privately.

When they had all gone, Ares looked pointedly at Henry, who was trying to remain inconspicuous by the window. Henry slumped, spreading his hands in appeal. "You have to let me stay, Ares. I know I'm just a Green, but—two should always share a watch," he repeated one of the maxims taught to the Green recruits.

Reflecting on that, Ares nodded. "You're right, Henry. Go bring you out some bedding to rest, and I will take the first watch." He jerked his head toward the bedchamber, neglecting to tell Henry that he had no intention of waking him to take a watch.

Encouraged, Henry brought out a couple of blankets and pillows, and lay down on the receiving room floor. A servant entered, offering to kindle a fire in the fireplace, but Ares dismissed him with the grate dark and cold. A few candles were still lit around the room, which was all Ares needed. Too much warmth made it harder to stay awake. As he would not eat, so he would not sleep till she was home.

Henry propped his head up on his hand so as not to fall asleep too quickly. Talking helped him pass the time and stay awake, so he introduced a topic: "I want to sit for certification, Ares. I'm ready. I can answer anything Giles throws at me."

Ares leaned forward, smiling. "Then you know that Giles' questions are not that important."

Dead Man's Token

"Well, even so, I have to know the answers, don't I?" Henry asked.

"Not necessarily. Nicole did not answer any of his questions right, and still passed," Ares observed.

Henry snorted, "That's because she's your—" His better judgment prevailed to silence him midsentence.

Ares regarded him with the same half-smile. "If anything, her being my wife made it that much harder for her, as I had to prove my objectivity." He paused. "Do you want to know why she really passed?"

"Yes," Henry said almost defensively.

"She wanted to know the Law for its own sake, for what it had to teach her, not because of what being certified would do for her, as far as any honor it would bring. She understood that she needed to *live* the Law, and not just know it, and that kind of understanding comes with time, Henry. Not necessarily from memorizing facts," Ares said, not unkindly.

"You're saying that I'm not old enough," Henry said dully.

"Yes," Ares replied.

"Then when will I be old enough?" Henry asked.

"I'll let you know."

Try as he might, Henry could not find that unreasonable. There was a long silence while Ares looked out into the night toward a road that he could not see from this window. Then Henry said, "Melva's story was almost too painful to listen to. . . . She was talking about her maid, Druella, wasn't she?"

Ares turned from the window. "Yes, Henry; I believe so."

"Yes. I remember her. It was a long time ago. Still, when she talked about being up on that platform, and watching people shout out bids for you . . . I felt all scared and weak all over again. I still have nightmares about the squirming maggots in the meal, and the bloody whips, and the dead bodies shackled next to me. Sometimes I wonder if I will ever get over the—the—fear."

Ares paused, feeling his own fear for his dove. It was like an open wound that oozed bloody pus at any touch. "Fear is useful, Henry." Ares' deep scar, a black chasm in his face, spoke most eloquently on that issue. "Use your fear. Let it drive you toward what you must eventually face."

Henry let his heavy head slip from his hand to the pillow. "But . . . Nicole wasn't taken by slavers, was she?"

"No. I don't think so," Ares said.

"Then we will find her. You found me, after I was taken. . . ." He closed his eyes and immediately fell asleep. By the faint yellow candlelight, Ares watched his face relax in unconsciousness.

Two years ago, Henry had taken a horse and run off in a fit of pique, only to be captured by the slavers. No one at Westford had any idea what had happened to him. He was sold to a noble family in Hornbound, and by sheer luck—or the grace of God—Ares was able to find him and bring him home. So now Henry seemed certain, as did the others, that Nicole would soon be recovered and this disgusting business of kidnapping put to rest. They did not know about the deadly potion. Nor did they have the fear that Ares had of this Polonti who had taken her.

Leaning back against the window casing to look at the shimmering stars and breathe in the cool night air, Ares thought about his faceless adversary. Isolated for the most part in Eledith, separated from the rest of the southern Continent by the Fastnesses, the Polonti were easy to spot whenever they did venture beyond Polontis.

The only Polonti Ares had ever known well was Chiacos. In transporting Melva and Druella from Hornbound to Westford, past slavers, wolves, and the Poison Greens, carrying a fabulous gold reliquary worth hundreds of royals, Chiacos had demonstrated the best attributes of his race—strength, hardiness, resolve, perseverance, and trustworthiness. Then after spending several days trapped in the secret passage, he had emerged to prove himself an able ally in the defense of Westford against Magnus' attack.

Since the Polonti had such a strong sense of honor and loyalty, few turned mercenary, where they sold their services to the highest bidder regardless of the task required—which usually involved bloodshed. Therefore, those Polonti who had no scruples about turning mercenary were doubly dangerous.

Just last year Roerich, the administrator of the palace at Crescent Hollow, had captured a notorious Polonti mercenary by the name of Chau who had terrorized the countryside for months. This man's arrival had caused such a panic in one village that the whole population, some seventy-five souls, fled to the church for safety. Finding them all so conveniently gathered, Chau barred them inside and then burned the church down around them. Thus he was able to spend the next several days looting the village at his leisure. When Roerich finally caught him, he had him drawn and quartered.

But there were more like him out there. For such a mercenary to seek out information about a long-sealed secret passage, then use it to enact a daring abduction, could only mean that someone was willing to pay him a large sum of money. Who? Which one of Ares' thousand enemies wanted his wife, the Surchataine of Lystra, in his hands?

The sudden agony of this thought drove him off the window seat to silently pace at Henry's head. *I must not lose control now*, Ares thought. *I must not be controlled by thoughts of what might happen to her*—But even as he resolved that in his mind, he was assaulted by the ferocity, the horror, of what twisted men would do to a beautiful woman out of sheer evil—"God!" he cried in distress.

Henry bolted up, but at the same moment came a pounding on the door: "Surchatain! They've found her! They're bringing her!"

"Dead or alive?" Ares shouted at the closed door.

"I do not know, Surchatain."

7

Ares opened the door with Henry at his elbow. "What do you know?"

The sentry reported, "A rider has just arrived. He is still downstairs—"

Without waiting to hear more, Ares left the receiving room for the first time in ten hours. He swung around the head of the stairway and descended at a pace that left Henry a dozen steps behind. Arriving in the hollow, echoing foyer, dark but for the low fire and sentry's lantern, Ares saw the scout bending over his knees, panting. At Ares' approach, he straightened, saluted, and gasped, "Fawler reporting, Surchatain."

"What do you know?" Ares asked. Henry came up behind him. Several other sentries approached with lights.

The soldier took a breath and began, "Halfway to Dansington we caught up with a wagon of wares and passed it, but something made Captain Crager turn back and demand to search the wagon. Just as he started to search, we were set on by renegades hiding in the trees along the road, and the wagon driver turned like mad back down the road.

"We gave chase halfway again back to Westford, fighting

renegades on our flanks the whole time while the wagon made for the crossroads to try to escape us. He might have! But there, by my life, was Oswald on his great bay blocking the whole dam' crossroads! Carts and riders backed up on every road, ever' one of 'em cursing 'im to get out of the way! But the Second stood firm, and the wagon had nowhere to go. We caught up to it, then.

"There was a short fight. I had my sword at work and saw nothing else until the Captain grabbed me and ordered me to ride back and report that the Surchataine was being carried home," Fawler finished. Henry looked back and forth between the soldier and the Surchatain, silently pleading for reassurance that she was being carried home alive.

"How is she?" Ares asked patiently.

Fawler opened his mouth. "I . . . jumped on my horse to ride when the Captain ordered me to, sir. I did not stop to question him."

"You did as you should. Where is the Commander?"

"In the courtyard, Surchatain," the rider said, jerking his head.

"Well done, Fawler." Ares then turned toward the great, iron-banded double doors that were held open by sentries. He trotted down the stone steps into the large cobbled courtyard, deserted but for the soldiers who stood on watch with torches. More soldiers manned the parapet above the open gates, watching intently down the road. Standing in between the gates, looking out into the deep darkness of a cloudy night, was Thom.

Ares drew up beside him. "They should be appearing momentarily, Surchatain," Thom said without inflection.

Ares nodded, gazing without focus. "Your men have done well, Thom."

"We will see," Thom replied.

They stood in the night, the torches behind them making the cobblestones blaze with reflected firelight. A light breeze lifted mingled scents of honeysuckle and lavender from the children's garden on their right, close to the gate.

That area had been a trash dump until Nicole had convinced him to have the refuse removed to a pit a good distance from the palace. Then she had gathered shovels and rakes, and all the children in the palace who desired to help, and began digging a garden.

The first several days only a few children showed any interest (none of whom was Bonnie or Sophie), but by the end of the week she had an army of helpers (including Bonnie and Sophie). She had done so much. . . .

Thom sucked in his breath. Ares felt it through his feet before hearing it—the pounding of hoofbeats coming down the road. Henry pressed forward and the sentries on the parapet held the torches high, so as to be seen from a distance.

The clattering of many hooves over the old wooden bridge reverberated in Ares' chest, and he closed his dry mouth, attempting to swallow. Thom gestured for him to drop out of the way as a wave of riders on sweating, panting, snorting beasts suddenly converged on the courtyard. There were shouts and confused milling, prancing horses that flung saliva as their heads were turned by riders looking for the Surchatain. He was searching dazedly for one slender form among the moving shadows.

"Here, now! There!" someone shouted, and Oswald on his huge bay gelding rode up toward Ares and Thom, solemnly saluting.

There was a dreadfully still, blanketed figure resting in front of his saddle; Ares' eyes fastened in recognition on the small white feet that protruded from the bottom of the blanket. The form moved, and a hand appeared that pulled the blanket down from a head of tousled chestnut hair. The hand then gathered the hair off a face which blinked as it weakly uttered, "Ares?"

He did not remember coming forward; all he knew was

that she was let down into his arms amid the respectful, gratified silence of the soldiers and the rushing of the blood in his ears. He rocked her, feeling the warmth of her body, then cupped one hand around her face to see her smile tiredly at him. Holding her, he could not speak a word for the wellspring of emotion.

Then he flung the blanket off her shoulders to look for injuries. "Ares!" she exclaimed in reproach while hundreds of eyes looked away. She bent to retrieve the rough woolen blanket and recover herself.

"Are you hurt?" he asked.

"No, but I beg my lord to regard that I am in my underwear," she whispered as if no one else knew. And she was, though the white linen bodice and bloomers were now soiled and torn.

Then Ares looked around as if waking from a nightmare. "Ring the bells to announce the Surchataine's homecoming," he ordered. "Stable these horses. Bring these men into the great hall. Summon Carmine to write commendations for them all—and wake the kitchen!" He was suddenly quite hungry.

There was a rush into the palace, stomping and cheering, congratulatory smacks on everyone's back and organized bedlam as lamps were lit and fires rekindled. "It will be so nice to bathe and eat," Nicole said tiredly. "I haven't had a bite all day."

"Nor have I." Ares paused at the foot of the stairs. "I promised to wake the girls when you were brought home."

"Please let me bathe," Nicole groaned.

Something behind them caught her eye, and she turned to see Henry. "Welcome home, Lady Nicole," he said, eyes full to brimming.

"Oh, Henry." She hugged his neck and looked over at Thom's approaching.

"There are many men who were not able to greet you on the road, Lady—myself included—and wish to do so," he said, jerking his head toward the proud, exhausted riders, some wounded. Doctor Savary's assistants were attending to them now.

"I must thank them all," she said, turning back toward the foyer.

Ares gestured to a servant. "Have Georges set up the table for these men in the great hall. We will have dinner now." The bells in the tower began tolling to wake the whole palace.

Someone muttered, "It will take an hour just for everyone to get into formal dress."

"Forget the formalities! Just—tell everyone to come in their nightclothes," Ares said crossly.

"Ares!" Nicole protested, shocked.

"They have robes! You have a robe. No one need be indecent," he insisted.

"Easy for you to say, my lord! There you are in your dinner dress!" Nicole laughed.

Impatiently, Ares stripped off his black jacket and white frilled shirt. "I will wear my robe, as you do yours. Come now." He would have carried her up the stairs, but she eluded him, running up the stairs by herself. It was a great relief to exercise legs that had been bound all day.

Word spread through the palace that, in the insanity of his joy, the Surchatain had ordered an immediate celebration in bed attire. He allowed Nicole the briefest bath before she donned her scarlet robe and put her hair up in a ponytail, as appearing in public with loose hair was too daring even for such an informal affair.

As promised, Ares stripped off his black boots and pants to put on his matching robe. Nicole had a dainty pair of silk slippers to wear, but Ares went barefoot, which, when he was seen, aroused talk that lasted for weeks. Everyone solemnly attested that Ares had never in recorded memory appeared barefoot outside his chambers. (No one remembered when Nicole was summoned to face the previous Surchatain straight out of the bath, and Ares escorted her in his breeches. But no one was looking at his feet at the time, for Nicole had only a sheet for covering.)

Dressed in scarlet, Ares and Nicole first stopped by their daughters' chambers. The girls, just now being roused and coaxed into their robes, cried out upon seeing their mother. They threw themselves at her, thwarting their maids' efforts to get them dressed, and could barely be persuaded to let go of her long enough to put their arms through sleeves. When they finally got sufficient reassurance that she was really home, the royal family descended the great staircase together.

The scene that greeted them in the great hall was unprecedented, so that the girls fell over themselves laughing. Since it was approximately two o'clock in the morning, the lords, nobles, and merchants of Westford who normally dined here were home in bed. Instead, the hall was filled with, first, the soldiers of the search party, who had cleaned up only minimally before swaggering into the hall. Attending them were maids in long-sleeved, high-necked nightgowns and menservants in long nightshirts and colored stockings. In the spirit of the hour, Georges wore a particularly fine tasseled nightcap.

Carmine appeared in his ermine robe, looking only slightly less pulled together than usual. Vogelsong showed up in an old, oversized nightshirt and baggy socks; Giles wore a gaudy nightshirt that matched his wife's nightgown. Doctor Savary wore an undyed cotton gown that he operated in, explaining that he usually slept so in case of nighttime emergencies. Melva appeared in a demure ensemble that, while modest, made a number of the soldiers look at her twice.

Renée made her standard grand entrance in a stunning, sheer silk robe, with her hair loose around her shoulders. But when she saw the rude, uncouth soldiers staring and drooling, she went back upstairs for a heavier robe and a cap. Her mother, Lady Vivian, declined to appear at all, considering the request obscene—so she later said, although others were of the opinion that she would have honored the request had Lord Notham been in attendance.

Poor Henry was the only one dressed, having bedded down in Ares' receiving room while still in his clothes. He could hardly strip to what he normally slept in, and had no immediate access to proper nightclothes. Worse, he looked with pained envy on Ben, one of the Surchataine's rescuers who carried the grime and sweat of the day like a badge of honor. But Henry was soon to forget his shame.

After Nicole had been warmly greeted by the palace occupants, she went around the table to thank each rider for his part in her rescue. She attempted to take their hands, but on her approach they fell to their knees and bowed their heads, so the most she could do was place a hand on their heads or shoulders. Then she sat at the head of the table with Ares and her daughters while the guests and soldiers lifted their goblets to her.

Ares stood, and the raucous table quieted immediately. "We will have accounts all around for what has happened today, but before I ask those questions, I have specific thanks and commendations. Have we an amanuensis?" he asked, looking around. The secretary with his quill, ink stand, and parchment stood up from his small table to bow. He wore a tasteful striped nightshirt and matching cap.

"Ah. Very good." Ares acknowledged him, then looked over the table again. "First, as we have no priest at this time, I offer my inadequate, unworthy thanks to my God and the Lord Jesus Christ, who saved my wife out of pity for me, knowing that I could not live without her. I commend those He used to carry out this gracious action: Commander Thom, for his unerring sense of the right course; Captain Crager, who led the party, and Lieutenant Derrick, who aided him. I commend these who fulfilled their vow to me most admirably—" and he began naming off those of the party, one by one, pointing them out. Those names he did not know were quickly supplied by voices on either hand.

"Finally," Ares said, "I have one to thank who shared the watch with me, and would not leave when I commanded everyone else to take their rest. Henry—you pulled your watch like a man." Henry bit his lip in a surge of grateful pride when Ares turned to him, and the table politely applauded.

"Now, I command all of you to eat." Ares waved, and the servants brought out all the odds and ends that the kitchen could produce at a moment's notice: potage, cold tongue leftovers, salted pork, gingered beets, asparagus, plums, frumenty with oat wafers, boiled chestnuts served with hot cream, and, for dessert, candied parsnips.

All those at table—especially the soldiers—ate greedily until their hunger was assuaged, at which point Ares called for their attention again. "Now we will piece together what happened, as best we can. Lady," he said, gesturing to Nicole, "will you please tell us how you were taken this morning?"

He noted her wary glance toward the amanuensis, waiting with poised quill. She began hesitantly, "I fear there is little I can tell you. While I lay in bed—it must have been after you left—I remember waking just barely, because of a draft in the room. Then someone took hold of me and pressed a cold, stinking cloth to my face. I felt like I was suffocating. I remember nothing else until I awoke, being thrown about in a small, dark space. After a while, I realized I was in some kind of box on a cart—and I knew it was not one of Coyle's that has the suspension.

"I was bound with ropes, encased in a burlap sack, and enclosed in something like a coffin. From the rattling noises on the lid above me, I knew that I must have been buried under metalware or weapons laid atop my coffin from head to foot! It was loud and unceasing."

She paused thoughtfully while the table sat listening. "It was very warm and stuffy, and I was groggy, but my prison rolled on for a long time—I have no idea how long. I was able to get my hands free, but that did no good, for I could not tear the burlap, nor untie the neck of the sack that was over my head. I could hear nothing but the wheels underneath me and the rattling above. However, I knew we were on a dirt road, and not the paved road to Crescent Hollow or Eurus, because the dirt that was thrown up underneath the cart made its way through the burlap. I got very thirsty, and I prayed. . . ."

Nicole shook her head as if to clear it, then resumed, "As I said, we were rolling for hours, when suddenly we stopped. And then the cart turned so sharply that I was sure it would roll. I was thrown against the side and the board above me shifted, so that I feared I would be crushed. But instead, a gap opened so that I could hear better. I heard many horses about, and the shouts of men and the clanging of metal. The cart began going faster than ever yet. I knew that I was about to be rescued or killed, so I held my soul in peace and waited for what was to come.

"The cart came to a halt so suddenly that I was thrown against the head of the coffin. I believe I have a knot here," she said ruefully, rubbing her head. "There was a great deal more shouting and violence above me, then all was still. Some moments later, I began to hear things being tossed out from above me. The lid was pried up, the burlap lifted and slitted with a knife. Then I was looking up into the most welcome face of Captain Crager." She smiled at him and he inclined his head with admirable poise.

"My dear husband's men took me out of the wagon and found a blanket to cover me. The Captain apologized for my discomforts and placed me with the Second Oswald, who brought me home again," she finished.

Ares studied her as a murmur of admiration went around the table and the riders sat basking in the satisfaction of the moment. Nodding, Ares replied, "Thank you, Lady. I am gratified to have married a woman as resilient as she is beautiful." He glanced at his daughters as if wishing them to take note. Both were gazing at their mother with an air of appreciation that they had not shown before.

"Now, Captain Crager." Ares turned toward the Captain, who was seated a few chairs down on his right. "I am looking to you to supply what information the lady lacks."

Crager nodded. "Surchatain, God was with us, directing us. That is the only way I can explain what happened. We proceeded out this morning under your orders, knowing only that we were looking for a conveyance capable of carrying a concealed person, conscious or not, on the road to Dansington. It was a great encouragement when Lieutenant Moeck spotted the banner thrown off in the trees, for that showed that we followed truly. We rode hard for several hours, but wasted valuable time searching two carts which were of no account.

"Late afternoon, we passed a peasant's wagon loaded with a jumble of old tin wares. There seemed to be no point in searching it, for it was a shallow wagon plainly filled with an assortment of loose pans and plates, like those that itinerant sellers carry from town to town. With the lateness of the hour, we were anxious to reach Dansington. But as we passed the wagon, I received a blinding flash across my sight." Crager leaned forward in attempting to convey the intensity of the impression. "At the same time, I seemed to hear someone direct, *'Look at his hands'*—those of the driver. His face was covered by a wide-brimmed hat.

"I turned back and saw the brown hands of a Polonti, so I ordered him to halt. When he did, I reached down through the wares to the floor of the wagon. When I discerned only a forearm of depth, whereas the sides of the wagon were twice again that deep, I realized it had a false bottom. As I raised the alert, the driver wheeled the wagon out from under me—I have rarely seen such bold driving!—and a mob of renegades rushed out of the trees upon us. It was clear that they had been escorting the wagon under concealment along the road.

"We drew our swords to defend ourselves. With the surprise of the attack, it was only by the grace of God, again, that none of our number was killed. But while we were thus engaged, the driver was escaping with his load back down to the crossroads, where with any luck, he might take one of five directions, his tracks being quickly obscured by other traffic, or ditch the wagon altogether and escape with his prize into the trees. This was my greatest fear."

Crager paused to take a drink while his audience waited to hear the rest. "At last we shook off the renegades to give belated chase, fearing the worst. But lo and behold, we approached the crossroads to find the Second Oswald sitting in command of it, holding up traffic each and every way, waiting for us to arrive like the host of a fest. With the straight road, he had seen our troubles from a distance!"

Despite admiring glances and murmurings, Oswald sat gazing straight ahead in the sweet composure of having performed what was required. Crager continued, "The wagon driver, seeing that he was blocked before and behind, leaped from his seat and quickly lost himself in the shallows of the Passage, where tracking him was impossible. But we had more pressing matters to attend.

"We quickly emptied the wagon and pried up the false bottom. The Surchataine, as she said, was wrapped in coarse burlap and bound tightly. But what a shout we raised when she looked up and said, in her way, 'I thank my husband's good men for their kind assistance.' The rest she has told you well enough, and I need add no more," Crager ended.

There followed scattered, subdued comments on the narrow rescue. Thom leaned to Crager to mutter, "Well done, Captain—only next time, see that your messenger knows that he is delivering good news." Crager stared at him, and Thom explained the deficiency of Fawler's message.

Then, sated with success, wine, and good victuals, the guests began to nod off with the weight of the hour. Looking around, Ares said, "Again, thank you all. You are dismissed." The rest bowed or saluted, depending on their positions, and the hall quickly cleared after Ares and Nicole had departed, he with a sleepy child on each shoulder.

Once they had put the girls to bed, Ares escorted his wife back to their own bedchamber, where they discarded their robes. In the quietness that followed, he rekindled a small fire from the solitary candle left burning. Nicole lay down on the soft pillow, murmuring, "My head aches so."

He straightened from the huge fireplace, where the low fire barely illumined the bed. "Will a draft of wine help?"

"Probably not, but thank you," she said.

Ares sat on the edge of the bed. "Now, Lady, be kind enough to tell me what you would not say in front of the amanuensis."

Removing her hand from her eyes, she smiled at him. "My lord is most perceptive."

"Were you molested, Lady?" he asked tensely.

"No, Ares. It was not that," she said, and hesitated. He waited without speaking. She sighed, rolling onto her front to rest on her elbows. "I heard more than I let on. As Crager said, there were a great many men involved. They were taking me to the inn at Dansington to hand me over to a representative of the man who had paid to procure me."

"Who was—?" he asked.

"That, I do not know." She shook her leaden head. "But there is something more. When I awakened to strange hands on me in bed this morning, I did not simply lie there and let him put me to sleep. I fought hard and made it almost to the receiving room before he subdued me—at least, I got the door open. And when I did, I had light to see him."

Ares looked at her, trying to divine what was so difficult for her to say. She finally got it out: "Ares, it was Chiacos."

8

Ares stared at her as his shock slowly deflated to crushed disappointment. "Chiacos? I can hardly believe it, and yet . . . I could not reconcile how any man, any Polonti, could have such thorough knowledge of the passage and the grounds. Why would Chiacos betray us in this way?" he asked, anger rising.

"There was a great deal of money involved," Nicole said sleepily, lowering her head back to the pillow.

"If Chiacos wanted money, he could have simply taken that gold reliquary he carried down here for Melva, and be set for life," Ares said scornfully.

"Something must have happened to him, Ares . . ." she drifted off.

"Quite," he snorted. After his anger had cooled somewhat, he reasoned, "While I do not see how we can ask him, we need to talk to Sophie tomorrow. She saw more than she realizes. We need to discover what she herself does not know yet. I understand that I must be gentle in questioning her—she is so easily bruised when I am harsh, though I don't mean to hurt her." He paused, looking down to see that his wife was insensible to anything more he had to say tonight.

Sighing, he lay down and nestled her protectively, though he could not sleep himself.

If it was Chiacos whom Sophie had encountered in the passage, did he know who she was? Chiacos had left when the twins were only toddling, but he could have guessed her identity. If his plan had been to take Nicole, then to kill or abduct the child would have ruined it. He could have threatened Sophie into silence, but it seems clear that he did not. It seems that his only objective upon encountering the child was to get away as quietly as possible. Hence she thought he had been a ghost. . . .

Only the sturdiest servants and administrators rose at their usual time a few hours later. One of them was Ares. Once he had shaved and dressed, the first thing he did was test the entrance to the secret passage, to see whether it was truly sealed shut. It was. In attempting to open it, he pulled so hard on the brass andiron that he bent it.

Nothing woke Nicole, so he exited to the receiving room and summoned Thom for conference. While he waited, his conscience reminded him of his need to confer with his own superior this morning, so he opened the receiving room window to receive fresh light on the new twists in this situation.

Some minutes later Thom appeared at the door, saluting, and inquired after the Surchataine. "Still asleep," Ares said, jerking his head toward the bedchamber. "I took for granted how satisfactory it is to see her sleeping safely in my lair." Thom mutely agreed and waited. "Do you remember Chiacos?" Ares asked.

A shrewd look came over Thom's face. "Yes," he said. "Do you mean—?"

"Yes. She would not say it in front of everyone, but she recognized him when he took her," Ares said, pacing.

"We need to send spies to Dansington, to see if we can

pick up a trail to him and his new master," Thom said.

"Do that. Circulate word quietly for those who might recognize him to keep an eye out."

"We should bring in all the Polonti men we find," Thom suggested.

Ares winced. "No, Thom—remember who we are dealing with. He must realize she recognized him; he will not be found in the open. We would show our hand with such bluntness."

"Of course," Thom conceded, glancing aside.

"Were you Chiacos—or his master—and you still desired, for whatever purpose, to have the Surchataine of Lystra in your grasp, when would you try again?" Ares posed.

"At the festival," Thom replied promptly.

"Let us keep that in mind, and see what your trackers find," Ares instructed. "You are dismissed."

"Surchatain." Thom saluted on his way out.

That done, it was still too early for Ares to talk to Sophie —besides which, he needed to think about how to broach the issue with her—so he attended some of the more urgent business that had piled up yesterday.

Most of it had to do with the upcoming festival: approval of entrance fees for merchants, booth locations, and types of permissible business. (Caged ferrets were allowed; prostitution was not.) Ares wanted to turn the whole business over to Carmine or Giles, but Carmine was already so encumbered with the logistics of the festival that further burdening could drive him back to drink.

As for Giles, approval of these matters required use of the Surchatain's signet, which only Ares, Nicole, Carmine and Thom carried. Ares was leery of what delusions of grandeur might seize Giles were he allowed to wield the signet. So Ares blew through piles of parchment as quickly as possible, but the task still required three full hours.

He paused to request some potage and smelts from the kitchen, which he took into the bedchamber to offer to Nicole.

But as she was still sound asleep, he ate them himself. Thus refreshed, he inquired after Sophie's whereabouts. Upon being informed that she was in lessons, Ares contemplated the unthinkable, then did it: he went to the library to interrupt the twins' studies.

When the door opened, they looked up in sleepy boredom; seeing him and sensing freedom, they scattered books and slates with happy cries on their way to his outstretched arms. "Oh, give us a day off from lessons, Papa, since Mama is home," Bonnie pleaded, imitating Renée's beseeching look.

To her enormous gratification, her father concurred, "That is a good plan. Since Mama is not up yet, you may go see when Aunt Renée can to take you to the dressmaker's shop. Sophie will join you in a moment."

With a triumphant squeal, Bonnie was off in a torrent of petticoats. Sophie grasped Ares' hand happily, pressing it between her two small ones, and he tugged gently: "Let's go for a walk, Sophie." He paused to nod to the tutor, who looked back in such exasperated displeasure that Ares almost apologized.

He took Sophie downstairs at a leisurely pace, then outside to the fig and plum orchard. It was a warm day with full sun. The two of them looked around the well-kept orchard, smelling the ripening fruit.

Ares asked, "Do you know how they tell which figs are ripe?"

"No, Papa. How?" she asked.

"They watch to see which ones the butterflies land on. See?" He pointed.

Delighted, she watched the iridescent blue and yellow butterflies swarm around the large-leafed branches spreading up from the ground. "I see!" she said, squeezing his hand.

"You are very observant," Ares noted, walking along with her. "I can always count on you to notice things that other people miss. For instance . . . we know now that it wasn't a ghost you saw in the passage, don't we?"

"Yes, Papa," she admitted, downcast.

By this time, they were standing in front of the sealed-up exit of the passage. He knelt before her. "But there must have been reasons you thought it was a ghost. Tell me everything you saw. Think about it," he coaxed.

She scrunched up her face to aid the thought process. "Let's start at the beginning," he suggested. "Tell me what you saw when the door opened. Tell me what it looked like opening."

Hesitantly, she said, "It . . . opened so slowly! Just the edge pushing out bit by bit."

Chiacos checking to see if anyone was watching, Ares thought. As she paused, he said, "Was anyone else around when it opened?"

"No." She shook her chestnut ponytail. "Just me myself."

"How far away were you standing?" he asked.

"About this far." She held her arms out to indicate no more than a yard. "I was trying to see what made it move, but I couldn't see a thing, so when it opened far enough, I went in."

On the verge of telling her that was a foolish thing to do, he bit his tongue. Instead, he asked, "Why did you go inside?"

"I wanted to see what was there. But as soon as I got in, it closed again," she replied.

"Did you hear anything? Close your eyes and try to remember," he urged her.

Obediently, she squeezed her eyes shut. "I heard something like a chain rattle. That made me remember what Doudney said about the spirits in fetters, so I thought I would move away from it."

Ares figured that she must have heard Chiacos' climbing gear clank together—his or his companion's. It probably frightened her enough to impel her in the opposite direction, toward the caved-in portion of the passage. "Then what? Did you hear footsteps after you?"

"No, Papa. When I got to the pile of rocks, I was pulling them down when the other door opened."

"Now tell me exactly what you saw," Ares said.

"The—thing went out then, so softly. It was all black, even its face under its hood. I ran out after it, but it just glided over the ground and jumped up on the wall with no trouble at all. I know that it must have been a real person, but it didn't look like one at all," she said stubbornly.

It crossed Ares' mind that Geurts had said essentially the same thing. "Was there anyone else in the orchard who might have seen it?"

"I don't remember. I don't think so," she murmured. It was not impossible for the trespasser to escape unseen through the orchard, even in daylight. The palace children delighted in playing hide-and-seek here.

Thinking, Ares studied his daughter. In exposing Chiacos, she must have very nearly ruined his plan. But he was so determined to carry out the kidnapping that he returned to the passage with a cohort to silence the guards. It was risky to the point of madness . . . and it almost worked. "Why wouldn't you tell me all this the first time I asked?" he said, slightly reproachful.

"I didn't think you'd believe me. You told Doudney to stop reading us ghost stories," she said glumly.

"Sophie, even if I thought you saw something different from what you thought you saw, I would still believe you if you said you saw *something*," he explained seriously.

She giggled in tentative confusion, then exclaimed, "The dead man's token! I forgot! Papa, it must have been a ghost after all, because it left a dead man's token!"

"What is a dead man's token?" he asked.

She assumed an air of authority in explaining to him: "Doudney told us all about it. It's a token that a ghost leaves behind to show something about who it was when it was alive or to show something about how it died."

"What is this token?" Ares asked with a shade of a smile.

"I will show you," she said smugly, marching toward the wall. "The ghost left it when it flew over the wall, and I buried it in the same spot so that the ghost couldn't come back for it." She walked along the orchard wall until she found a line of small stones. "I marked the spot," she informed him. Kneeling, she dug down a small ways, then triumphantly handed up to him a gold coin.

Ares brushed dirt from the coin to study it. It was a gold crux—a Scyllan coin corresponding to the Lystran royal. But this one was about ten years old, having been minted during the reign of Magnus' father. This was, quite possibly, part of the payment Chiacos had received for kidnapping Nicole. Had he accidentally dropped it? It hardly stood to reason that he would be carrying around a bunch of gold in the execution of his task. Or, had he been intending to leave this coin as a message once he had taken her? Who would be paying him with old Scyllan coins?

"This is significant," Ares admitted, glancing down at her.

"It proves it was a ghost," she said, vindicated.

Ares studied her. Why was it so important for Sophie to believe that the intruder was a ghost? Correction: why *this* intruder was a ghost. A ghost could not have kidnapped her mother—that had to be a real, live man. So if what Sophie encountered was a ghost, and not a living man, then she had not contributed to her mother's harm by remaining silent about it.

"You may be right, Sophie," he said, pocketing the coin. "Go on, dear one. Aunt Renée and Bonnie will be waiting for you."

"All right, Papa." She reached up with puckered lips and he bent down for her to kiss his cheek. Satisfied, she skipped back toward the palace while Ares made a detour to see that the oak branches that had been overhanging the wall were now lopped off, chopped up, and drying for firewood.

From there, he went to the palace foyer to summon Thom again. The Commander emerged from a side corridor to salute: "Surchatain, trackers were sent out to Dansington hours ago, led by Moeck. I was just now meeting with my Seconds in Command. Would you care to join us?" He nodded toward the corridor that housed his chambers.

"Gladly." Ares walked the old, familiar corridors and paused at the open door of the spartan stone room. This had been his home for years, until he had finally been persuaded to move upstairs to the Surchatain's suite.

Ares had been reluctant to move because of the garderobe in this room, created when engineers broke through the wall to discover an underground stream that ran just beneath the palace. From there, it was a simple matter to build a closeted latrine. They had attempted to route water to other rooms by means of a water wheel, which succeeded only in raising a small portion of the stream to the top of this garderobe. A trough hanging over the garderobe doors could be swung out to divert a portion of the stream into a wash tub, which in turn drained back into the garderobe. Until Ares had the cistern on the roof and conduits built, this garderobe was the only one in the palace equipped with running water.

When Ares entered Thom's quarters, Seconds Oswald and Rhode turned from a small table to salute. The Surchatain returned it, glancing around at shelves littered with correspondence and maps. On the floor next to the bed (the same one that Ares had rebuilt for his and Nicole's comfort) were piles of new weapons and gear that Thom was in the process of testing out. Remembering when this room had been cluttered with dresses instead of battle paraphernalia, Ares asked Thom, "Does Deirdre not object to war councils in your chambers?"

Thom smiled, jerking his head in unconcern. "Since she

spends most of the day in the nursery with Ryle"—their three-year-old son— "she contrived to seize a side room off the nursery for her own use, and lets me wallow in my pig sty here."

Ares noted, "So you require a sty, now? And you used to be so organized, Thom." Oswald chortled and Rhode coughed, but Ares' gaze settled contemplatively on the garderobe doors. He crossed the room to open them and look inside.

Starting from a point about a foot above his head, the stream cascaded from the hidden water wheel down the graded rock on the back side of the garderobe between the ledges of the closet where the user would crouch. From there, the flow disappeared through a roughly circular, four-foot-wide opening in the garderobe floor, rejoining the main stream underground.

Ares knelt to look down the drain tunnel as far as he could. The water came to a foot or so within the roof of the tunnel, allowing for plenty of air space as far as he could see. "Did Chiacos know about this garderobe?"

Following a stricken silence, Thom said, "I do not know."

Ares turned. "Has anyone attempted to swim it?"

"Not that I know of," Thom answered tensely. "Should I call for a volunteer?"

Ares stood, closing the doors. "Not unless it becomes imperative. I don't want to lose a man in the process. But you might start bolting it."

"And have him waiting in there the next time Deirdre tries to use it?" Thom asked.

Ares glanced back at him. "I doubt it, somehow. Even if he knew about it, he would not know any more than we where it surfaces outside, if it does."

Rhode broke in, "If I remember aright from Coyle, the underground stream diverges and empties into the waterway on one hand and Willowring Lake on the other, both miles from here."

"Making it a highly unlikely passage," Ares said. Thom glanced doubtfully at the closed garderobe.

"Well." Ares returned to the table, reaching into his pocket. "Tell me what you make of this. Sophie said her 'ghost' dropped it while going over the orchard wall." And he tossed the gold coin onto the table.

Thom picked it up while Rhode and Oswald leaned over to look at it. "It's a crux with Ossian's stamp," the Commander noted.

"I haven't seen one of those in years," Rhode marveled. "After Magnus took the throne—what?—nine years ago?—first thing he did was recall all of his father's coinage, have it melted down and reminted with his stamp."

"He missed some pieces," Thom noted, flipping the coin to gauge its weight. "It's genuine."

"Someone's had it hoarded, and they're just now paying it out," Rhode observed.

Ares looked at him. "Yes. That would explain it. Who?"

No one offered any guesses. Then Oswald grunted, "We need to find Chiacos."

"Quite," Thom agreed, then asked Ares, "Was he the one who took Sophie into the passage?"

Ares exhaled, "It must have been. The hobnail in the boot definitely belongs to the kidnapper, and Nicole says it was definitely Chiacos. But unless he was flying over the wall at the same time he was kidnapping my wife, then he had an accomplice whose boot nails are all intact."

Thom shrugged impatiently. "In a way, it does not matter. If there were two, they were acting as one. Chiacos is still responsible."

"What if his accomplice is someone in the palace, Commander?" Rhode asked.

"Then he will be found out and dealt with," Thom said.

They covered some other matters, particularly those related to security at the upcoming festival, then Ares left them to go upstairs, tossing and catching the crux as he went. Noting the sentries at the head of the Surchatain's wing and more sentries standing guard at his own chambers, he passed through the empty receiving room and opened the door to the bedchamber—to find it also empty.

His heart constricted and his hand clenched the door handle. But as his eyes swept the dim interior, he found it all in relative order. So he went back out to address one sentry at the door: "Have you seen the Surchataine?"

"Sir." He saluted. "She left word that she will be in the apple orchard."

"Good," Ares said, breathing again. He took the back stairs down to the large orchard on the south side of the palace where apple, pear, peach and persimmon trees grew. Nicole had a personal garden of herbs and flowers here, too. She loved gardens. The ground seemed to erupt in green under her feet.

Following a pebbled path through the soldierly rows of trees, Ares spotted her at once in a long-sleeved work dress with a large, floppy hat shielding her from the sun as she worked. A basket hung on her arm in which she deposited daylilies, ferns or rosemary cuttings that suited her purposes. Ares paused to watch her, comforting himself with the sight after staring at a wretchedly empty bed all yesterday.

Approaching her from behind, he slipped his arms around her waist and she turned, hampered by the large, flat basket. "I had rather a start when I found you out of bed," he complained.

She made a show of indignation. "As if I rarely got out of bed? As if my whole purpose were to wait for you in bed?"

"What more should there be?" he asked, deadpan.

"Getting ready for the festival?" she suggested.

He groaned, "I am sick already of the festival. I would cancel it except that Giles and Renée would send me to the block. Giles would wield the sword himself."

Unsympathetic, she turned back to her task. "You've lost any sense of entertainment, my lord."

"No, Lady, I haven't. I've merely lost the need to purchase it," he said, stroking her shoulder. She laughed at him, and he regarded what he could see under the great brim: her full lips spread over clean teeth, her neck and upper chest white in the shadow, her auburn ponytail glinting red-brown in the sunlight. "Well," he said, "I have had a most illuminating discussion with Sophie about ghosts."

"Ghosts?" she said, lifting the brim.

"One in particular, who has a habit of leaving tokens." He opened her hand to place the crux in her palm. While she studied it, he told her everything that Sophie had said, as well as his discussion with Thom and his Seconds.

When finished, he let a few seconds pass without talk, then said, "Nicole, we must take precautions so that you are not snatched away from me again."

He watched her chest expand in a reluctant sigh. "At the festival?"

"I believe that would be an opportune time for another attempt," he admitted.

She looked up at his scar. In the harsh sunlight, it stood out in all its ugliness: jagged, discolored, disfiguring. But she had long ago learned to love it, for it was the mark of a man who had suffered to attain his calling. Even as a child, he had borne the assaults to his heritage—his right to rule. He had to fight for it. And she was his wife. . . . "I will not hide in our chambers, Ares," she said softly.

"I knew that," he muttered.

Dinner that evening was held as a celebration of the Lady Nicole's dramatic rescue, the highlights of which were circulated in great (and ever expanding) detail. The nobles and merchants of Westford were appropriately exuberant and wise enough to pretend that they were glad over her return and not simply because their dinner privileges were reinstated.

But their relief went deeper, for no one doubted that had the Surchataine turned up dead, or not at all, plans for the festival would have died as well. Since discovering a windfall in last year's festival, the participating merchants had made themselves dependent on a repeat performance this year. Only a few moneyhandlers, among them Giles, were wise enough to resist banking everything on it.

While braised goose fringed with escarole was served, Captain Crager was pressed to recount for the hundredth time how he had been compelled to go back and search the unassuming wagon his men had just passed on the road to Dansington.

In hearing him tonight, however, his listeners from the early morning might have discerned a difference: he now implied that something furtive about the driver's manner prompted Crager's search—not that he was Polonti. The fact that the driver was Polonti was omitted entirely. Few hearers noted the discrepancy; those who did, such as Carmine, knew that it was a prudent omission. While Thom's men had no desire to harass innocent Polonti in Lystra, their principle motivation for looking quietly was that they did not wish to spook their quarry.

Midway through dinner, while Renée had the table inescapably locked in a story about the dresses she had bought for the twins that afternoon (which she refused to describe, citing some thrilling innovation of Lord Preus'), a sentry entered the hall almost invisibly to speak in Thom's ear. Thom blinked, then wordlessly excused himself from the table with a bow to Nicole and a brief salute to Ares.

Nicole only glanced at him before returning her attention to Renée, but Ares intently watched Thom leave the hall. The scouts had discovered something. That was the only thing that could prompt the Commander to risk the social disapproval of leaving the table in the middle of dinner.

Ares badly wanted to know what they had found—it was imperative that he know—but if he got up during Renée's story, it would infuriate her enough to insure some imaginative, effective retaliation on her part.

Nicole suddenly turned to him. "My lord, I am highly desirous to have your approval of these dresses. As our dear Chataine wants to keep them from public view as of yet, will my lord be kind enough to go upstairs and look at them?"

It was such an absurd request that those at table were left smiling in amusement or disbelief. Ares blinked at her—then read the knowing expression in her eyes as they flicked in the direction of Thom's exit. Ares lifted her hand to kiss it. "I will certainly do what the lady requests. Please continue with dinner in my absence."

When Ares rose and left the hall, Renée tossed her head smugly at the unexpected credibility offered her. Once he saw the dresses, he would have no choice but to approve them. That was a certainty.

In the foyer, Ares spotted Thom conferring with two of the scouts—Lieutenant Alphonso and the new man, Fawler. They saluted him as he approached, whereupon he demanded, "What do you know?"

Thom replied, "Surchatain, Alphonso and Fawler have come across separate reports that Chiacos is dead."

Ares lifted his chin to keep his balance in the suddenly unstable room. "As of when?"

Thom paused reluctantly, so Alphonso filled the gap: "Years ago, Surchatain."

Ares asked, "Did your informants see him die?"

Fawler shook his head and Alphonso replied, "No, sir. But they both gave it happening in the same circumstances: he was murdered by a mercenary of his own race."

"Where did you hear this? You've not had time to go to Dansington and back," Ares said irately.

"No, sir. I talked to Bagur, the Polonti potter in Westford.

His shop is something of a clearinghouse for all things Polonti, especially information," Alphonso said.

Ares turned to Fawler. "And who was your source?"

The man replied, "Sister Agnes, Surchatain. Ever since the Polonti in the area learned she will take in Polonti orphans as well as any other at the abbey, they talk to her."

Ares inhaled, looking around distractedly. "Well—somehow—your informants are wrong. Keep looking." With that, he returned to the great hall and sat at the table, frowning abstractly at the poached pears in front of him.

"Well?" Renée demanded triumphantly, and Ares looked up, blank.

"What does my lord think of the dresses?" Nicole prompted him cautiously.

He studied Renée with equal parts gravity and bemusement, then said, "You have bested me on this, Chataine. I don't know what to make of them."

9

The days leading up to the festival passed so quickly as to flow together in a frenzy of preparations. Nicole's ordeal was promptly forgotten in the excitement—except by those who were charged with seeing that it not happen again. In all that time, Ares asked only once: "Lady . . . are you *sure* it was Chiacos who took you?"

The question took her aback mostly because of its excruciatingly bad timing: earlier that day, while looking over some selections that Lord Preus had brought to the palace, Nicole had found a gorgeous silk robe, very alluring, that screamed *Renée*. But the Chataine was criticizing other garments at the moment and missed seeing this one. So Nicole, in a fit of daring, bought it. Tonight, while waiting for Ares, she had bathed, arranged her hair, and donned the robe. She was positioning herself in bed when Ares walked in, looked at her, and—voiced the question about Chiacos.

Nicole was shocked speechless for five full seconds before she sputtered, "Yes, Ares! How could I say it, knowing it would mean his death, if I were not sure?" Growing angry over his lack of appreciation for her pains tonight, she flounced out of bed to her wardrobe.

"Did he speak to you?" Ares asked, following her. He never saw the risqué robe before she threw her scarlet robe over it, ending her attempt to emulate the Chataine.

She set aside her anger long enough to think back. "No. It seemed as if he wanted to, but, he could only moan and mutter. I could not understand him at all."

In thought, Ares looked at the fire burning low in the grate, the flames reflecting lazily off the bent andiron. Still wearing the robe, Nicole dropped into bed and drew the heavy covers emphatically over herself. Ares looked back at her. "What is wrong?"

"I am tired. Good night, my lord," she said, and closed her stinging eyes. She was even more chagrined when Ares accepted that, undressed, and lay down at her back to fall directly asleep. Only then did she realize that not only had she wasted a rare opportunity for intimacy, but she should be glad that he never even noticed a garment that looked just like something Renée would wear.

The spies that Ares had sent out kept looking all the while, of course. They brought back reports that a stranger had been seen waiting in the common room of the inn at Dansington on the evening of Nicole's abduction. He was reliably described as not Polonti, finely dressed in a vaguely northern Continental fashion, quiet, mannerly, and moneyed. Significantly, he had also paid for the night's lodging with an old crux, which, gold being gold, the innkeeper accepted without hesitation.

However, the scouts had been unable to unearth anything about Chiacos beyond what Alphonso and Fawler had discovered on their first attempts. He had been conclusively seen nowhere; his death could be conclusively established by no one.

Nicole herself treated the matter as if it were some huge, unlikely mistake. Since she rarely traveled outside of Westford anyway, she refused to allow her activities to be further curtailed by any supposed threat. Of course she would go to the festival. Her daughters expected to accompany her, and a number of the merchants were hoping for a condolence visit from the Surchataine Nicole if the Chataine Renée failed to grace their booths with her presence. No slight to Nicole's status was intended; it was only so because Renée was known to spend as much as a whole clan.

By sunrise of the opening day of the festival, the fields south of Westford had been teeming with activity for hours. Scores of merchants had arrived, erected tents, and unpacked merchandise all by torchlight. Giles had been on site since the afternoon before, masterfully overseeing all aspects of registration and setup, even through the night. When he looked around and saw torches being extinguished upon the advent of daylight, he collapsed in a fit of exhaustion. After a few hours' dead sleep, however, he arose renewed for the commerce of the day.

As opening time approached, hundreds of customers were held behind barricades until Ares arrived to inaugurate the festival, his dress blacks presenting a stark contrast to the colorful flags and banners that cracked in the morning breeze around the main gate.

With Nicole and his daughters following, he mounted steps onto a temporary wooden platform to face the excited crowd. They applauded in anticipation as Ares congenially raised his hands. "I, Surchatain Ares and my family, Counselor Carmine, Steward Giles, and all the skilled craftsmen of Lystra welcome you to the June festival of Westford!" he cried, and they cheered.

He pointed to the soldiers manning the gate, and with fanfare, it was opened to permit the crowd to thread their way through a series of turnstiles to the grounds crowded with tents, booths, and stages. The necessity of restraints at the gate had been made clear last year after a few people were trampled in the inexplicable rush to get in. "What is the mad hurry? The festival lasts a week!" Ares had vented, distraught over the injuries.

So while the crowd was allowed to trickle in, Ares and his family stayed on the platform to wave, nod, and exchange pleasantries with their guests. The girls drew many admiring comments, as they did indeed look precious in their new dresses. One dress was a reverse color pattern of the other: while Bonnie's dress comprised elongated blue diamonds on a rose background, Sophie's had rose diamonds on a blue background. As befit the girls' tender age, the dresses were short, reaching just past the knees (their legs being covered with white hose). But the innovation which Renée had found so compelling was in the attached petticoats.

Multiple stiff petticoats were necessary to make any dress stand out properly, but wearing them on a warm summer day, especially outdoors, was almost too much to ask of any little girl, even a Chataine. Therefore, Lord Preus had designed a petticoat with a hem sown of sheep bladders (disguised by lace) that could be inflated by mouth and stoppered. The inflated rim held the skirt aloft with a fraction of the weight and bulk of regular petticoats. Bonnie was thrilled, and even Sophie was persuaded to wear the dress without complaint. However, she had to be reminded to keep secret things secret when she was spotted lifting her skirt to show off the innovation to anyone interested.

This morning, the girls were all proper and decorous in their roles as welcoming royalty. Nicole, of course, was radiant in the morning, with the sunlight glinting off the famous chestnut hair that cascaded down her back behind the rose-colored cap. Tales based on her abduction were still circulating around Westford, but the spin on newer versions was that she had been kidnapped for romantic purposes because of her beauty.

Two travelers who had heard of the affair now studied her

as they passed through the turnstiles. "Aye, she's a looker, wouldn't you say?" offered the first.

The second paused to turn sharp blue eyes up at the graceful lady on the platform, now only six feet away. "Quite." Prudently refraining from staring, he lowered his eyes to the ring of soldiers stationed between the platform and the crowd.

"I waited on her at the cheesemonger's. I can introduce you," the first offered.

His companion glanced back to the platform, to the man in black beside the lady. "And arouse her husband's interest? I'd rather not meet her until I've placed myself in his good graces."

"As you say, Fancsali—but why so cautious all of a sudden?"

"To study the lay of the land, Cratch. I want you to tell me everything you know about the good hosts of this festival," the lord murmured, watching Ares direct a word to two sentries who began moving off through the crowd. Fancsali assumed an air of vacuous interest as he entered the festival grounds, but, like the soldiers, he paid more attention to the people than the merchandise—especially certain people whom Cratch pointed out.

The memorial honoring the Greens had been set on a stone close to the entrance, so that the lines coming out of the turnstiles had to literally flow around it to reach the booths. Watching, Ares was gratified by the number of patrons who stopped to read it or have it read to them.

The last line of the commemorative, composed by Vogelsong, read, "Therefore, let Westford remember with gratitude the faith-fulness of those who died defending her and offer thanks to God that their sacrifice was not in vain." Ares was so struck by the wording that he had a derivative inscription cast in bronze and placed inside the front doors of the palace, where it would be seen whenever the doors were shut at night: "May the Lord God regard the sacrifice of this day, that it not be offered in vain."

The new priest made his debut at the festival. His name was Father Birondo, and Ares set him up in a nice little booth in a prime spot under a shade tree to read Scripture aloud or sing Psalms because he had a nice voice. To encourage listeners to tarry, there were benches set in the shade, cool water to drink, and free oat wafers. The new priest was all Ares had hoped for—besides being pious and learned, he was anxious to please to the point of nervousness, having heard something about what happened to the previous priest.

Ares was taut as a bowstring all that day. Besides the incidents that would normally occur when so many people, goods and money are gathered in one place—the pickpockets, fights, thefts, and accidents—Ares was distracted by his daughters' running pell-mell from booth to booth, taxing the endurance of their guardians. He was further dismayed by Nicole's refusal to have more than two soldiers accompany her on her rounds. As it was, Renée successfully upstaged her by attending the festival in a litter carried by four liveried servants.

Riding thus in luxurious, shaded comfort, Renée was guaranteed to draw a crowd to whatever booth she chose to visit. The moment the litter was placed on the ground, and the curtain drawn aside for her exit, a circle of respectful, intensely curious fair-goers would gather to watch her alight and enter the fortunate merchant's tent. If the booth was open-sided, and the merchant amiable, nonbuying patrons who wished to attend her shopping would crowd in under the stern eye of her Lystran bodyguard. Her selections would then be paid for by one of Giles' assistants and immediately taken back to her quarters.

Periodically, she would ask to see the list of her purchases, to refresh her memory as to what she had bought and what she needed to buy. Unknown to her, Giles had instituted an incentive program for his staff to help the Chataine manage her accounts: if they neglected to record a purchase which she did not remember, it was possible for the item to be diverted to the treasury. Upon each successful transaction from the Chataine's possession to the treasury, the subordinate would receive a bounty of five percent of the purchase price. Of course, if she did remember a purchase that had mysteriously disappeared, the repercussions would be almost too horrific to imagine.

Like everyone else at the festival, Fancsali and his companion were arrested by the sight of the litter. Curious, they followed it a ways, until it stopped at the silversmith's booth where a fine selection of mirrors was on display. The bearers set the litter on the ground, then one leaned forward to lift the curtain and extend his hand for Renée to alight. She did, exposing a slender ankle, and looked up indifferently into the interested eyes of Lord Fancsali.

The Chataine was used to being stared at—some say she courted stares—but Fancsali's look was something rather different. She expertly appraised him at a glance: his clothes were good quality, not foppish nor extravagant, but definitely those of an outdoorsman. He was trim and groomed, with shoulder-length hair and a short beard. His only adornment was one prominent ring on his right hand, which was sufficient to communicate both wealth and authority.

Above everything, his features conveyed sharp intelligence and generous self-confidence. As her limpid blue eyes lingered on him for a fraction of a second longer than necessary, he smiled rather inscrutably and bowed slightly. Before she could respond, had she chosen to, he turned away through the crowd and was gone.

His companion caught up to him, sputtering, "Where're you going? You had her eye!"

"I have all their eyes, good Cratch," he replied with a trace of boredom.

"But that one's different. That's the Chataine Renée, and I hear tell that she gets a new proposal every month, at least," Cratch argued.

"Which makes her high maintenance," Fancsali observed dryly. "Were I inclined to invest that much in a woman, it had best be someone who could guarantee a good return."

The other gaped at him a little stupidly. "How?"

Fancsali lifted his brows. "Oh, well, I would require someone who would continue to be, shall we say, stimulating after she was married. Like the Surchataine, for instance. Someone seems to have a great desire for her company for some reason . . . a reason I would like to know very much," he ended on a murmur, and his friend studied him.

Despite a predictable range of opening-day problems, the commencement of the festival was a great success. Bonnie and Sophie lasted until late afternoon, at which time they were carried home for a nap before dinner. At sundown, soldiers began moving through the fields, herding customers toward the gate. Only registered merchants and their hirelings could stay on the fields at night, sleeping in their tents to protect their merchandise. Lystran soldiers stood watch around the perimeter of the grounds until the gate was opened again the following morning.

Although Nicole's bodyguards kept Ares apprised of her whereabouts constantly throughout that first day, he was unable to relax until the palace gates were closed for the evening with her safely ensconced in their quarters. At that time, he provided a tolerant audience while she brought out all the various little items she had bought—mostly books and miniature paintings. She also liked cunning boxes with hidden compartments and sliding panels. Since there was nothing very costly, and nothing that Giles' assistants had to keep track of, she got to keep everything she had bought.

When she had shown him everything, he nodded contemplatively, stirring. The question must be asked:

"Nicole, did you . . . see him? Did you see anyone who looked . . . out of place?"

"No, Ares," she sighed. "I tell you, no one paid the least bit of attention to me except the merchants who hoped I might match Renée's spending. Were anyone still determined to snatch me—which I doubt—he would be insane to attempt it around so many people. There is no place to hide! Everything is all out in the open!"

"True," he admitted. "True."

The second day of the festival was even better, with bigger crowds. It was also overcast, but without any rain to ruin merchandise. Feeling lazy, Renée arrived at the festival late—almost noon—and was just stepping out of the litter at the perfumer's booth when she caught sight of the intriguing stranger with the lordly bearing and rugged clothing.

Again he was watching her, and she straightened imperially under his eye. His bow to her this time was lower, with more flourish, and she responded with the barest inclination of her head. Then he disappeared into the crowd again, and she felt distinctly peeved.

Today, the twins reverted to their standard mode of dress: Bonnie in a fashionable dress with mounds of petticoats and Sophie in a play dress with no petticoat at all. Walking along hand in hand as their guardians trailed them, they paused to watch a thrilling puppet show and receive candy from the hand of a puppet for a copper pence.

A strolling flutist dressed in motley came by, bowing for them to place a few pences in his hat. Acrobats performed daring leaps, somersaults, and tumbles that caused Bonnie to squeal and Sophie to try a flip or two before being apprehended and set firmly on her feet by her guardian.

As the girls walked, they talked about the problem of the ghost which remained to be solved. Sophie informed her sister, "Papa said the dead man's token was really—really—" she couldn't remember the word he had used, so she substituted, "important. And it proves it was a ghost all along."

Bonnie looked troubled. "How could a ghost take Mama out of the palace?"

"It didn't. That was someone else," Sophie pointed out.

"But . . . how do you know that the ghost left the token, Sophie? How do you know it wasn't a real person?"

"I know what I saw," Sophie said stubbornly. "I've never seen a real person float like that."

"Then who took Mama?" Bonnie whispered, looking around nervously. "Oh, look at the dolls!" she cried. And so their discussion was suspended while Bonnie ran into the dollmaker's tent to look over the many lovely dolls made of cloth, wood or painted clay, with braided horsehair on their heads and little dresses of cotton or satin.

She selected a new companion for her many other dolls (which the guardian paid for out of his purse) but once outside the booth, resumed her previous line of thought: "Sophie, if the ghost didn't take Mama, who did? And what did the ghost have to do with it?"

"I don't know," Sophie admitted, hanging her head. "I know Papa had to seal the passage up, but I wish he didn't have to, because ghosts always return to—" She broke off, staring.

"Return to what? What is it?" Bonnie asked, following her eyes.

"There it is!" Sophie gasped. Without further explanation, she darted through the crowds to the back side of the potter's tent. She stopped, looking all around. There was nothing here but the back sides of numerous tents a few feet away from the temporary fencing that enclosed the festival grounds. A road that was little more than a trail ran beyond this particular stretch. "It must have gone over the fence," she panted.

Clutching her new doll, Bonnie caught up to her. "What was it?"

"The ghost," Sophie said solemnly.

"Are you sure? In daylight?" Bonnie asked doubtfully.

"Yes!" Sophie wheeled on her sister. "It was in the same black coat and everything! I saw it in daylight the first time, remember?"

"If you say so," Bonnie shrugged. "But if you saw it again, you have to tell Papa."

"I know," Sophie admitted reluctantly. "I will." And they came out from behind the tent while their guardians scolded them and Bagur the potter watched curiously.

True to her word, Sophie went off in search of her father while Bonnie asked her guardian to find Aunt Renée, in hopes of being allowed to ride in the litter with her today. (Yesterday, Renée had declined permission, given all the concentrated shopping she had to do.) So the girls parted.

Sophie had a good idea where her father would be. There was a large tent near the entrance with lots of guards and moneyboxes, and where the Steward sat at a table to write in big books. Sophie knew that her father had a table of his own in that tent, so she went in, and there he was, head in one hand, reading lots of papers. As Sophie approached his table, he looked up and smiled. She loved it when he smiled at her. The whole world grew bright and happy.

"Hello, Sophie. Are you having fun? You haven't bought anything yet today," he observed.

She reached over to pull on his hand. "Come out with me, Papa." There were too many people in here for her to share her secret with him.

He balked, "Dear one, your poor Papa has so many papers to look at—"

She would not take no for an answer. "Papa, come out with me," she insisted, still tugging on his hand.

With a bemused frown, he allowed her to drag him outside, where they began walking aimlessly while she kept looking all around. Her guardian followed at a discreet distance. When she was satisfied that no one else was within earshot, she pulled him down to her level and whispered, "Papa, I saw it again today."

"Saw what?" he whispered back.

"The ghost," she confided, and was gratified at how quickly his expression changed.

He straightened. "Where?" he asked aloud.

"Over there, behind the potter's tent," she pointed.

He paused. "Which potter?"

"I'll show you." He seemed anxious to get there, so she began trotting toward the general area of the potter's tent. But it wasn't close by, and she couldn't remember exactly where it was. She slowed uncertainly, finally coming to a complete stop to look around.

Ares knelt beside her. "Sophie, do you remember which potter? Was it the Polonti potter?"

"I think so," she said doubtfully.

"Describe the ghost, dear one. What did he look like?"

"Just the same, Papa. That's how I knew what it was. It was long and black, with no face, and went along very quietly."

Ares stood, beckoning to a nearby soldier to issue quiet instructions to him. Then Ares knelt again to tell his daughter, "Thank you for coming to me this time, Sophie. You did well. Unless your ghost vanishes into thin air, we will find him. Now—please go see what your sister is buying."

"All right, Papa." Satisfied, she kissed his cheek and ran off, her guardian trailing her doggedly. Shortly thereafter, hundreds of soldiers were unobtrusively searching around the perimeter of the field for a man dressed in a long black coat, or anyone who appeared to be trying to hide his face or cloak his appearance.

Soldiers also searched Bagur's tent thoroughly on the pretext of looking for a missing child. And in minutes, also according to instructions, Nicole was brought to Ares.

She came in haste and concern. "What is it, my lord? What is wrong?"

"I . . . wanted to know that you were safe," he murmured, bringing her fingers to his lips.

"Why?" she asked.

"Sophie spotted her ghost on the grounds," he told her.

Nicole exhaled. "Ares, that's preposterous. We both know that there is no ghost."

"No, but there is Chiacos, and she recognized him. Nicole—please—will you please go back to the palace?"

She looked at him in gentle reproach, which was the worst kind. "And live the rest of my life in fear of a ghost? Ares, I will take seriously the warning that Chiacos has been seen. I will be careful to stay within sight of my bodyguard. I will use all discretion in where I go. But please—do not ask me to hide."

He lowered his eyes to the fingers he still held, then released them. "Be sure to show me what you have bought tonight."

"Certainly, my lord." She curtsied, smiling, and he let her go. And no one found Sophie's ghost, or anything like it.

The third day of the festival was a washout, literally. The rain came down in torrents, precluding all but the most determined from setting up shop to sparse, mostly juvenile crowds. Renée, unreasonably angered by the weather, kept pacing to the nearest window to see if the rain might let up enough for her to go out.

This attitude astonished a number of people, none of whom had ever seen the Chataine brave bad weather for anything. Moreover, they thought she would be bored with the festival by now. Ares, for his part, was relieved to see Nicole having to stay inside and do needlework.

The next several days fully made up for any losses the merchants might have incurred due to the weather, for when the rain left, the crowds came back in force to enjoy the new sweetness of the air and newly washed tents. Moreover, those who had to travel to reach the festival finally arrived, bringing new money. Although Giles did not handle individual merchants' monies, he was frequently asked to authenticate foreign coinage, and did so happily. He saw plenty of cruxes, but none minted prior to Magnus' reign.

Sophie's ghost did not make another appearance either. Since the second day when it was spotted, Ares had taken to walking the grounds, greeting festival-goers and just looking. On one such stroll, he was canvassing the field when he spotted a dashing figure in hunter's cloak and cap.

Ares paused, watching him, and the lord turned to find himself the object of the Surchatain's scrutiny. Not lacking courage in the slightest, he was still mildly startled by the scar fixed in his direction.

So he bowed, and Ares addressed him with reserved civility: "I have not had the pleasure of an introduction. I am Surchatain Ares."

"Surchatain, you are well known for your hospitality to weary travelers. I am Fancsali of Eviron," he replied with a salute.

The lord was genuinely surprised at the sudden recognition in Ares' face. "You do yourself a disservice, omitting your title, Lord Fancsali."

"It seemed insignificant, comparatively speaking," the lord answered with a hesitant smile.

"Hardly. It was well earned through exemplary service to Magnus and your fellow man," Ares said warmly.

Fancsali took a step toward him almost involuntarily. "You are too generous, Surchatain."

"Nonsense. I have been looking for an excuse to have you to dinner. Now I find you have fallen into my festival, which gives me reason enough. Only—" Ares hesitated, then uttered a laugh. "Only, I have a bizarre request of you."

Fancsali strode to his side. "This grows more interesting

by the moment. Please proceed, Surchatain, knowing that whatever you ask of me is granted."

Ares shook his head wryly. "This may teach you to restrain yourself from rash oaths, Fancsali. Here is the matter: our dear Chataine Renée, whom you have certainly seen riding in a litter these past several days—"

"Unmistakable," Fancsali agreed, nodding.

"Yes—well—our Chataine has been the victim of a heartless joke. A prankster has sent a marriage proposal to her in your name, so . . . when you arrive for dinner, Renée will be under the impression that you have proposed to her. While I hardly expect you to honor a hoax, we do not wish to embarrass or humiliate her," Ares ended in a warning.

"Indeed," Fancsali said softly. "I am intrigued and flattered, Surchatain."

His response being more good-natured than Ares had hoped for, the Surchatain was quick to offer him an out: "It will be quite easy to disentangle yourself gracefully of the obligation. All you need do is propose to remove her from Westford to a one-room bothy on your estate, where she will prove her worth in hard work and endless childbearing. I assure you that she will turn you down flat. But with an appearance of great reluctance," he was quick to add.

Fancsali laughed. "But what if I choose to honor the proposal, Surchatain?"

Ares paused, then admitted, "I had not thought of that. You . . . have not met our Chataine."

"Then I look forward most eagerly to the opportunity," Fancsali said, and Ares studied him.

10

Ares finished a hurried, whispered narrative to his amazed wife, "And so—there stands our situation with Lord Fancsali." They were standing in the anteroom preparatory to entering the great hall for dinner. After having met the lord that afternoon and issued the invitation to dinner, Ares had forgotten all about it until just an hour ago. So he had to quickly alert Georges that they would have a prominent guest that evening.

Worse, until Ares and Nicole were descending the stairway moments ago, he had forgotten that she knew nothing of Giles' forged proposal to Renée. Therefore, Ares had to hasten to cover himself on all fronts.

"Surchatain Ares and Lady Nicole," Georges announced. Nicole came out of her shock, placing her hand atop Ares' for him to escort her into the hall as the guests at table bowed.

When all had taken their seats and Ares gestured to the wine steward, he glanced at Fancsali to his left, where Sophie normally sat, and Renée to Nicole's right, in Bonnie's place. The twins had been excused to the kitchen for dinner, which outraged Bonnie and suited Sophie, as long as she got her father's lap after dinner.

"Well, I trust that Lord Fancsali has been properly announced, so we need only make introductions," Ares said. "This is my wife, the Surchataine Nicole."

Fancsali inclined his head to her as she nodded. "The lady is famous," he noted, and she paled, the words of welcome dying on her lips. No proper lady wanted attention amounting to fame—that was opprobrious.

"Uh—yes—" Ares said, glancing at her. "To your left is Counselor Carmine."

"Whose negotiating skills are renowned, though you've had your share of sticky wickets, eh, Counselor?" Fancsali said genially.

Carmine raised his brows slightly. "And which of my modest exploits merits the attention of an adventurer such as yourself, Lord Fancsali?" he wondered.

"The Chataine Renée," Fancsali said as if in answer, looking at her across the table, and everyone wondered if he knew that Carmine had once been married to Renée. For her part, she studied Fancsali coolly, saying nothing. As always, she was gorgeous, with shimmering golden hair bundled in a tiara that complemented the most fabulous gown Lord Preus had ever constructed, but there was particularly high color on her cheek tonight.

"The very one," Ares said, watching Fancsali. "Next to her is my Commander, Thom, and his wife Deirdre." Thom leaned forward as if daring Fancsali to make some comment about him, but the lord only cleared his throat. "And next to Counselor Carmine are the Steward Giles and his wife, Genevieve," Ares added.

Genevieve smiled and inclined her head, but Giles sat there sweating, eyes popping out of his head, in utter terror that his ploy was about to be exposed. Ares winced inwardly, wishing that he had remembered to inform Giles of Fancsali's promised cooperation. The last thing Ares needed was for Giles to be incapacitated in the middle of the festival.

"Yes, good Steward, we are two of a kind, you and I, what?" Fancsali said amiably. He was watching the roast swan, cooked whole and upright, being positioned on the table as a centerpiece, steam issuing from its beak. At the same time, carved portions of another roast swan were placed on gold plates in front of the diners.

"We—are—you and I?" Giles croaked, and Genevieve went rigid in embarrassment, eyes fixed on the middle distance.

"Yes, you and I," Fancsali said heartily. "Our only aim is to serve our master well, eh?" Helping himself to the meat before him with his fingers, Fancsali delivered a rascally wink to Giles. The Steward breathed a weak, unconvincing laugh in reply.

Studying Fancsali with a mixture of amusement and wonder, Ares leaned back in his seat as buttered ramekin and parsley-stuffed artichokes were set before him. Who in his right mind would accept the invitation of a Surchatain in order to provoke his highest administrators—and the Surchataine!—with jesting insults?

In concern, Ares glanced at Nicole beside him; placated, he picked up his fork. Far from being traumatized, Nicole was directing evaluative glances at their guest. Having been alerted to his brand of humor, she would not be caught off guard again.

The table lapsed into wary silence as all began eating. To prevent further slights, Ares issued no further introductions. A glance at Renée, however, gave him startling insight into Fancsali's motivations. She was gazing at the rogue lord in undisguised, utter infatuation. Here, at last, was a tongue to match her own in sharpness and wit. Ares was mildly awed by Fancsali's prescience: how could the lord have known that his taunts would elicit her admiration?—if that had been his intent.

"Lord Fancsali," Nicole opened with a benign smile,

"some days ago Steward Giles was championing your name at this table, telling us of your heroism in holding a large band of slavers captive—" Here she paused so Fancsali would know that he had abused a friend in impugning Giles. "So now, if it please you, I would be highly desirous to hear of the matter from your own lips."

"Hear, hear," some voices seconded.

Ares looked at Fancsali expectantly. "Yes, let us hear if you truly served Magnus as well as Giles serves me," he said with as friendly a face as his scar and his own grave nature would allow. With such dazzling praise from the head of the table, Giles blinked rapidly, as if about to burst into tears.

"It was a trivial undertaking, hardly worthy of my lady's attention," Fancsali scoffed.

"Indulge me," Nicole said with a cold smile—the closest she had ever come to issuing a command as Surchataine.

Fancsali sighed reluctantly, elbows on the table, picking meat from a rib. "As you wish, though I'll be guilty of boring the most celebrated Surchataine on the Continent. Here is the simple matter: The daughter of a friend of mine had gone on an outing with a lady from Magnus' court, and they had gotten themselves rather too far from Eurus, into old Gargus' territory.

"Well, his band lit on them like horseflies, of course, but one servant escaped to run in a blind panic to my loggers. They came to me. I had been looking for a reason to impale Gargus' ugly head on my gates, so I sent the servant back to Eurus to inform Magnus, then collected my men and went after the scoundrel. We were able to split company, half pursuing him from the south, half taking a shortcut to Falcon Pass, so as to encircle them when they arrived at the Pass.

"From then, it was child's play to pick them off while they hovered between hell on the north and the devil on the south. They thought to threaten the hostages if we didn't stand down!" Fancsali laughed. "But when the rascal who held the knife to the lady's throat got himself shot in the head, the lot of them lay down like sheep. So they were resting under our hooves when Magnus arrived, and I do recall that he was aggravated that none were left in any condition for him to chastise in his torture chamber. So you see, while the ladies were retrieved whole, my own part in it was less than satisfactory," Fancsali ended regretfully.

"So Magnus awarded you a title and an estate merely out of the goodness of his heart?" Nicole asked.

"To be truthful, Lady, that was the Surchataine's doing, as the lady we regained was a favorite of hers," Fancsali admitted.

"Druella? How is she?" Melva asked wistfully. One seat down from Genevieve, Melva had not been introduced, nor had she spoken before now.

Fancsali looked down the table in keen interest. "The last I saw her, Lady, she was flowering and radiant—though not to compare with the royalty here," he replied, glancing back at Renée. Returning his attention to Melva, he observed, "You ask as one who knows—"

"Well, it is quite evident that, whether it was Magnus or his wife who rewarded you, it was justified," Ares said, as though unaware that Fancsali had been speaking. Seeing that many of the diners had finished their dessert of peaches and cream, Ares asked, "Do you dance, Fancsali?"

"I? Pshaw," he demurred, which led everyone to believe that he was an outstanding dancer.

Ares gestured for the musicians. "Then someone can surely be found to teach you. We dance solely for pleasure. There is no consequence at all for failure to perform on the floor," he said grimly.

Having uttered not a word all evening, Renée stood and said, "I shall be your tutor tonight, Lord Fancsali. Do not refuse me"—as if any man could. He promptly rounded the table to face her. Taking her outstretched hand, he bent low to kiss it, then straightened to lead her out onto the floor.

While he was thus distracted, Ares turned to Carmine. "Have Melva taken upstairs. I do not want him to know her identity."

"Agreed," Carmine uttered, gesturing to a servant.

Ares rounded on Thom. "Send a team of spies to his estate. I want to know as much about him as he seems to know about us."

"Gladly," Thom concurred with a light sneer. He turned on his heel to depart the hall, thus leaving Deirdre to find a dance partner among the nobles.

Then Ares bowed over his wife's hand preparatory to joining the line dance that was presently forming. "What do you make of him?" he murmured in her ear.

She expelled a breath in exasperation. "I don't know! He is certainly most cocky and irritating."

"Which seems to be his design," Ares noted, glancing at the lord folding his right arm behind his back while his left hand supported Renée's. As the music signaled the start of the dance, every eye in the hall was on the guest. To Nicole's relief, he was actually a mediocre dancer, but Ares watched Renée determinedly tutor him.

For the rest of the evening, Renée and Fancsali held their own private counsels. She was clearly smitten as she had never been before. Fancsali was clearly encouraging her, which clearly disturbed several people.

Watching them, Carmine began hoisting one cup of wine after another. When Vogelsong noticed his red-rimmed eyes and flushed face, he went and spoke a word to Ares on the dance floor. Leaving Nicole stranded on the floor, Ares returned to the table and leaned down at Carmine's side. "Counselor, I require your presence upstairs."

"Shurchatain," Carmine mumbled, weaving to a stand.

Taking him discreetly by the elbow, Ares walked with him to the foyer staircase. With Carmine leaning heavily on his arm, Ares assisted him up the long, curved staircase. Ares started to speak several times, then curtailed each comment in the effort to say only what would be profitable. He finally uttered, "He is playing with her, Carmine."

"Eh?" The Counselor focused on him as if just now aware of his presence.

"Fancsali does not intend to marry our Chataine. She is his patsy," Ares said.

Carmine tittered, "So the player becomes the plaything."

"Yes. But we who are charged with defending her honor must keep ourselves alert and watchful to plan our steps. We must stay sober to deal with this Fancsali, Carmine."

"You are right, Ares," he replied, drawing himself up at the head of the stairs.

Ares took him to the door of his quarters to hand him over to his personal attendant, Hauffe. But before closing the door, Ares dragged Hauffe out into the corridor, leaving Carmine alone in the room.

The servant bowed as well as he could with Ares' fist clenched on his collar. "You are to see that your master receives nothing stronger than peppermint tea from now on," Ares breathed. "No ale, no beer, no wine. If he abuses you for this, you will be rewarded. If he dismisses you for this, come to me. And as soon as he is awake and alert tomorrow morning, you will tell him that I have summoned him."

"Yes, Surchatain," Hauffe replied in perfect comprehension. Ares released him to attend his master and turned back down the corridor with heavy steps. Once before, he had lost years of Carmine's service to the wine—that blackout being precipitated by Renée, as well—and Ares was determined never to lose him that way again.

Returning to the great hall, Ares was met by Nicole. "What is wrong with Carmine?" she whispered anxiously.

"He could not make it through the evening without numbing himself," Ares muttered.

"He hasn't started drinking again?" she asked in dismay.

"Where are Renée and Fancsali?" he asked.

She looked past the expanse of floor toward the double doors opening into the garden. "They went out to the garden, I believe."

Ares gestured to a sentry, who ran over. "You—" Ares began, then stopped. "Geurts?"

"Yes, Surchatain," he saluted, pleased at being recognized.

"You are healed already?" Ares asked.

"Mostly, sir. The doctor won't let me ride yet, but I can stand guard as well as ever," Geurts said.

"Very good. You are the Chataine Renée's chaperon tonight. You will keep her and our guest in sight at all times, and you will allow them to see that you are keeping them in sight. They are presently in the garden," Ares nodded.

"Surchatain." He saluted and made haste for the garden doors.

Ares took his wife's hand to resume their dance. "Where are the girls?" he asked, glancing around.

"Up to bed," Nicole sighed. "They're both tired and cross from so much excitement. Bonnie threw a most unladylike fit that Renée finds the lord's company so much more interesting than hers. I wish . . . Renée had taken a moment just to tell her goodnight, but . . . she would not be bothered."

"Wait a moment. With Geurts standing over them, the Chataine may be throwing her own fit," Ares predicted.

Shortly thereafter, the two lovebirds emerged from the garden, Renée tossing a withering glance in Ares' direction. Dancing with Nicole, he pretended not to notice. While Fancsali returned to the table to quench his thirst and sport with Giles, Renée interrupted Ares and Nicole to coolly inquire, "As tomorrow is the last day of the festival, Lord Fancsali is to be our guest tonight, I assume?"

"Of course, Chataine," Ares said solicitously.

"You will not put him in the lower corridor, will you?" Renée asked darkly.

"Of course not. He shall be lodged in the guest quarters on the third floor," Ares said.

Glancing toward Geurts standing off a pace, Renée added, "I do not require the guard, Ares."

He straightened. "The courtship of a Chataine is bound by strict rules and conventions which I intend to relax for no one. To do so would slight you and me."

Since he phrased it that way, Renée could hardly quibble with special treatment. "As you wish," she said stiffly, and swept toward the table on the other side of the room. As Giles slunk away, Fancsali met her laughing, spinning her around for a dramatic dip and kiss. Geurts shot a questioning look at Ares, who gestured him over.

"We will not interfere with what they choose to do in the sight of all," Ares told him. "The lord will be staying the night, and probably several nights following, in guest quarters on the third floor—Georges will show you which. When Fancsali is in his room and she in hers, you will post two guards at each door. There will be no commerce between the rooms, nor any wandering of corridors in the dead of night."

"Surchatain," Geurts grinned, saluting. Then he sprinted off to make these orders known, and perhaps revel in his newfound status. Then Nicole and Ares bid goodnight to all their guests, and went up to console their disgruntled daughters.

The twins were fighting like magpies when the royal parents entered; looking over to see who dared interrupt their game, they squealed and bounded off the bed. Sophie, of course, rushed to her father's arms, and Nicole was privately thrilled that Bonnie went to her as eagerly as she ever did Renée.

The girls babbled out their separate complaints to the parent who had their ear. Bonnie was still angry over being left in Fancsali's wake. "I *saw* him, Mama! He's not dashing or nice or anything like the man Aunt Renée said she was waiting for. He just has this stupid grin and he doesn't smell very good! He's just like all the other men she makes fun of!" Bonnie wailed.

"What . . . kind of man is Aunt Renée waiting for?" Nicole asked, intrigued.

"Well," sniffled Bonnie, "she always said she wanted some-one smart, and witty, and handsome, and—I can't remember the words—someone who could talk well and dance well."

"That sounds like Counselor Carmine," Nicole observed.

"She says she's tired of him. She wants someone new," Bonnie said.

"Well, even people you have known for a long time can surprise you, if you're paying attention," Nicole said.

"Is Aunt Renée tired of me?" Bonnie asked in a small voice.

"I can't imagine anyone being tired of such a charming girl," Nicole said, offended. Bonnie snuggled down in her mother's skirts and very soon closed her eyes.

With two sleepy children tucked into bed, Ares and Nicole left the chambers, nodding at the guards who stood watch. As they crossed the corridor to their own apartments, Nicole asked, "What was Sophie telling you about?"

"Her ghost," he muttered pensively.

"Is she still afraid of it?" she asked.

"She's not so much afraid of it as determined to catch it," he replied, opening the door into the receiving room for her.

"She is her father's daughter!" Nicole said with a laugh.

The dense darkness of the chambers was unrelieved by the solitary candle that burned low in its holder on the table. Ares picked up a new candle to light it from the first one and carry it with them into the sleeping chamber. There, he extended the candle toward the cold, lifeless grate, with fresh wood and kindling stacked nearby, then he turned to her with a pointed look. "You can do better than Ursula, Lady."

Nicole uttered a chuckle, standing beside the wardrobe to begin undressing. "Because you won't have a manservant to light the fires? Because Ursula is afraid of the fireplace now and won't go near it?"

"You could do with a more competent maid," he grumbled, setting the candlestick on the hearth to begin stacking the kindling on the grate.

"No, I need Ursula," Nicole said. "Help me with this, please." He stood and she turned around for him to unfasten the long row of buttons down the back of the dress—a task in which he had become quite proficient.

After returning the dress to the wardrobe and depositing the rest of her underclothes into the basket, she dropped herself into the sunken tub. It was fed by a continuous trickle that cascaded down the rock, sending droplets on the massed ferns around the edge. "Oh, it's chilly. Hurry," she urged, shivering.

He piled on the rest of the wood and lit a stick of kindling from the candle. Applying that to the lowermost twigs resting on the grate, he wondered, "Why do you need an incompetent maid?"

"She keeps me humble," Nicole said. "She teaches me patience. Oh, Ares, please hurry! I'm freezing!"

With a wry smile, Ares stripped quickly and lowered himself to the tub to surround her with his warmth. It would take at least a half hour for the fire to warm the rock enough to make the water comfortable. "If you had a maid who kept the fire going, then the water wouldn't get so cold," he murmured into her neck.

"If you would condescend to have a manservant to keep the fire going, then I would not have to release a dear girl who is only a little dense," Nicole returned, closing her eyes. Her eyes popped open again when she realized, "I haven't bought her anything at all from the festival! And when she finds out about the puppet I bought for Eleanor, she'll be so hurt that she won't speak to me for a week. I will have to get her something tomorrow—"

Ares stopped her mouth with his. And before the water had hardly any time to warm up, he lifted her from the tub to lay her in bed. But then Ursula knocked on the door belatedly to light the fire, and by the time they got rid of her, Captain Yonge, who was in charge of security at the festival, appeared bearing a list of miscreants that he desired to publicly ban from any future festivals. That meant publishing the list before the end of this year's festival, and as some of those at the top of the list were related to prominent Westfordians, the Captain required the Surchatain's seal. Even though Ares transferred the responsibility of ratifying the list to Thom with all due haste, Nicole was asleep by the time he finally crawled into bed.

By the next day, the last day of the festival, the strain of nonstop entertainment had begun to tell on everyone. Giles looked like walking death, but was out on the fields early to avoid Fancsali. Following the rotation of sentries, Ares received the night watchmen's report: after retiring in the wee hours of the morning, Fancsali stayed put in his room. The Chataine attempted to leave her quarters once; being denied permission to roam and knowing that her actions would be reported to Ares, she did not make a second attempt.

The twins slept in, rebelling against lessons, so Ares gave them the day off to attend the festival, but they did not go right away. Ares was told that they were playing together in the vegetable garden; in fact, they were looking for further clues as to the ghost's whereabouts. Sophie was convinced that it was in some way bound to the passage that was now sealed in concretus. "But then what was it doing at the festival?" Bonnie asked.

"I guess we had better go find out," Sophie decided, so they set out for the festival with their guardians in tow. As usual, Bonnie was dressed nicely, with curled hair, while Sophie wore a ponytail and play dress that made her look like any middle-class child.

By this time it was late afternoon, and the crowds were sparse. The last day of the festival was allotted for booth takedown and departure, as the fields had to be cleared by early tomorrow. Therefore, most merchants had already been packing for some time. A few of the more cautious had already left to avoid nighttime travel, which was unwise even in Lystra. Many tents were already coming down, although some would stay up to shelter their owners overnight. But with the banners furled, the decorations packed, and the shelves bared, an air of sad finality pervaded the place. The end of a holiday, when the gaiety gave way to mundane life, was almost unbearable for children.

The twins were shuffling through the trodden meadow, sighing as if bereaved, when Sophie stopped and cocked her head, looking at the tent in front of them. Bagur the potter came out, then turned to shake the hand of a man remaining in the doorway. "Thank you, sir, you've been a great help. I'm honored to learn from a master craftsman," Bagur said.

"No trouble, my good man," his host replied with a wave.

As Bagur departed, Sophie gripped her sister's hand and sidled into the tent. Its occupant, a potter, was directing the packing of pots, plates, cups, and pitchers into crates padded with straw. They were almost done. Bonnie shrank back from the dirty, sweaty laborers, but Sophie began an intent exploration of the tent. She happened upon the money table, where the merchant's wife sat counting out receipts. There on the table was a short stack of cruxes, which Sophie recognized.

The woman, seeing the common-looking child staring at her money, spat, "What d'you want? Get away!"

Sophie met her eyes defiantly, but began backing away. The potter looked up from his packing to see the little girl flee to the front of the tent where her sister anxiously waited. Through the open flap, he saw the pair of bodyguards standing outside. And he knew whom his wife had just chased out of their tent.

"Woman, have you lost your mind? Why are you abusing the Surchatain's child?" he cried. Uncomprehending, she looked up from her receipts, and he moaned, "We'll be thrown out of next year's festival . . . if they catch us. Hurry up with those," he suddenly urged.

Sophie, straining to remain calm, took Bonnie's hand and began walking quickly back toward the palace. "What is it? Whatever did you see?" Bonnie asked in a whisper.

Her sister glanced back at the bored soldiers trailing them. "*That* was the tent—the one I saw the ghost behind—and it's not Bagur's tent! And they had lots of dead man's tokens! We have to go tell Papa right away." She paused to fix the location of the tent—everything about the vicinity—in her memory, to be able to tell him where it was.

At that moment, Nicole was finally making her way to the festival to pick up something for Ursula. Although vexed by the delay, this was the soonest she could get away, as Renée had held her hostage for several hours with gushing talk of Fancsali. The more Renée had talked of him, the less Nicole liked him, and she could not say why. He just seemed . . . false.

When Renée had finally begun her elaborate toilet for dinner, Nicole was able to escape before every booth at the festival closed. Hence she barely paused to grab a purse before literally running out of the courtyard down the mostly deserted path toward the festival grounds. It was already nearing twilight, with the booths' shadows lengthening into one great shade.

Nicole knew that she should have taken the time to

summon a bodyguard, but the continual coddling chafed her. Also, whispered reports that Chiacos was dead reached her ears, sealing out any thought that she might still be in danger. Above all, in a small corner of her mind she was still a peasant girl from Prie Mer, unworthy of such fuss. So the only precaution she took today was to inform the doorkeeper where she would be.

She wandered over the grounds in some anxiety, seeing that the best merchants had closed up already. Then she paused at the belated realization that they would certainly open up again just for her, should she request it. But she did not wish to inconvenience merchants as Renée would, requiring them to unpack merchandise for her inspection and then walk off without buying. So she was walking, trying to remember the location of the confectioner's booth, when she heard someone crying.

Startled, Nicole looked all around; the grounds were practically empty. She saw no one but a few people loading boxes in carts or pulling up tent stakes. Then she heard it again —it was definitely someone crying, or moaning, and it seemed to be coming from behind a tent that was being taken down.

Thinking someone to be hurt, Nicole hiked her skirts and ran to the rear of the tent. There, she drew up in surprise, murmuring, "Chiacos."

II

Sophie and Bonnie passed out through the festival gate minutes after their mother had entered, narrowly missing her for the stream of outgoing wagons and conveyances. In great haste, the twins arrived at the palace and went about inquiring where their father might be.

First, they were told that he was with Giles inspecting the festival records, but when they finally located the Steward at the door of the fourth-floor treasury, their papa was not with him.

Inquiring again, they were told he was entertaining Lord Fancsali with a tour of the palace, but they found the lord not with Papa, but with Aunt Renée on the south balcony overlooking the apple orchard. Moreover, he and she were engaged in such close physical contact that Bonnie screamed, "Ughh!" and ran away with tears in her eyes.

After consoling her sister, Sophie decided the best place to look for Papa was probably his receiving room. As they approached to enter, the sentry stopped them. "Is Papa in there?" Sophie demanded.

"Yes, Chataine, and he left orders not to be disturbed," the sentry replied.

"But this is *important*," Sophie stressed.

"It will have to wait, Chataine," he insisted. So wait they did, as he was unmoved by tears or threats and would not grant them entrance.

Inside, Carmine stood rigid and pale, facing the table while Ares paced behind him. "I can't lose you again, Carmine," he said through gritted teeth. It had been almost exactly two years ago that Carmine had climbed out of a deep alcoholic haze to resume his duties as Counselor. From that time until last night, he had drunk nothing alcoholic. But last night—

"No one can replace you!" Ares shouted, slamming his fist against the window shutter, splintering it. Carmine flinched. "No one can do what you do! No one knows as much as you do! . . . No one suffered with me under Talus and Cedric as you did," he finished in a whisper, standing at Carmine's ear. The Counselor opened his mouth slightly, but knew that mere words would not suffice to answer for what Ares considered a personal betrayal.

"I have prayed to God to show me how to keep you sober, knowing that it is beyond my ability to do so. But this He showed me," Ares continued to whisper at his side. "This will be my command, and you must decide what you desire. If you so much as touch another drop of wine, I will banish Renée from Westford forever."

Carmine's head jerked toward Ares in utter shock. "You —how can you—"

"She will be provided for the rest of her life, but not here. As you have never been able to unbind yourself from her control, I will do it for you. If Renée causes you to drink, then she must go," Ares said coldly.

"But—Fancsali—" Carmine stuttered.

With a wry look, Ares walked around the table to throw

himself back into the chair. "Lord Fancsali is out to see what sport he may have with her while he is here, but he will not marry her. Thom reported to me moments ago that there is a lady ensconced at his estate who purports to be the mother of his three children, and his wife." Carmine closed his eyes, staggering as if a knife had been thrust between his ribs.

"Have you had enough of her, Carmine? Then you have the power to be done with her for good. But I make my word binding to you before God on this matter: if you imbibe anything that intoxicates—one drink!—then Renée will be sent away forever, though my own dove hate me for the rest of my life," Ares said, his scar purple and throbbing.

"May it never be," Carmine whispered, trembling.

"As you wish," Ares said, standing, and Carmine was shaken to his bones to see tears in the Surchatain's eyes.

Outside in the corridor, the girls looked up when Counselor Carmine exited, white as death. Sophie slipped past him to dart to her father, who sat holding his head at the great table covered with papers and maps. "Papa, I found it," she whispered urgently.

With effort, he raised his head from his hands. In a sigh, he asked, "Found what, dear one?"

"I found the tent that I saw the ghost behind. It was a potter's tent, but not Bagur's. And there were the dead man's tokens there, too!"

He froze momentarily, then stood. "Do you remember where it is?"

"Yes. I made sure to know," she said.

"Lead on, Chataine." He gestured, and she shot out of the receiving room ahead of him. In the corridor, he caught her shoulder, and she turned. "We do not run unless it is a matter of life and death, Chataine," he reminded her.

Nodding, she slowed her pace, and Bonnie caught up to

them. "I know where it is, too!" she said.

Ares held out his hand. "Then come, Chataine."

He trotted down the staircase, gripping their little hands to stabilize them on their rapid descent. They crossed the foyer to the great doors, then he stopped so suddenly that the girls almost fell backward. Blinking once, he asked the doorkeeper in a low voice, "Do we know where the Surchataine is?"

He saluted. "She left for the festival about an hour ago, Surchatain."

Ares stepped out to look south, where darkness was spreading over the meadow. "And she has not returned?"

"No, Surchatain."

"Did she take bodyguards?" he asked tightly.

The doorkeeper paused. "I did not see any, Surchatain."

Ares nodded, eyes south. "Initiate a search for the Surchataine in the palace environs. And summon the Commander to the fields."

"Surchatain." He saluted again.

Taking a torch from a sconce by the door, Ares nodded at his daughters. "Lead me, dear ones." Now they did run, all three of them.

Arriving breathless at the field, they stopped in dismay, and Bonnie started crying. There were a few random tents still up, and a few wagons yet being loaded, but most merchants had learned the previous year that it was best to go ahead and leave during the last day, because the Lystran soldiers did not stand guard around the field after sundown of the last day.

The soldiers were not here now. Very few people were. Ares could look over the whole field from where he stood and see that she was not here, unless she was in one of the dark tents.

While the three of them stood gazing over the meadow, a cadre of riders approached from the palace behind them.

Without looking back, Ares said, "Thom, has the Surchataine been located?"

The Commander could not bring himself to answer the question directly. "We are looking," he replied.

Ares nodded down at his daughter in the deepening darkness. "Can you still find where the ghost's tent was, Sophie?"

"Yes, Papa," she said decidedly. He angled the torch forward and down to illumine the uneven ground before them, and she set off at a confident trot with Ares at her side and Bonnie just trailing them. Behind them rode Thom, Oswald, and several other soldiers.

Sophie led this train on an angular route around patches of dead grass where tents used to be, then she made a straight shot toward the temporary fencing that separated the field from the road ten feet beyond it. Ares felt a raw squeezing in his gut at the sight of the new moon rising over the road.

"Here," she proclaimed, stopping and spreading her hands. "Here is the tent that was full of dead man's tokens, and I saw the ghost behind it here. Between the tent and the fence."

Ares jerked his head back toward Thom. "Get Giles out here with his logs to tell us who had this space." Thom gestured to a soldier, who spurred back toward the palace at a gallop. Then Ares walked over to what had been the alley behind the tent and knelt with the torch to examine the ground all around. Sophie and Bonnie followed him to watch. While he was thus engaged, a few other riders approached. One told Thom, "Commander, no one has been able to locate the Surchataine."

Ares heard him, but did not react. He picked up something small from the ground and asked, "Bonnie, what dress was your mother wearing today?"

"The lavender with silver flowers, Papa," she answered promptly. "It has the silver belt and the purple drape rimmed in silver."

"Silver like this?" he asked, extending a scrap of fabric toward her.

She took it in her hands and cried, "Yes! This is from her sleeve! She didn't like the bell sleeves because they were always getting caught on things and ripping!"

"I see," Ares said, continuing to move the torch methodically over the ground. "Thom." The Commander dismounted and knelt by his side while Bonnie, weeping, showed the scrap to her sister, who comforted her in whispers.

Meanwhile, Thom and Ares were carrying on their own dialogue, pointing to various indentions in the ground. "Here are her footprints. And here is our ghost," Ares observed.

"The same square-toed boot as in the passage, with the protruding hobnail in the right heel," Thom said.

"He's limping."

"She struggles."

"She was dragged to the fence." They examined the cracked top railing of the fence, then hopped over it to scrutinize the ground between it and the road. "A horse was waiting."

While they were studying the hoofprints, another rider careened up to the scene and dismounted in great haste. Before anyone could stop him, he had leaped the fence to stand beside Thom and Ares. Ignoring him, they continued their discussion. "Look at the calks. The farrier in Dansington does that," Ares noted.

Thom replied, "True. And the rider's heading west, toward Dansington."

"No," Fancsali interrupted. Only then did the other two look at him. "No. Look," Fancsali reiterated, kneeling. "The animal's been fitted with backwards shoes, acting as rockered toe eggbars. Look at the extra nail holes and spacing of the prints. He's headed east."

In unison, Ares and Thom looked back down at the prints, and slowly pivoted from the west to the east, eyes on the tracks. Disbelieving, Thom followed them on hands and knees for a few yards, then sat up to grunt, "He's right."

Ares breathed, "That makes no sense! Heading west on this road will take you to Eurus, Dansington, Crescent Hollow, or Prie Mer. But eastward, the road peters out to a sheep trail! There's nothing eastward, but—"

"Eviron," Thom said, standing. He and Ares evaluated Fancsali.

"All the more reason I must go with you to search for the lady," Fancsali said. "If he has brought her anywhere near my lair, then I will hear of it."

Hesitantly, Ares asked Thom, "Who is the best tracker we have?"

The Commander thought for only a moment or two. "Lieutenant Moeck."

"Summon him."

"He is still in Dansington, Surchatain," Thom said reluctantly, and they both looked at Fancsali again. Tossing his cloak over his shoulder, the lord took the torch from Thom's hand and began following the hoofprints on foot, head down.

"Get us horses," Ares instructed Thom. "Select five riders to accompany us, and arm a unit to follow us." While Thom was carrying out these instructions, Ares turned to his two little girls huddled together in the midst of the men. Kneeling, he opened his arms and they rushed to him.

"You both did very well," he said, looking from one to the other. "Without your help, we never would have known what happened. But because of what you told me, we can find her."

"Are you going yourself, Papa?" Sophie asked.

"Yes, dear one. This time I am going myself to get her back."

"Then I know that she will be all right," Sophie said in calmness of heart.

"Yes. And I will find your ghost, and put him to rest," he said, then added, "You must go home now, and go to bed, for it may take a while. Several days."

"Yes, Papa." They each kissed his cheek, one on either side, then Ares stood and made eye contact with a pair of soldiers. They presented themselves, saluting, and he surrendered his daughters to them without a word. They knew what to do.

Thom rode up, leading two horses. Behind him followed Oswald, Fawler, and three other soldiers, all mounted, armed, and carrying lights. Ares swung himself up on one of the horses, and Fawler extended a scabbard with sword to him. As Ares strapped it on his hip, they began following Fancsali at a walk.

During daylight, it was possible to follow a trail on horseback, but at night, someone had to lead on foot. Going so much slower than one's quarry could be a severe disadvantage—except if the quarry was unaware of pursuit. Eyes on Fancsali's back, Ares reasoned that no one must have witnessed her abduction behind the tent. And as no one raised a cry, her captor had no reason to suspect that anyone would follow.

Sucking in a breath, Ares brushed aside thoughts of recrimination or punishment. Nicole was Surchataine; if she left the palace without requesting a bodyguard, no one would stop her and demand that she take one. Why had she not?

Even as he posed the question to himself, he knew the answer: She would have none of special handling. *Why?* This he did not know.

Fancsali suddenly knelt to pick up something. Turning to Ares on horseback, he handed up a ladies' silk pouch. "Do you recognize it, sir?"

"Yes," Ares said. "It is hers." He only had to heft it to know it was still full of royals.

"It would seem that our thief was not interested in her purse then," Fancsali noted, turning back to the trail. A glance passed between Ares and Thom, and the Commander silently concurred that Chiacos was expecting payment of another kind upon delivery of the goods.

Shortly, the dirt road that they followed faded into grassland. Although Fancsali's confident step hardly wavered, Thom dismounted to assist him. Dry grass would stay down once trampled, but green grass, as this was, would spring back only hours after being walked on. By that time it would be much more difficult to find signs of passing. Private prayers were raised from several minds that there would be no rain tonight. Rainfall would obliterate any trace of a trail.

It was not long after Thom had joined Fancsali that contention arose between them. While Fancsali stepped one way, Thom objected, "No! The trail goes here." He pointed in the other direction. Fancsali barely glanced over before dissenting, "You are mistaken, my friend. That is nothing but the resting of a covey."

"Surchatain—" Thom turned back with gritted teeth to appeal.

While his horse weaved restlessly, Ares refused to dismount to look for himself. If he could not trust his trackers, he might as well stop right where he was. And of the two, he suspected that Fancsali was in the right. So Ares told them,

"We cannot separate to follow every possibility. You must be in agreement."

"Check the ground again, Commander," Fancsali urged politely, kneeling to part the grass to its roots. "There is the left rear hoof. See?" Thom bent to look, then grudgingly nodded. Fancsali stood. "Then let us not waste time haggling." He continued on a straight line, and minutes later Thom remounted in defeat.

In pursuit of the trail, they passed Willowring Lake on their left. As they were miles south of the shore, only glints of its black surface were visible here and there, but it stretched for quite a ways.

Then they came to the eastern fork of the Passage. This stream was so much shallower and narrower than the western fork, or the waterway that used to be the Village Branch, that it merited little attention, being unsuitable for all but the smallest boats. Still, their arrival at its rocky edge caused a ripple of concern, and Oswald began muttering to himself. If Nicole's abductor chose to obscure his trail by riding even a short ways downstream or up, it would be all but impossible to find the resumption of the trail on the far bank at night before it was washed away.

Without hesitation, Fancsali plunged straight into the water. Torch held aloft, he waded across, and the water came no higher than his waist. The party on horseback stayed on the far bank out of the stream, lest their entry cause ripples that would obscure a crucial print.

From forty feet away, Ares watched the torch swing this way and that when Fancsali reached the edge. Moments later he was scrambling up the bank, turning to wave the following party forward by torchlight. "Our foolish thief thinks himself safely away!" he shouted back at them. With that encouragement, the riders plunged into the stream after him.

"We're in Magnus' territory, now, Surchatain," Oswald said, riding at Ares' left. Ares nodded pensively; the Passage marked the boundary between Lystra and Scylla. Why had Nicole's abductor taken her into Scylla this time? To throw pursuers off? Or . . . was that closer to his final destination?

By this time, a unit of fifty men had caught up to them with weapons and provisions. Taking a drink from a water bottle, Ares paused to think. He did not know how much farther into Scylla the trail would lead. He did not know all the purposes behind this abduction—and he wondered, all of a sudden, where Lady Auer had gone after she had been banished from Lystra. So Ares gestured Fawler forward and told him, "Take two with you and return to Westford. Collect the Blue Regiment to follow us at once."

"Yes, Surchatain," Fawler saluted. Wheeling his horse, Fawler peeled two other riders from the unit and they disappeared into the night.

Returning to the head of the formation, Ares called, "Fancsali! Do you need a drink?" He had been pursuing the trail at a trot for hours now. Soaked from the waist down, Fancsali waved back over his shoulder, head down, to indicate no. Not wishing to distract Fancsali with the news that many more Lystrans would soon be occupying Scyllan soil, Ares muttered to Thom, "I have summoned the Blue." Thom nodded assent.

So they pressed on through miles of meadow, and Fancsali slowed only once or twice to confirm his direction by parting the grass. Other than that, he made neither stop nor detour while the new moon rose higher and the stars slowly etched their way across the sky.

After another few hours of painstakingly picking his way through grassland dotted with pine seedlings, Fancsali began to slow. The trail certainly had to be fading by now. They had been tracking for over six hours, and it could have been as long as eight hours ago that she was taken. Thom, astride his horse, leaned over to whisper to Ares, "He's lost the trail and's too proud to admit it." Ares only shook his head, whether in disagreement or despair.

Then Fancsali threw himself to a sit, gesturing. Riding up to him, Ares was surprised to find himself suddenly on a dirt road running vaguely north-south. Even from the saddle, even in the wavering torchlight, he could see the unmistakable backwards hoofprints leading north. "A draft from your skin would be welcome, Surchatain," Fancsali said, and Ares tossed the water bottle down to him.

After a generous swig, Fancsali wiped his mouth. "This is the road to my estate. The rascal has got himself into grave trouble now, for he's added trespassing to his crimes," he said in grim levity.

Stubbornly disbelieving, Thom dismounted to look closer at the trail. Shortly, he was forced to climb back into the saddle with a disgusted sigh. "Right again. He's uncanny. Unless—" He turned with sharp eyes. "He knew where they were going all along."

Ares shook his head. "Even had he known, Thom, it would not enable him to track them so reliably in the dark." He smiled wanly at his longtime friend. "I know you don't like him. I don't care much for him myself. But he is a first-rate tracker."

"Hmph. Moeck can do as much," Oswald said, sniffing.

As Fancsali got to his feet, Ares said, "There's no point in your walking as long as our thief has kept to the road, Fancsali." He gestured to the spare horse.

Handing off the torch to Thom, Fancsali said, "I'll take you up on your kind offer, Surchatain. Not as young as I used to be," he grunted, swinging a damp leg over the saddle.

This road had seen so little recent travel that the newest prints stood up in stark relief. The party was able to follow at a lope, which they sustained for almost an hour. The meadowlands gradually gave way to trees—first pines, then oak, ash, and black walnut.

Here, evidences of Fancsali's logging came into view, what with the broader road rutted by heavy wagon travel and the stumps of trees here and there. Although Ares could not see much beyond the torchlight, what he saw told him that Fancsali was smart enough not to clearcut his land and thus destroy his livelihood. He felled trees selectively, allowing for new growth. He also thinned trees back from the road to deprive robbers of their hiding places.

The greyness preceding sunrise was spreading in the east when Fancsali and Thom both called: "Stop!" "Hold up!"

Reining up, Ares could see that the trail of prints had vanished from the broad dirt road. "Where—?" He turned his horse in circles, looking, and groaned at the sight of the fifty-odd riders following him who would have thoroughly obscured any turn-off that Fancsali had missed.

"Here," the lord said calmly, retreating on horseback ten feet to a nearly invisible path that broke off from the main road. "The rascal decided not to come to my front door, after all." Fancsali seemed to have a definite idea where their prey had gone, for he spurred to a lope on the narrow path through thickening woods. Ares and company followed.

Minutes later, Fancsali held up his hand in a signal for the party to stop. Dismounting, he glanced at the ground. "Aha," he said in satisfaction. "Surchatain, leave the lights and men here, and follow me."

Ares had hardly lifted his right foot from the stirrup before Thom and Oswald had landed on their feet, wordlessly indicating their intention to accompany them. "You, also,

Commander," Fancsali said generously. "And your charming subordinate." Oswald curled his lip.

The four of them proceeded down the path on foot. All carried swords except Fancsali. "This leads to my warden's old cottage," he whispered. "It is a mean, windowless hut, so months ago I moved him and his family to better quarters closer to my house. The hut should be empty now—but I'll warrant that it is not."

The hoofprints they had been following all night led reliably to a clearing in which stood a dark wooden hut with a thatched roof. Seeing no horses, nor any movement around the hut, the four soundlessly approached the lone door. With the gradual lightening of the sky, Thom bent to study the ground. Standing, he whispered, "He stopped and unloaded her here. Then he took off again that way." Thom waved in a northerly direction quite apart from the path.

"I will venture to say that the Commander is correct," Fancsali said, without looking for himself.

Ares looked over the door, which had a newly installed iron latch securing it—from the outside. While Thom and Oswald drew their swords, Ares raised the latch and pulled the door open.

12

The interior of the hut was intensely dark, so that Ares stood exposed in the doorway for several seconds before he could see a thing. There was a sudden exhalation and a rustle—Oswald, behind him, raised his sword reflexively, but Ares put a hand back to restrain him. He knew the sound of a woman's skirts.

The next moment Nicole was in his arms. He closed his eyes, pressing his lips to the dirt and sweat on her temple. For some minutes she could only cry, and he did not speak. Then she whispered, "Ares, I am so sorry. I was too proud to take a bodyguard. My pride would have been the end of me, but for the miracle of your coming."

"Are you hurt?" he asked, drawing her out of the hut to look at her in the ever-brightening morning.

"No, my lord." She shook her head, tears dropping from her lashes. She was disheveled and exhausted, her silk bell sleeves hanging in shreds.

"Bring the men forward." Ares gestured to Oswald, who hurried back down the path to apprise the unit of their success.

Nicole glanced at Fancsali, then self-consciously put a hand to her disorderly hair. Bowing, he said, "Surchataine—"

"We are relieved to find you whole, Lady Nicole," Thom said, preempting him with the title she preferred, and she squeezed his arm in tearful gratitude.

Soldiers began pouring out of the woods to see the object of their search standing with her husband, and they nodded to each other in satisfaction. "How in heaven's name did you know where to find me?" she asked Ares.

"Sophie showed me where she had seen her ghost earlier in the week. Bonnie identified the scrap from your dress. And Lord Fancsali tracked you here. This is part of his estate," Ares replied, unnaturally calm.

"Then I am in your debt, Lord Fancsali," Nicole said, distinctly uncomfortable.

"It was a great pleasure to make myself useful to you, Lady," he replied.

"Now, Lady," Ares said, "tell me what happened."

She sank against him. "I went to the festival—it would be yesterday afternoon—because I remembered that I had not gotten anything for Ursula. I was walking around, looking for any booth that might still be open, and I heard someone crying. So I went in back of a tent, where the sound seemed to be coming from—and it was Chiacos, weeping! He seemed to be truly in pain. But he seized me, and when I saw him bringing out that stinking cloth again, I promised I would go with him quietly if he would not use it on me.

"So he put me on his horse and brought me to this place. He left me here with a trencher of bread and a pitcher of water, then rode away. I could not get out, and grew hoarse with calling." Her voice was still rough.

Thom and Ares looked at each other, eyes glinting in apprehension of the same fact. "He has gone to fetch his master," Thom said softly.

Ares almost smiled. "Who will find a surprise when he comes. Oswald," he summoned, and the big man came forward in anticipation. "I commit the lady to your

Dead Man's Token

safekeeping once again, to see her home. Take as many men as you need."

"Surchatain!" Oswald saluted and lowered himself to one knee. "The lady's servant awaits."

She began to accompany him, then stopped at the sight of the vast number of soldiers in Lystran blue who seemed to occupy every space between the trees. "Why so many men?" she gasped.

"We will endeavor to preserve the lord's woods," Ares said with a glance at Fancsali, "but I am making war on Chiacos' master."

Nicole closed her eyes and nodded in dismay. "I am so sorry, Ares—"

He cut her off. "The blame does not rest with you, Lady. Chiacos was evidently determined to take you whenever possible. I am glad that it happened now and that my meeting with his master is at hand."

With a final kiss of comfort, he placed her on Oswald's great bay with the Second, who then departed with a salute and a generous contingent of arms. Ares turned to the property owner. "Lord Fancsali, as the lady said, we are in your debt. I release you from further obligation to me."

Fancsali looked pained. "You would dismiss me without allowing me to see the end of this affair—on my property, yet? That is not grateful or even nice of you, Surchatain."

Ares barely smiled. "Then go snatch some grub and rest. Someone will wake you when anything happens worth seeing."

Fancsali saluted. "Then I am grateful to *you*, Surchatain."

Thom watched him go claim a pouch of foodstuffs, then told Ares, "He still may have known she was here."

"If he did, what can he do now, but watch it play out? I will take Nicole's place," Ares said, swinging the door of the hut full open to examine the interior in the morning light. It appeared to be exactly as Fancsali described: mean and abandoned. There was no wood in the small earthen fireplace, but there was a cot, a blanket, and the provisions Nicole had described, which she had not touched.

Sitting on the cot, Ares ate the bread and drank the water. "Lock me in," he said, stretching out and pulling the blanket over himself and his sword. "Conceal the men in the woods—steer clear of the path Chiacos took leaving."

"Surchatain," Thom agreed, then hesitated. "I fear that you may fall asleep and be discovered, to your disadvantage."

Conceding that it was a real, if unflattering possibility, Ares took the pitcher and got up. "Then I will set a sentry." He nodded to the door; Thom exited and closed it behind him. Moments later Ares heard the latch clank into place.

Bending, he placed the pitcher at an unsteady angle against the door so that the moment it was opened, the pitcher would fall against the rocky threshold. Then he lay down on the cot again, his sword in his hand, and pulled the blanket over his head.

He did not sleep, but fell into a reverie of half-wakefulness, his mind wandering over the past seven or eight years. Chiacos had come to Westford with Melva and Druella eight years ago, only months after Nicole herself had arrived. A week later, Magnus announced his father Ossian's death and himself as new ruler of Scylla. With the passing of another week, Renée and Carmine were married, and on the night of their wedding, Magnus had piggybacked his attack on that of the Qarqarian usurper, Ulm. While Ulm was out to kill Melva, the legitimate heir to the Qarqarian throne, Magnus wanted to marry her—but wound up being tricked into taking Druella instead.

But, as Melva's story indicated, apparently Magnus found all that he needed in Druella—their son, Bondurant, was born several months before the twins. In the years since, Magnus had made no attempt to discard her or secure Melva, the true Chataine. But immediately upon attaining the throne, he had collected all of his father's coinage and reminted them under his stamp.

But he missed some. Some of the old coins of his father had escaped his grasp . . . and Chiacos had been paid with these coins to kidnap Nicole. There was a link, a connection somewhere there that Ares was missing. What was the link between Chiacos, Nicole, and old cruxes?

Eyes closed, Ares let his thoughts drift. *Old cruxes.* . . . The link was somewhere in the past. It was someone from the past who knew Chiacos, knew Nicole, and had the opportunity to amass and hoard cruxes for emergency use years later. A rich Scyllan who had a grudge to pay out against Ares. A Scyllan who wanted Nicole—

"Trench digger!" Ares' eyes sprang open as he made the connection. He knew now. He knew who Chiacos' master was —although how the man had induced Chiacos to betray Nicole for mere money was still a mystery. Was there more to it? Was that why Chiacos was weeping when Nicole found him?

Ares heard a footfall outside, and the latch lifting. Gripping his sword under the blanket, he lay still as he listened to the creak of the door opening on rusty hinges and the pitcher breaking on the threshold, which startled the incomer so that he paused.

A shaft of light from the open door fell across the cot, allowing Ares to look up through the thin blanket and see the shadow of a figure approaching. There was a whispered, "Nicole" as the blanket was lifted—

The next instant Ares had the tip of his sword pressed under the man's bearded chin. "Nicole could not stay, but I am here to greet you," Ares breathed, rising as he forced the man backward step by step by means of the blade at his throat.

"You!" he gasped. "Trench—" he bit his tongue. "But you are Surchatain now. And Chiacos has betrayed me."

"Do not blame the dead, Tancred," Ares said, evaluating him in the light of the doorway. Magnus' younger brother was no longer the eighteen-year-old boy Ares remembered from eight years ago. He had a lean, hunted look; his eyes were red and a tooth was missing. His hands trembled from fatigue or nerves. He wore old, very worn clothes that were probably new when Ares first met him at Westford.

Just days after Nicole and Ares were married, and months before Melva arrived, Magnus and Tancred had come to Westford, ostensibly for Magnus to court Renée. There, Tancred had fallen in love with Nicole, and coerced her into coming to Eurus to be presented as his betrothed to his parents.

But he had been the patsy, for Nicole convinced him to return her to Westford to present a petition of divorce to Ares, which he simply tore up. Thus Ares kept his wife, and Tancred had vowed revenge.

"I hear you have been a thorn in Magnus' side," Ares said. "He will be happy to see you again."

"Fool! You don't understand!" Tancred shouted.

Sounds of fighting outside distracted them both. Shortly, Thom came to the doorway to report, "His men have been contained. We are holding them for your instructions."

Thom paused, staring hard at Tancred, trying to place him, so Ares enlightened him, "This is Magnus' younger brother, Tancred."

"Ah. Well done, Surchatain. Excuse me—I am being summoned." Thom directed a last look at Tancred, which said: *You are a dead man.* Then he withdrew from the doorway.

"Just out of curiosity," Ares said, the tip of his blade toying with Tancred's collar, dingy grey that used to be white. "How did you compel Chiacos to kidnap Nicole? I cannot see how any amount of money would suffice."

Tancred stared at him, and there was something pathetic in the sudden droop of his shoulders. "Because Chiacos was never divorced from Druella. I threatened to expose her if he did not help me."

"What?" Ares blinked at him.

"Druella married Chiacos when they were both in service to Melva's father. When my brother took her, they were still married. Magnus' marriage to her has never been legitimate, nor is their son," Tancred said dully.

"But...."

"Chiacos was always loyal to her, and would never betray her. So when I found him at the inn in Dansington, I knew I had a way to get a message to you," Tancred continued.

"What ... ?"

"My brother killed our father and mother to gain the throne!" Tancred shouted. "He did not have to—he was the Chatain; all he had to do was wait! But he slaughtered them in their beds as they slept, then came after me! Had I not already been awake at that hour, I would have died with them. But my father's man ran to warn me, though it nearly cost him his life. I escaped with the clothes on my back and a few friends.

"I was content to let Magnus rule—I sent messages to that effect, but still he pursued me. These eight years since he has been hunting me like a criminal. The one time I tried to go to Westford to ask your help, I was shot the moment I was recognized." He yanked open his shirt to expose the old, jagged scar of an arrow that had pierced his shoulder and been ripped out again.

"But when I found Chiacos, I found hope of getting your ear. If I could get Nicole away from the palace, I could tell her my story, and send her back to you. As God is my witness, that was my plan," Tancred said.

Ares' blade had been sinking lower and lower as he listened, his gut coiling in distress. Tancred's story was all too plausible—Ossian's death had been so sudden and suspicious, few at Westford doubted that Magnus had a hand in it. But after Druella went to join him, Magnus became distinctly more friendly toward Lystra, eventually proving an able ally against the slave trade.

But a rulership attained by murder, even by a Chatain, was morally invalid—many rulers across the Continent would refuse alliances with such. And Tancred was correct that if Druella was married to Chiacos, and that fact became known, then she and her child would cease to be recognized as Surchataine and Chatain. The scandal would be as damaging as adultery. "How can you prove what you say?" Ares demanded.

"One of my father's servants saw Magnus emerge from my mother's bedchamber with a bloody sword. Magnus left without seeing him, so he ran in and found her hacked to death—he went to alert my personal man, who ran down to stop me before I ascended to my death in my bedchamber. Both of those men are with me today—if your men have not killed them," Tancred said in a low voice.

Expelling a troubled breath, Ares sheathed his sword. "What about Druella's marriage? Who can verify that?"

"Chiacos would never tell," Tancred observed. "But if Chataine Melva is still with you, she should know of it."

"How did you come to know?" Ares asked.

"Even after I fled Eurus, I had friends there. Druella unknowingly sent one of them, a messenger, to Chiacos with a letter and a great deal of gold. As soon as my friend made the delivery, he came to tell me—and so ended his service at the palace," Tancred said wryly.

"What did her letter say?" Ares asked.

"She urged him to wait, and they would be reunited. She was sending him the gold as a pledge. My man memorized the message, if you care to hear it word for word," Tancred said, gesturing outside.

"So how did the both of you manage to lay hands on all these cruxes before Magnus reminted them?" Ares asked.

"What?" Now Tancred looked confused.

"The old cruxes. You had a store of old cruxes," Ares said.

"I—look at me!" Tancred shouted. "I told you, I ran with nothing but the clothes on my back! I've had nothing to pay my men, or buy arms or travel or feed myself with!"

Ares noted his priorities in listing his needs. "Then how did you pay the men with Chiacos?"

Tancred shook his head. "I paid him nothing. I used only the threat of exposing Druella to force his hand. Whatever help he had, he paid for himself—no doubt with the money she sent him. My friend said the evening she gave him the letter to deliver to Chiacos, she took him down to the treasury where all the old coins were stockpiled and had him take two bags. My friend knew why she required him to handle the bags: so if the theft was discovered, it would be blamed on him, and he would be put to death for it. So my friend kept one crux as proof of his story before he made his delivery and escaped to me in hiding. Ask him!"

"In good time. But even if all you say is true," Ares said in a low voice, "do you really expect me to believe you took Nicole only to get my attention?"

"Look at me," Tancred repeated in a voice that cracked. "She is Surchataine. How could I induce her to love me now, when she would not all those years ago when I had wealth and privilege? Yes, I wanted to see her again, but if I would not take her by force when I had the chance then—and I did not—I certainly would not now. But if I could get anyone in Westford to listen to me, it would be she."

Ares looked out of the hut, his mind spinning. But when he saw Fancsali watching Ares' men standing guard over their prisoners, his thoughts took a new tack. "Do you know Lord Fancsali?" he asked Tancred.

"One of my brother's staunchest supporters," Tancred said bitterly.

Ares cocked his head. "Do you know whose land you are on?"

Tancred shrugged. "Anywhere in Scylla is death to me. It

no longer matters. I am tired of running. I am ready to die. My only regret is that my companions will also die, when their only crime has been to keep me alive."

Ares almost groaned. Stepping to the doorway, he called, "Thom!"

The Commander came running. "Surchatain?"

Drawing him inside, Ares asked, "Did you tell the others what I told you? That Tancred is here?"

"Yes," Thom said, his face clouding. "Should I not have?"

Ares chewed his lip, thinking. "No matter. Fancsali is likely to guess, and as long as he is with us, he cannot do anything."

Thom watched him with furrowed brow, waiting for some word of enlightenment. So Ares told him, "Tancred tells me that Magnus assassinated his mother and father to gain the throne, and further, that Druella was married to Chiacos when Magnus took her. He says that Magnus has been after his life these eight years. We . . . must preserve him until we can assess the truth of all this."

Thom glanced outside. "And Fancsali is bosom friends with Magnus. I knew I hated him," he vented. Tancred's eyes began watering.

"Suggestions?" Ares asked.

Thom looked outside contemplatively. "Yes, Surchatain. Let us send Fancsali straight to Magnus with word that we have Tancred." Ares studied him, and he went on, "We get Fancsali out of the way, for we do not need him to guide us back. At Westford we can protect Tancred until we discover whether he is telling the truth or not. If he lies, we can deal with him how *you* shall choose—not Magnus. If he tells the truth . . . then Magnus shall know we are sheltering his worst enemy."

Ares straightened slightly. "Thom, I underestimate you."

"I know, Surchatain," he replied.

Ares turned to Tancred. "Put your hands behind your back as if they are bound." Tancred did so immediately, and Ares instructed Thom, "Bring him out after me."

Striding out of the hut, Ares glanced aside at the group of twenty-odd ragged men who stared back at him defiantly, their sorry horses standing nearby. Ares went straight to Fancsali, who preempted him with, "Is that truly Tancred?" He was staring hard at the man Thom was steering out of the hut by the shoulder.

"Yes. Lord Fancsali, you have proved your worth. I have one more task: ride immediately to Magnus and tell him who I have in my keeping," Ares said, gesturing for a horse.

"Bring this prize to Eurus without delay, Surchatain," Fancsali urged, straining to see Tancred.

"Pardon, Fancsali, but *my* prize waits in Westford, and I will go to *her* without delay," Ares corrected him.

Hardly listening for excitement, Fancsali exclaimed, "Then let me take him!"

"Before I have had the opportunity to punish him for taking my wife?" Ares asked coolly.

Fancsali coughed. "Forgive me, Surchatain. I forget myself," he said, displaying appropriate chagrin.

"I am content to let you receive Magnus' commendation for this capture," Ares said mildly, taking the reins of the proffered horse to hand over to Fancsali.

"You are most gracious, Surchatain Ares." Fancsali mounted with a leap. He paused to regard Tancred one last time, then took off at a run.

"Well, now." Ares watched him go in satisfaction, then he turned to Thom. "Is the Blue here?"

"Yes, Surchatain. Almost a thousand," Thom said with justifiable pride.

"Good. Then we shall not be harassed on the return trip. You and your men mount up," Ares said, nodding to Tancred.

"Thank you, Ares," Tancred replied in a near whisper.

Ares glanced at him, then told Thom, "Keep them to the inside—just in case—but you ride with me up front." Thom saluted.

Weary as he was, Ares would not risk resting in Magnus' territory, so after eating from the packs of bread, cheese and figs, he led the men at a fast pace back to Westford. On the return trip, they took the shorter route north of Willowring Lake.

However, the four-hour ride was lengthened by the necessity of rest stops to accommodate Tancred's weak horses. Other than that, there were no delays. Although no one really expected Fancsali to appear up the road with men and arms to demand the prisoner, Ares did not relax until they had crossed the old wooden bridge and pounded into the cobbled courtyard of the palace at Westford.

He left instructions for Tancred and his men to be fed, bathed and dressed, with the attentions of Doctor Savary, if necessary. Then, attended by congratulations from every courtier he passed, he wearily mounted the stairs to his chambers.

Nicole was waiting for him in the receiving room. Upon his entrance she rose to greet him, clinging to his neck. "Ares, I—"

"No more apologies," he reminded her, closing his eyes in the fragrant dampness of her hair. Newly bathed, she wore only her scarlet robe. "Did you see the girls?" He wanted them to know that their faith in him to find their mother had been justified.

"Yes, I went to them straightway," she said bemusedly. "They were glad enough to see me, but—rather—matter-of-fact about it all. Bonnie was more upset by the condition of my dress, and Sophie was keen on finding out whether it was her ghost who actually kidnapped me."

Smiling tiredly, Ares sank onto the bench next to the sunken tub to begin undressing.

"Ares." She knelt beside him, hand on his knee. "Who was it?"

"Tancred," he replied, glancing at her. "We brought him back with us." He pulled off one boot and dropped it wearily, looking at his sodden, muddy socks.

"Oh." Her face clouded in dismay.

"I will tell you what he told me. See if it rings true to you." While stripping off his sweat-soaked dress blacks and easing himself into the tub, he relayed all that Tancred had told him about Magnus, Druella, and Chiacos. Nicole listened quietly, without interruption.

By the time he was finished with his bath, he could hardly keep his eyes open. Nicole dried him off and put him to bed. After dressing herself quickly, she summoned a manservant to wake him at the appropriate time to dress for dinner. Then she went out to interview Chiacos' master herself.

13

Before Nicole left the receiving room, she deliberated a long time over the best way to get to the truth in this situation. She would speak with Tancred, but she must have some counterweight to his arguments, to test their truthfulness. As she pondered this, all at once she knew who would provide that balancing view.

With that course in mind, Nicole went to the Surchataine's receiving room and from there summoned Melva. The girl entered in a rush and flung herself on Nicole's neck. "Oh, Lady, how glad I am to see you! The Surchatain is a great hunter to find you not once, but twice."

"Thank you, dear Melva. I agree—Ares is very stubborn about not losing things. Please sit." She gestured, and they made themselves comfortable on the plush velvet bench. "It occurred to me, Melva, that we have all been very stupid in this affair."

"What do you mean?" Melva asked, growing still.

"Well, from the first moment we knew that Chiacos was involved, we should have come to you to ask about him. You knew him before you came to Westford," Nicole observed.

"Only a little," Melva murmured.

"A little of what you knew is more than what we knew. I believe that you can help us understand a lot about him—such as how he could ever be moved to kidnap me. I know it pained him, Melva. Do you know how I know?" Nicole asked, and Melva shook her head. "He cried," Nicole replied. "When he laid hands on me at the festival yesterday, it was with respect and sadness. It grieved him." Melva lowered her head.

Nicole stood to pace, as it was easier for her to assemble a chain of thought that way. "Then we found the crux he had dropped in the orchard while fleeing the secret passage, and it was an old one, minted before Magnus took the throne. And we could not understand how Chiacos came by old cruxes . . . unless someone gave them to him. Do you know who could have given him cruxes, Melva? A great many of them?"

"No," Melva said in a small voice.

Nicole sat abruptly beside her. "Whom are you loyal to, Melva?" The girl looked at her with wide eyes. "Do you feel any loyalty toward me and my husband, who have sheltered you and protected you since you came to us eight years ago?"

"Of course!" Melva said.

"Then help us understand the reasons I was kidnapped, twice. What is the relationship between Druella and Chiacos?" Nicole asked. Melva hung her head and said nothing. "Are they married, Melva?"

"No," the girl replied in a hard voice—but without the indignant surprise such a question should have elicited.

Nicole stood with a sigh. "There is someone who disagrees with you." Going to the door, she quietly ordered the sentry, "Summon Tancred."

As Nicole resumed pacing before the bench, Melva asked in guarded alarm, "Who?"

"I have summoned him," Nicole replied. Melva watched her pace, then jumped when the sentry knocked on the door. "Enter!" Nicole called, turning.

In came the sentry with Tancred by his side. Clean,

shaved, and dressed, he looked less wild, but certainly sad and weary. Seeing Nicole, he stood agape, then fell to his knees. "Forgive me, Surchataine. I was a desperate man."

"Stand up, Tancred," she ordered, though her eyes watered on seeing his state. When he did, she asked, "Do you know who this is?" She paced over to stand in front of Melva.

He looked at the Chataine hard, but finally shook his head: "No, Surchataine." Melva looked between them in apprehension, not knowing what Nicole was about.

"This is the Chataine Melva of Qarqar," Nicole said.

"Ah," Tancred said, appraising her again.

"And Melva says that Druella and Chiacos are not married," Nicole stated.

Tancred looked at Melva. "Then for her loyalty to Magnus, I am to die," he said. Melva looked startled.

Nicole turned to Melva. "Tancred says that he was able to persuade Chiacos to kidnap me by threatening to expose Druella, and meant me no harm. If Tancred lies, and paid money for my kidnapping, then he will die for it. If he tells the truth, then Druella has been false to us all—and Magnus really did murder his parents."

Melva gasped, but Nicole continued to pace with mounting resolve. "So here we are at an impasse where lives hang in the balance. We must know the truth, whether it is what we would like to hear or not. Are Druella and Chiacos married, or not? Tancred says yes; Melva says no. I say that we three will not leave this room until the two witnesses agree on one answer." And she stopped pacing to look at them both.

Tancred said, "I have spent the last eight years of my life being pursued like an animal because of that fact. I will not deny it now. They are married."

Melva silently hung her head. Tancred asked her, "Do you think that I am the only one who knows? Do you not realize that, whether I live or die, the truth will come out? Then how will Surchatain Ares look on you, who kept this news locked up even to the harm of his wife?" he asked.

"Yes!" Melva cried, bursting into tears. "Yes, they are married! But Druella made me swear to never tell."

Nicole sat beside her and put an arm around her shoulders. "An oath to keep a lie safe is false, dear Melva. Have you not read that in the Law of Roman?"

"I haven't been paying much attention," Melva said tearfully. Tancred watched her.

"Nonetheless, you have done well now," Nicole said, standing. "You are both dismissed." When Melva rose unsteadily, Tancred offered his hand for support. She declined it, glancing away.

As the sentry opened the door, Nicole said, "Tancred." He gave her his full attention. "Dinner is at eight."

He seemed to let out a breath, then bowed. Melva curtsied and they withdrew, but before the door was closed, Nicole heard him say, "Thank you for saving my life, Chataine." Melva looked up at him, and then the door was shut.

Before anything else, Nicole informed Georges that Tancred would be a guest at dinner that evening. Then she summoned Counselors Carmine and Vogelsong.

When they came, she invited them to sit on the bench while she paced in front of it, deep in thought. "I have just interviewed Tancred and Melva," she told them. "They both told me that Druella and Chiacos were married in Hornbound and never divorced."

"What?" gasped Vogelsong. He looked at Carmine, who straightened just slightly.

Nicole paused. "I may have gotten ahead of myself. Did you know that Ares and Thom brought back Tancred? That he is the one who hired Chiacos to kidnap me?"

"No," said Vogelsong.

"Yes," Carmine said quietly.

Glancing between them, she said, "Then let me tell you all that my husband told me."

When she had covered that bit of news with them, Vogelsong sat speechless, but Carmine asked, "And what of Lord Fancsali, Lady?"

Nicole paused. "I—do not know. Ares did not mention him. Did Fancsali not return with them?"

"No," Carmine replied, standing. "If you will excuse me, Lady, I will make inquiries." He went to the door of the receiving room, spoke to the sentry, and returned to the velvet bench.

"All this has left me rather dazed," Vogelsong said with an uneasy laugh.

"I imagine so. Would you care for a draft?" Nicole picked up a golden pitcher of wine and held it over a matched cup.

"Yes, I would, Lady; thank you," Vogelsong said, reaching for the cup.

"Carmine?" Nicole asked.

He cleared his throat. "Dear Lady, I believe you are unaware of the Surchatain's word to me about this. If I have another drink, he will banish the Chataine Renée from Westford."

Vogelsong looked as if the world had gone mad, but Nicole quietly set the pitcher down, perceiving that Ares was resorting to drastic measures to keep Carmine sober.

Even as she realized this, and understood it, the temptation to use this knowledge to her personal advantage blindsided her—wasn't she tired of always being overshadowed by the Chataine? How long must she sit back and watch Renée try to supplant her in the affections of her husband and daughter? How long before Ares succumbed to Renée's continual attempts to seduce him? Well, the situation need not go on another day. It would establish her power and prestige once for all to simply command Carmine to raise his cup. He would do it, if she commanded it. And he would understand why.

This terrible inner struggle ensued for a fraction of a

second, which seemed days to Nicole. At last, she rejected the action without any conscious reason other than that it was foreign to her nature.

Tossing the temptation out on its pointy ear, she murmured, "I see. Thank you for telling me, Carmine. No one but the wine steward need know." And that was all she said. Vogelsong stared briefly at the cup in his hand, then set it hastily on the table, still full.

Moments later Paramore, Captain of the Blue Regiment, appeared in response to Carmine's summons. He bowed to those in the room and stood at attention.

Carmine said, "Thank you for your promptness, Captain. Am I correct in assuming that you accompanied the Surchatain and the Commander in tracking the lady's kidnapper to Eviron?"

"In essence, Counselor." Paramore inclined his head. "The Regiment received orders to follow after they were underway. We caught up to them at the terminus of the search."

"The warden's hut?" Carmine asked.

"Yes, Counselor."

"And did you witness the Surchatain's confrontation with Tancred?" Carmine asked.

"No, Counselor. That occurred inside the hut. We were later told that Tancred had made several accusations against Magnus: that he married a woman who was not legally available; that he assassinated his parents for the throne; and that he had pursued his brother with intent to murder him for his knowledge of these actions. A while later the Surchatain brought him out as if a prisoner, and sent Fancsali off on horseback," Paramore replied.

"Do you know what was said to Fancsali?" Carmine asked.

"The Commander informed us that Fancsali was dispatched to tell Surchatain Magnus that we had captured

Tancred. But our imperative was to transport Tancred in safety to Westford and keep him safe until the veracity of his claims could be established," Paramore replied.

"So Fancsali is at Eurus?" Nicole asked.

The Captain paused. "If he continued at the speed with which he set out, he should be about halfway there by now."

"Do you think he set out intending to go straight to Eurus?" she asked carefully.

"Oh, yes, Lady. Certainly," Paramore said. "He was most desirous of taking Tancred. The next best thing he could do was take the news of his capture."

"Thank you, Captain," Carmine said. "Unless the Lady has further questions—" he glanced inquiringly at Nicole, who shook her head. "Then you are dismissed."

Captain Paramore bowed and withdrew, and the three sat in contemplative silence. Clearing his throat, Carmine mused, "The next step, I believe, is to interview Tancred's associates, to see what they know of Ossian's death."

"Yes. But we must wait for Ares to do that. Clearly, he wanted to hear them himself," Nicole said. "Where are they being held? In the prison?" she asked in dismay.

"No, no—we are better hosts than that," Carmine assured her. "Our guests were allowed the use of the great room off the barracks kitchen, where there is room for them all. They are watched, but not held, and none seems to show any inclination to run. Until the Surchatain can interview them, I doubt that we can accomplish much more." Carmine stood as he said this, and Vogelsong also stood.

"You're quite right. Thank you, Carmine, Vogelsong." Nicole nodded at them, unable to use the words to dismiss Carmine, whom she still considered her superior. They bowed and departed.

Nicole returned to the Surchatain's quarters, and Vogelsong retreated to his fourth-floor library. He was in the process of moving all the old documents he had found from their insecure storage to better housing in the new library, as some of them were rare and valuable manuscripts.

Since cataloguing and organizing these various records was such a large project, he had conscripted Chataine Melva to assist him. She was willing, as long as she could do it when she would otherwise have to attend class.

Upon returning to his quarters, Carmine paused in the corridor to send a sentry after his servant, Hauffe. When the man arrived at the Counselor's quarters, Carmine gestured to the pitcher of unfermented cider. As Hauffe poured his drink, Carmine asked, "What has our dear Chataine Renée been told of today's events, my good man?"

The neat little man squinted thoughtfully. "Well, now, judging from what Eleanor tells me—not that I know all that is in the Chataine's mind, of course—she knows only that Lord Fancsali was successful in leading the party to the Surchataine and did not return with the others, Counselor."

"Ah. Then be sure to whisper to someone in the hearing of her maid that he has returned to his wife and children in Eviron, Hauffe."

"Yes, Counselor."

"And raise a quiet lament over the penalty which shall be incurred if I drink," Carmine continued.

"In her maid's hearing?" the man asked.

"That is the whole point of saying it, my good man."

"Yes, Counselor. Now?" Hauffe inquired.

"If you have time," Carmine said dryly. His servant bowed genially and withdrew. Sipping the cider, Carmine winced and then sighed, "I suppose I had better get used to it."

Ares was awakened with enough time before dinner to hear about Nicole's discoveries of that afternoon. While he expressed appreciation for her initiative, the news did not please him. He was willing to overlook almost anything to maintain stability on the Scyllan throne—but murder. And if Tancred was telling the truth about one matter, it increased the likelihood that he was correct about the other, more serious matter.

Shrugging on a clean black shortcoat, Ares muttered to his co-conspirator, "I won't interview any of his men tonight, however. It will have to wait until tomorrow."

He looked at her, fresh in a yellow silk dress, and smiled. "Did I welcome you home again, Lady?"

"Yes, my lord, quite adequately." She nestled in his arms, and he kissed the top of her head, where her hair was bundled in a gold and yellow snood.

"The dress reminds me of one your father made," he observed, stroking her shoulder. It was finely cut and luxuriant enough, but of simple lines and a downright modest neckline.

She smiled a little sadly—her father Robert, a tailor, had died shortly after she had come to Westford. "My clothes seem to be changing. I tend to pick out things that look more and more like what he made."

"They become you," he murmured, and as she reached up to his lips, the bell tolled the dinner hour. With a sigh, he took her hand to lead her downstairs. Entering the great hall upon Georges' announcement, the royal couple saw at a glance the restrained mayhem at the table.

Bodies in motion froze at their entrance; exclamations hung dying in the air. The reason for the disturbance was manifest: having no instructions regarding tonight's dinner guest, and given the absence of last night's dinner guest, Georges had placed Tancred in Fancsali's seat of honor across from Renée. When she had entered to see this kidnapper and interloper seated across from her—well, it was good that Ares was not there to witness the main outpouring of her fury.

By the time he and Nicole entered, Renée was in the midst of deep, indignant breaths and her cheeks were practically scarlet. Tancred appeared wary but resolute; Melva had tears streaming down her pale face; Giles looked blanched and dazed, as if he were somehow at fault for the travesty.

Ares looked across to Carmine, who appeared unperturbed, and at Thom, who was smiling vaguely. The children were not at table.

The ruling couple took their places at the head of the table and everyone hastily sat. Ares motioned for the wine steward, who brought forward his pitcher and began to pour. "So has Tancred been introduced?" Ares asked innocently.

"How could you, Ares?" Renée asked. Looking at Nicole, she demanded, "Are you so spineless not to be insulted that he treats as an honored guest the man who took you?"

There was a collective gasp at the comment. Nicole began to reply archly, then thought better of it and said, "I appreciate your concern, dear Chataine, but you do not know everything that I know. Tancred is supplying us with a great deal of information."

"Will he be so useful when Magnus attacks us because of his presence here?" Renée asked scathingly. Some of the nobles looked seriously to Ares for an answer.

"Why should Magnus attack? I sent Lord Fancsali directly to him with word that we were holding Tancred. Should I debase myself by the ill treatment of the Surchatain's brother, regardless of his present status? I did not treat you so ill, Chataine, even when others urged me to after the death of your father," Ares said. Renée looked away.

"I wonder why you defend Magnus, after what he did to you," Tancred said to her. He remembered quite well how Magnus had married her only to reject her days later. The taunt "used goods" had played a large role in that public humiliation.

"I care nothing for Magnus," Renée sputtered.

"Oh?" Tancred said, and no one enlightened him as to whom she did care for.

As stuffed cabbage and duckling in wine were served, Carmine cleared his throat to dispel the heavy silence around the table. "There are a number of points about the

Surchataine's ordeal that still baffle me, if Surchatain Ares will permit a question or two to our guest—?" Carmine looked inquiringly to Ares, who hesitated before nodding.

"Thank you. I promise not to bring the graciousness of this court into disrepute by conducting an interrogation during dinner. Chatain Tancred, I was wondering if you told Chiacos your reasons for requiring the Lady Nicole," Carmine said.

Tancred paused. "No, not directly."

"So, Chiacos did not know what you intended to do with her?" Carmine asked.

"No. I never told him that I needed her to get a message to the Surchatain," Tancred said.

"I see. That explains what the lady told us of his apparent dismay. I understand he was weeping, Lady?" Carmine asked.

"Yes," Nicole confirmed.

"It also may explain why Chiacos took no trouble to obscure his trail," Carmine continued.

"Are you saying that he wanted us to find her?" Thom asked.

"It may have eased his conscience to think that he was leaving a clear trail for you to follow," Carmine allowed.

"That was not so much Chiacos' doing as mine, Counselor," Nicole said quietly. "He was nervous and hasty, so never noticed the purse I dropped."

"Well done, Lady. That gave us a starting point to find you," Thom said.

"It was unnecessary. You would have received her back whole," Tancred said to Ares, color rushing to his face.

"So why didn't you tell Chiacos what you were about?" Thom asked, popping an olive into his mouth.

"Why should I trust him? For all I knew, his only loyalty was to Druella," Tancred said.

Something wrong as Ares listened to this exchange. He muttered, "I do not understand why you chose that hut to hide her in, Tancred. The game warden's hut on Fancsali's estate."

Tancred uttered a dry laugh. "*Fancsali's* estate? That used to be my property, until my brother came after my life. He did not wait until I was dead before disbursing my property to his cronies."

Ares admitted, "Well, there was cause. That was no mean feat, to dispatch the slavers—"

Tancred broke in with sudden wild laughter that had half the table gaping at him. "Don't tell me that you *believe* that tale! 'Old Gargus had captured two ladies of the court, so I had to ride after him, fa la la'—"

"What do you know differently, sir?" Carmine interrupted with a touch of severity.

"I know that old Gargus died in a trader's dispute with old Dorn and lost all his slaves to him!" Tancred said scornfully. Turning to the head of the table, he pleaded, "Seriously, Surchatain—did you ever have any independent witness as to what happened, or did you just take Fancsali's word for it?"

"We received an announcement from Magnus, which I had no reason to doubt," Ares said without inflection.

"Of course. Why should you doubt him?" Tancred asked, venting years of pent-up anguish, fear and frustration. "Why should you doubt when he says his brother Tancred is warring against him for the throne? Why should you doubt the reasons for the honors he bestows on his spies and henchmen? Fancsali gets what once was Tancred's estate; Juscen gets Tancred's inheritance; Auer gets Tancred's stables—"

"What?" Ares asked sharply. "Who?"

Tancred blinked, bringing himself under control. "Ah, Lord Juscen received my share of the inheritance from the treasury—"

"The last name you mentioned," Ares prompted him.

"Lady Auer received my stable of horses to sell for the care of her nephew. He was badly injured in some kind of accident, so Magnus has provided them a house in Eurus," Tancred replied.

14

Staring hard at Tancred, Ares uttered, "How do you know that Magnus is providing for Lady Auer and her nephew?"

The young man was slightly flummoxed. "I still have friends in Eurus who tell me what he is doing, at peril of their lives," he said.

Ares leaned back slightly, and Tancred looked around in alarm. All the guests save one were silent and rigid, staring at safe nonentities. But Renée sat with her hands in her lap and her proud head bowed. Hearing her newfound lover so roundly scorned seemed to quash her normally robust spirit. While Tancred did not understand the precise reason for her humiliation, it still dismayed him. "Forgive me, Chataine," he whispered. "I mean no harm—I speak only what I know."

"What do you know of her nephew's accident?" Ares asked him in a steely voice.

Adrift in ignorance, Tancred shook his head. "It was never described to me, Surchatain."

"And what do you know of Lord Backvold?" Ares asked.

Tancred blinked rapidly. "The name is unknown to me, Surchatain—nor why Lady Auer's receiving gifts from my brother should disturb you so."

Carmine leaned forward. "No one holds you responsible for these developments, Chatain. Only, can you tell us how long Lady Auer has been receiving benefices from Magnus?"

"N-no, Counselor," Tancred stammered. "Her name was not known to me until I was informed that she had received my prize horses . . . stalwart, worthy animals. I had spent years searching for the hardiest strains, breeding strength to strength to attain beasts who could survive the most punishing runs. And so he gives them to an old woman and to Fancsali's wife to ride to market." He ended on a pained laugh.

The silence around the table deepened, only all eyes turned toward Renée, who looked up with an ice-white face. Carmine gritted his teeth briefly, wondering if he would have to find yet another personal servant who would do what he was asked to do. Carmine could not know at this time that the fault for Renée's embarrassing ignorance lay not with Hauffe, but Eleanor, Renée's maid. For once, Eleanor could not bring herself to repeat to her mistress the devastating news she had overheard. She had been planning to break it to her gently during her bath tonight.

Passing a hand over his brow, Ares gestured to the dinner master. "Georges, summon the musicians. If there is any more talk at this table tonight, I fear it will end in war." The dinner master bowed, and straightway the musicians were sent in to play for the duration of dinner.

Exhausted from recent events, Ares and Nicole went directly up to their chambers after dinner. Ares had not yet received an accounting on revenues from the festival, but all such trivialities would have to wait another day (to the displeasure of the administrators awaiting disbursements). As soon as he and she had undressed, however, and were making themselves comfortable in each other's arms, a sentry knocked.

Sophie and Bonnie were granted entrance into the Surchatain's bedchamber. When Bonnie ran directly to her mother yet again, Nicole began to wonder if the kidnappings had awakened her to the fact that she really did love her mother more than her "aunt." While Nicole was not ready to acknowledge any gratitude for such ordeals, she could appreciate the unintended side effects.

Sophie, as usual, went to her father. The question that plagued her tonight must be put to rest once for all. "Papa, there wasn't ever really a ghost, was there? It was just a man all along, wasn't it?" she asked, braced to hear the worst.

Ares lifted her onto the high bed and sat her on his lap, considering an answer. "Actually, Sophie, it was a ghost. But it wasn't the kind of ghost like Doudney told you about. It was a different kind of ghost."

Nicole looked over with brows raised, Bonnie clinging to her neck. Sophie snuggled closer to her father in grave interest. "What do you mean?"

"Doudney had you believing in a kind of vapor that used to be a man—something that floats in graveyards at night and evaporates in the sunlight. Whether such a ghost exists or not, I do not know. Chiacos was—is—another kind of ghost. He had a life once. He had our respect and trust; he had usefulness and belonging. But then he was faced with making a hard choice, and he could not make it. He had to take one of two paths, and he could not choose which way to go," Ares explained.

"What was the choice he had to make?" Sophie asked.

Ares paused, not wishing to explain divorce or adultery to a seven-year-old. Chiacos' choices lay in divorcing Druella, thus giving her up—which evidently he could not do—or exposing the fact of their marriage after she was supposedly married to Magnus, which Chiacos also could not do. Since he did not have the courage to take one route or another, he was forced into a third path, thornier than the others: cooperating with Tancred.

Ares phrased it this way for his daughter: "He had to

choose to either tell the truth or lie, and live with the consequences either way. He was so torn between those choices that he became a shadow of what he was. He lost any life he had to wandering and aimlessness, so that what you finally met in the passage was really nothing more than a ghost."

Thinking hard on this, Sophie dug a forefinger into her nostril. Nicole reached over to gently remove the finger. Then Sophie observed, "Henry said that Chiacos had been trapped in the secret passage once before."

"For several days," Ares said. "He might have died in there had Melva not spoken up."

"That's why he came back to it. Because he knew it," Sophie said intently.

"Yes," Ares said.

"So part of him is still trapped there," Sophie insisted.

"You could say that," Ares allowed.

"That's sad. I feel sorry for him," Sophie said.

Bonnie sat up. "I don't feel the least little bit sorry for him! He took Mama! He should be whipped!"

Sophie looked at her beautiful mother, who smiled and brushed her cheek. Ares shifted Sophie on his leg and observed, "Your sister has a good point. We can pity Chiacos, but what did he do? He came through the secret passage and took your mother from her bed. He used the same potion on her that he, or his companion, had used to kill a man earlier—although we think he did not mean to kill him. He tied her up and took her by force. What kind of person kills and steals? But Chiacos chose what he would become—whether he would be a real man or a ghost—by *not* making a choice. The only choice that means anything is when we choose to do the right thing, no matter how hard it is."

Sophie studied him, taking in every knot and discoloration of his scar. "I think I understand," she said hesitantly.

"Very good," he said. "Good night," he added firmly.

Kisses were exchanged all around, then the girls were escorted back to their quarters. Ares buried his face in Nicole's chest with a sigh. Stroking his head, she murmured, "We hold Chiacos accountable for kidnapping me, as we should, yet Tancred. . . . I tried to be kind in inviting him to dinner, but it wound up looking as though he were an honored guest. Why is that?" Renée's taunt may have had a belated effect.

Raising his face to her lips, he breathed, "My dove, we are pumping Tancred for whatever information he may provide. Do not confuse guest with patsy." Still exhausted from the nightlong trek, he sank into her softness and went to sleep.

Meanwhile, Renée had just now sent Eleanor away after receiving the gossip she had to deliver, belatedly. The Chataine never cried in front of her maid if she could help it, and tonight she had many bitter tears to shed. Alone in her bedchamber, she buried her clean face in the feather pillow and cried until it was soaked through.

Men were beasts, all of them—Fancsali, Carmine, Ares—to a man, they were treacherous, lying, and evil. At last, at last, Carmine had the upper hand on her. All he had to do was lift a cup to his lips, and she was banished from her beloved Westford forever. The terror of it overwhelmed her, for she was nothing outside this place. How could Ares be so vengeful? Thinking of him, she rolled onto her back.

She thought back ten years ago, when he was still Commander, before Nicole had come to Westford. She remembered the hours she made him dance with her, teasing him with kisses. The ugliness of his scar was fascinating. It was erotic, and thrilling in a small, wicked way, to feel the jagged flesh on her face and neck when he kissed her. She remembered the tension in him that caused him to tremble, strong as he was, when he held her on the dance floor. And she remembered the night that she tried to lure him to bed with her. In his agony to have her, he gripped her and whispered, *"Marry me, Chataine. Darling Renée, marry me."*

A Chataine marry a soldier? She had laughed in his face. He was so much fun to play with—he took everything with patient good humor, yet he felt everything deeply. She could cause him anguish or joy by merely a flickering glance. But when she laughed at him that night, he turned to stone in the corridor. He refused to enter her receiving room—so she had dismissed him and sent for Carmine instead. Carmine came, and entered, never knowing that he was her second choice. And after that evening, Ares never spoke to her of marriage again.

Then the fates had played strange tricks on her. By Renée's own invitation, Nicole had come to Westford, and in her sweet beauty Ares found all he had ever desired. Then by unbelievable circumstances—the fates throwing her world upside down—Ares had become Surchatain. He now ruled a province far larger than her father had ruled, with far greater wealth and power. Who could have imagined that the Commander would one day rule? And had Renée not laughed at him that night, she could have shared all that with him, instead of being a debtor to his good graces.

What was worse, he no longer lusted after her. She had tested him—teasingly, to be sure—numerous times over the last ten years. There may have been a flicker of interest from him at first, but even that weak flame died completely after Nicole had run away to the abbey. In the extremity of his sorrow, any remaining lust was flooded away, never to be rekindled.

So what was left for her now, growing older with no husband and no prospects? Carmine, who was made a eunuch because he believed her when she said she loved him? Watching Nicole's children grow up and supplant herself as Chataine?—for she would never be Surchataine of Lystra. She was now reduced to considering marriage with persons of lesser rank than Commander, who had previous wives as well.

Renée looked toward the secret drawer where she kept the small, jeweled dirk. But even that option had been spoiled—she had no desire to shed her own blood after having seen and smelled real blood pouring from gaping wounds, draining the life away. But what else was there for her?

She thought of her half-brother, Henry. She almost envied his being taken by the slavers, because that gave Ares the opportunity to rescue him. With such manifest proof of Ares' love for him, Henry had no difficulties accepting his debasement from Chatain to Green recruit. He threw himself into serving Ares, and Lystra, with a pride that bordered on ferocity. He had found his worth in offering himself completely to Ares' service, however he would be used, or not.

Thinking on this, Renée lowered her head back to the damp pillow, and soon closed her eyes.

The following morning, Ares faced a full workload. First, Giles brought him reports of revenues from booth rentals for the festival, which were impressive—up eighty-seven percent from the year before. Giles also informed him that the proprietor of the booth behind which Chiacos had taken Nicole was a respected Scyllan potter named Fassnacht. "He is a master craftsman. I cannot believe that he had any knowledge of or involvement in the despicable business of kidnapping the Surchataine," Giles argued.

"You're probably right," Ares allowed, studying the festival totals.

"Furthermore—" Giles continued, then caught himself upon realizing that the Surchatain was in agreement. With that point settled, he moved on. "The Westfordian merchants are requesting another expansion next year, as well as a denial of permit to Eugenian dealers."

Ares looked up. "Are you willing to forego the revenue?

And incite Klar to retaliate by blockading Lystran trade into Eugenia? If you accede to this demand, what will the Westfordian guilds demand the following year?"

Giles had opened his mouth, raising his eyes to the ceiling in consideration, when Ares handed the stack of reports to him. "All that is for you to decide. You handled this festival so admirably, next year's is yours alone. I leave it entirely in your hands. You are dismissed."

"Thank you, Surchatain!" Giles exclaimed, greedily gathering up the account books. "I shall endeavor to prove myself worthy of your trust in me," he effused on his way out, bowing repeatedly over his armload.

In the quiet aftermath, Ares sighed, "That feels good. I should have turned this year's festival over to him."

A sentry announced the arrival of Carmine, whom Ares gestured into the receiving room. With a short bow, the Counselor said, "We are ready to interview Tancred and his men at your pleasure, Surchatain."

Ares leaned back in the chair, drumming his fingers on the table. "You and who?"

"Vogelsong, Thom, and myself await you, Surchatain," Carmine said.

Ares shook his head. "You three are quite capable of getting out of them whatever you want to know. And this is what I want to know: Do you believe, from what they tell you, that Magnus assassinated his parents? I want testimony that will hold up to a Council hearing."

The only indication of Carmine's surprise was a slight widening of the eyes. For such a crucial question, he fully expected Ares to take the lead in the interrogation. But as Ares stood, the briefest look communicated his expectation that his administrators were capable of arriving at the truth. There would be no thought, much less talk, of any debilitating influence operating on them . . . such as wine. "Surchatain," Carmine said, bowing, and he, too, departed with a mission.

That left Ares alone to stand at the open window and look out over the fields green with summer wheat. The mill was not visible from this window, being south of the palace, but Ares saw it in his mind's eye turning, ever turning, driven by the flowing of the Passage to the Sea. The mill was as old as the bridge, and under constant maintenance and repair to keep its great stone grinding out the wheat into flour, grinding. . . .

The demands of a responsible daily life were grinding, but from under the stone came the stuff that sustained many lives. So Ares lay his life under that stone, one moment at a time, to nurture the lives in his care—his family, his administrators, his subjects. As he was laid down daily, so daily he had to seek restoration of his life from the Bread of Life—or there would be nothing left to give. With his schedule cleared this morning, he leaned on the windowsill to pray.

War with Magnus? Ares could hardly conceive it. It would wreck the prosperity and peace of both provinces, leaving tens of thousands of people easy prey for the slave trade—not to mention poverty, famine, disease. But to turn a blind eye to ascension by murder would bring the curse of God on his own house and rulership. "God, help me," he whispered, sagging on the sill.

Over the next hour, alone in his receiving room, Ares wrestled with the hard choices that were laid before him. After preaching to Sophie last night about the necessity of making such decisions—and standing by them—he perceived the irony of his own position. He was a veteran soldier. He had seen up close the horrors of battle, especially on the innocent and the defenseless. He recoiled from the thought of subjecting his people to that. But he also knew that whatever peace came from tolerating evil was short-lived. The devil always came to claim his own.

With no resolution in sight, Ares sat back down with a sigh to attend the lesser matters that cluttered the table in front of him. In short order, he sent messages to the heads of the more powerful guilds in Westford congratulating them on their part in making the festival a success and informing them of Giles' complete authority over next year's event. He placed his seal on the final findings of the appropriations council. He reviewed and approved Thom's request for replacing several hundred sets of tackle. But finally, he was reduced to sitting at the table, staring at his folded fingers.

He held up four fingers. There were four of them—the Horsemen of the Apocalypse in the vision of St. John. Ares ticked them off on his fingers: the white horse of Conquest, the red horse of War, the black horse of Famine, and the pale horse of Death. Ares had heard them described collectively as a succinct history of the human race. But—were they inevitable? Would the power struggle between Tancred and Magnus unleash the dreaded Horsemen on Lystra?

The sudden knock at the door startled Ares out of his contemplation. "Enter!" He straightened when Carmine, Vogelsong and Thom all came in. "Sit," Ares said, nodding toward the spartan, straight-backed chairs along the wall. The three drew out the chairs, placing them around the table, and sat.

Ares looked to Carmine as the spokesman. He said, "Surchatain, here is how we proceeded with our investigation. Counselor Vogelsong, Commander Thom and myself each privately interviewed Tancred and the two associates he specified as witnesses to the murders of Surchatain Ossian and Surchataine Danae. We asked specific questions as to time, sequence, incidental details, other witnesses, and such. Then we met afterward to compare our findings. And what we find, Surchatain, is that the accounts have been carefully rehearsed and coordinated and are not reliable."

"What?" Ares asked, dumbfounded.

"They made their stories match up," Thom said, somewhat impatient with Carmine's precise manner. "They were very careful to tell us all exactly the same thing. If we'd had the chance to question them the night after it happened, or a week after it happened, or even a month after it happened, we might have had a chance to find out what really happened. But eight years later, they've had so much time to make their stories all line up that other corroborating details have been lost."

Stupefied, Ares looked at Vogelsong, who concurred, "In cases of this type, Surchatain, one looks for individual differences in the accounts that do not contradict the main facts, but indicate that the witness is giving his own viewpoint, and no other. One person will notice the torn bed coverings, another will see the stained rug. One will note the spilled wine, another that the dog is missing. We found no individual reminisces at all. There is no way for us to judge conclusively whether Magnus killed his parents—with or without the collusion of his brother."

Ares caught his breath. "You think Tancred was involved?"

Vogelsong replied, "He could have been, Surchatain. That is one of the possibilities we were forced to look at."

"Then why would Magnus pursue him?" Ares asked.

"A falling-out among conspirators," Carmine suggested. "Tancred might have lost his nerve at the last moment or not held up his part. Nor do we know, either, that he took the Lady Nicole for the reason he gave. He may have, and Magnus may have acted alone in killing their parents, but . . . we do not know."

Ares looked out the window, seeing a great burden fly from his shoulders. If he could not prove that Magnus killed his parents, then he could not justify making war on him. As for the legitimacy of Magnus' marriage, Ares now regarded that as none of his business and unworthy of investigation. "Well," he said, returning his attention to his administrators, "then we shall see what reason Magnus gives for the return of his brother. Meanwhile, we do nothing. Agreed?"

"Yes," Thom said.

"Certainly," was Carmine's word.

But Vogelsong said, "What about Magnus' support of Lady Auer?"

Ares leaned back in his chair. "Ah, yes—I had almost forgotten about her. So in addition to everything else, we must know whether Magnus was working behind my back for my overthrow or if the lady came to him with some cockeyed story that he swallowed without scrutiny. That we will address whenever we hear from Magnus."

Vogelsong was expressing his satisfaction with this plan when the sentry entered in considerable excitement. "Surchatain, the most amazing thing! Fawler has found Chiacos!"

15

Ares rose part way from his chair. "How did Fawler find Chiacos?" With such a turn of good fortune, he half wondered if he was but dreaming it all.

"Fawler said he was impressed with how unique the hoofprints were that you were tracking to find the Surchataine, with the backward shoes and all," the sentry explained. "So this morning, he just set off on the main roads looking at all the prints. After a few hours he ran across some prints that looked similar coming in from the northern road. He followed them to the Dancing Bear, went in and made inquiries, and was told that a Polonti who paid for his lodging with an old crux was in his room at that time. Fawler just went in, woke him up, and brought him back!"

"Send them up," Ares said, settling back to his seat. After the sentry had left, the Surchatain told his officers, "We will see if it is really he."

Some minutes later, Fawler brought in a dirty, haggard Polonti who slumped as if he had no bones. "Look at me," Ares ordered. When the man raised his face, Ares recognized him. He was older, thinner, and decades more careworn, but he was Chiacos.

First, Ares nodded at the soldier. "Well done, Fawler. Thom, see that this man receives a commendation."

"Certainly," Thom replied. Fawler saluted and stepped back, leaving the unfortunate Chiacos to face the Surchatain he had betrayed.

Ares let some silent minutes pass while they all studied the drifter. Then he asked, "Why did you take her, Chiacos?"

At first it did not seem that he would reply, but finally he sighed, "What does it matter? I am a dead man."

"You can save your life with your answers to me now. We most desire to know why Magnus is contending with Tancred."

"They are brothers of blood . . . united in death and blood," Chiacos moaned, his head drooping again.

"What does that mean?" Ares asked.

Again Chiacos sighed. "In the end there is only death." Which is where he certainly seemed in spirit.

"Chiacos! Answer my questions. How did Tancred persuade you to take Nicole for him?" Ares said sharply.

Unable to look Ares in the face, Chiacos repeated, "It is but death."

"He is mad," Thom said under his breath.

The sentry knocked again, and Ares called for him to enter. "Surchatain," he said, saluting, "our lookouts report an army of several thousand on the march from the north."

Thom stood. "Magnus comes for his brother."

"Probably. Go see," Ares instructed. "And see that Tancred and his men are secure." Ares then ordered Fawler, "Put Chiacos in prison with bread and water."

Fawler left with his prisoner, and Thom went out to issue orders for the Red and Blue Regiments to gear up and ride out. While the city's defenses were being brought together, another rider approached the gates alone. After explaining his mission, he was taken up to Ares, still in conference with his counselors.

The messenger, dressed in purple livery with the insigne of a bear on his crest, bowed before Ares and presented a small scroll wrapped in gold cord. Untying the cord, Ares broke the seal and unrolled the scroll. Then he uttered a dry, humorless laugh. "It is a marriage proposal from Fancsali to Renée."

"What nerve!" Vogelsong exclaimed. Carmine, mindful of the messenger's presence, only blinked.

Ares nodded to the sentry who had escorted in the messenger. "Summon the Chataine Renée."

She came at once, radiant as always, but subdued in her manner and still rather pale. Vogelsong, who knew little about women, thought it appeared that she had been crying—a lot. She made a token curtsy to Ares, saying nothing. But she noted everyone who was in the room, especially the messenger.

Ares waved to the messenger. "Wait outside." When the man had stepped out, bowing, Ares rose from behind the table to present the scroll to Renée without a word. She unrolled it and read it, blinking rapidly. Then she raised her face. "What does this mean?"

"Lord Fancsali is offering his estate to you in marriage." Ares stated the obvious, brows drawing down.

"Why a second proposal?" she demanded.

"Oh." Ares let out a breath in remembrance, and Carmine glanced away in distress at the revelation that must be forthcoming. Ares reluctantly explained, "The first was a . . . forgery, Chataine. Giles was having trouble coming up with enough suitors when they all knew you would turn them down."

Renée stared at him, her lips parted in shock. Vogelsong stared at the floor and Carmine kept his eyes trained on the middle distance.

Only Ares looked her in the eye, and that matter-of-factly. "All that is irrelevant now, Chataine. The genuine proposal must be dealt with immediately, as it affects other matters. What is your reply?"

Gazing at him, Renée suddenly thought of her father. He would have not hesitated to order her to do what suited him, banishing her from Lystra had she not obeyed. But Ares acted as if she must decide her own course . . . except when it came to Carmine. Staring at Ares as he waited for her decision in all seriousness, she apprehended that this was not the action of a vengeful man. "What would you have me do?" she asked.

"Chataine?" The question caught Ares unprepared.

"Fancsali proposes marriage, when I know he is already married. How do you desire me to reply to this? What is best for Lystra?" Renée asked.

Vogelsong murmured, "Very good, Chataine! Excellent," and Carmine straightened, looking at Ares.

"Well—" Ares cleared his throat. "You never cease to surprise me, Chataine. What do you think, Carmine? How should our Chataine reply?"

Gravely thoughtful, Carmine said, "A man's toying with the affections of a lady is a serious offense, Surchatain, but how we respond should take into account the Chataine's feelings for the lord. If she would truly desire to marry him, then she should ask straightforwardly when he plans to divorce his wife, and what kind of provision he will make for her and her children from his estate. Only if our dear Chataine is not interested in marrying him would we play it to a political angle."

"Chataine?" Ares looked at her, as did the other men. "Would you marry him?"

Her large blue eyes went to the window, and for some moments she did not reply. Then she asked softly, "Do you think he would make a good husband, Ares?"

"Ask his wife, Chataine," Ares said with some bite.

"It may be that is what I deserve," she said hazily, being twice married and divorced already.

"You deserve to be happy, Chataine," Carmine (husband number two) said indignantly.

She looked at him quickly. Although tears loomed under the surface, she kept her composure. Returning her gaze to Ares, she said, "I do not wish to marry him. What then shall I say?"

"Carmine." Ares gestured eagerly, clearing off a space on the table for a small sheet of fresh parchment.

The Counselor began to pace. "So many ways, so many ways we might work this. The overriding question is, how much influence does Fancsali carry at Magnus' court, and can we leverage any of that?"

"I've never had any spies at his court. It would be nice to have spies in Eurus," Ares said petulantly.

"Well then—that is what we will ask for." Carmine turned to Renée. "You will play with him, dear Chataine. Tell him that he interests you, but that you know nothing about him. Ask him to send highly placed persons *from Eurus* to tell you all about him. If he does, then of course what you will ask them will be designed to tell us more about Magnus than Fancsali. We will supply you with questions."

"Very well," Renée said, brightening. Playing with people never failed to cheer her up.

"Here, Chataine. Please sit," Ares said, drawing out the chair and dipping the quill for her.

So with Carmine dictating, Renée wrote out a reply to Lord Fancsali. When it was all blotted and sealed, Ares opened the door and put it in the hand of the messenger, but told him to wait. "We had best see what Magnus does before we send you off," Ares said, and the man looked apprehensive.

Before Ares went downstairs with the others, Renée held him back for a private word. "Chataine?" he asked warily as she closed the door between themselves and help on the outside.

"Ares, I . . . wish to make it known—unofficially, of course—that I will entertain no more proposals in the foreseeable future. These men seem to think it some kind of game, and I will not be handled lightly," she said.

"Of course, Chataine," he said. She paused, and Ares said restlessly, "I must go out to meet Magnus now, Cha—"

"So . . . was Fancsali the first that Giles . . . forged . . . a proposal from?" she asked with difficulty.

Ares looked at her, wanting to lie more than anything in the world right now. But he said: "No."

She blinked. "How many . . . ?"

"I don't know, Chataine," he said, reaching around her for the door handle.

She blocked him. "So how many others—besides the Counselor, of course—knew . . . ?"

"No one," he said hastily. "Giles was very clever about it, since he knew you would decline them all. And no one who was in this room today would dare speak a word about it."

"Of course not. That is all," she dismissed him, and he left in relief.

By the time Ares got downstairs, two forerunners from the advancing army had arrived at Westford's gates. They were indeed from Magnus, having come with the demand that Ares give up Tancred and his cohorts at once.

Ares' response to the forerunners was, "Magnus and I are friends. I will come talk to him. Wait here." And he left them in the courtyard while he went back into the foyer to summon Thom and three horses.

When Thom arrived, he reported, "The Blue and Red are ready, Surchatain."

"Good. Deploy them only as far as the north shore of Willowring Lake. You and Carmine will ride out with me to talk to Magnus."

Carmine, standing nearby, startled. "I? Ride out?" No one could recall the last time the Counselor had gotten on a horse.

Ares looked at him levelly. "Yes. If we can't get the information we need out of Tancred, then we will have to interrogate Magnus. With his army backing him, he may feel disinclined to talk, so I will need your help."

"Surchatain. . . ." Carmine weakly smoothed his embroidered surcoat with a trembling hand.

"Don't worry, Carmine. We will go slow for you," Thom said solicitously, hand on his shoulder. Ares turned back as if to retort, *No, we won't*, but refrained from saying it only to avoid the appearance of contradicting his Commander.

Shortly, the three of them were mounted and heading out of the gates with the forerunners from Magnus' army. Carmine, pasty white in the sunlight, gripped the saddle with both hands and both knees. True to his word, Thom kept his horse to a gentle lope. Ares matched his pace, which left the messengers pulling out farther and farther ahead. This was intentional, as they wished to report Ares' coming before his arrival.

Several miles north of the lake, the outgoing party spotted the lines of Magnus' archers stretching for what appeared to be miles in either direction. At front center, with the standard bearers and trumpeters, were Magnus and his Commander in full armor. Even their horses were armored. Having given their message, the forerunners turned to stand beside their Surchatain and wait.

The Lystrans arrived with Carmine flagging only slightly between Ares and Thom. Ares reined up, calling, "Greetings, Magnus! How have I offended you, that you bring your army against an old friend?"

"The army will go home again when you hand over Tancred!" Magnus shouted.

Ares made his horse trot forward to come alongside Magnus on his great warhorse, burdened with a hundred pounds of steel. As usual, Ares wore only his dress blacks. Soberly, he replied, "I had to question Tancred about why he hired someone to take my wife, so he's not in much condition to ride."

"Dead or alive, I care not. Just drag out his carcass," Magnus instructed.

"What is this about, Magnus?" Ares asked. "We are friends and allies. I think you should be able to tell me why you want him dead."

Magnus stirred, then took off his helmet (much to Carmine's relief). Although only thirty, Magnus was looking more like his father every day, with the greying of his temples and the widening of his girth. He also sounded much like Ossian as he grunted, "Tancred has been a gadfly to me for years, flitting about the country spreading the most vile lies, undermining my character and my right to rule—and that of my wife as well, who has never been anything but brave and virtuous."

"What has Tancred been saying?" Ares asked.

"If you questioned him, then he told you. I'll wager he talked your ear off, and that you listened," Magnus spat, a touch of the old hothead returning.

"How did your parents die, Magnus?" Ares asked. Carmine and Thom were back a few paces on their horses, still within earshot.

"They were slaughtered as they slept!" Magnus erupted. "I was roused from bed by the cries of the servants. I emerged from my chambers to their babbling, so I armed myself and went to my father's room. He was dead, hacked to pieces. I ran from there straight to my mother's chambers to find the same.

"But there was a trail of bloody prints leading out of her chambers down the stairs—I looked down to see Tancred in the midst of those villainous friends of his—scheming, worthless idlers and liars. I called out to him and he fled. He would not stand and answer for where he had been or what he had seen. He robbed the treasury of hundreds of cruxes and then disappeared to slander me relentlessly from that moment on."

"I see," Ares said. Then, squinting up in the bright sunlight, he added, "Please allow me to confer with my officers a moment, Magnus." With a flick of the reins, he turned his horse and trotted back to Carmine and Thom.

"What do you think?" Ares asked in a whisper.

"Who can say?" Thom replied. "God alone knows what happened that night."

"God and Chiacos," Carmine said.

"What?" The other two turned to him.

Shifting in his unaccustomed seat, Carmine said, "I believe Chiacos told us what happened. He said they were brothers united in death, in blood. I believe both of them shared complicity in their parents' death. Druella found out about it after she went with Magnus. Since she knew, Chiacos knew. She must have used him in some capacity—probably to pay out hush money to others who knew what happened."

"The old cruxes," Thom said, nodding.

Ares asked, "Could it have been blood money, in payment for their murders?" The four Horsemen loomed up again, terrible and bloody, in his mind's eye.

"Blood money?" Carmine repeated in a whisper. "Can you see Magnus paying anyone to hack his parents to death when a simple sword thrust would have sufficed?—for all of the witnesses say that the parents were butchered. No, the ferocity of the murders attests that they were personal acts of vengeance. But Tancred must know more about it than he says, else he would have brought his brother to trial years ago."

"What went wrong, then?" Thom muttered.

"That, we do not know. Perhaps Tancred lost his nerve or suffered remorse—Chiacos certainly did. I believe the guilt of his knowledge has been haunting him ever since," Carmine replied.

"Then what do we do with Tancred?" Thom asked.

Carmine glanced over at Magnus. "Whatever that is, we must decide quickly. Magnus does not care for this extended conference."

Concurring, Ares spurred back to Magnus. "Begging your patience, I have one more question for you."

"Speak," Magnus barked.

"Why would Tancred kidnap my wife?" Ares asked.

Magnus laughed hoarsely. "Are you such a fool that you do not know? After you snatched her away from him, playing him for an idiot? Do you not know how he has burned for revenge? What he would not give to lie with her and then send her body back to you in pieces!" *Hacked to death as Ossian and Danae were?* Thom wondered.

As the echoes of Magnus' grating laughter died away, Ares held his peace, watching him. Whatever he thought of Magnus' answer, his face showed nothing but attentiveness. Carmine and Thom were silent as well. Finally, Magnus said, "Enough of this parley. Go fetch him, or I shall come get him!"

Ares lowered his head, then looked up again to say, "Tell me why you are protecting Lady Auer."

"Who?" Magnus screwed up his face.

"Lady Auer and her nephew Athian have received benefices from you. Tell me why," Ares said.

Exasperated, Magnus turned to scan the subordinates flanking him. One leaned over to whisper to him, then Magnus relayed to Ares, "The lady enrolled as a dependent with relations in Eurus on our benefices roll. She's received no special treatment from me—I do not even know the name. What has this to do with Tancred?"

Ares replied, "Lady Auer put up her nephew to challenge me for the throne. I spared his life, but banished them both. Tancred tells me that you are harboring them."

Magnus almost ground his teeth. "Sagar!" he barked, and

a rider presented himself. "Ride back to Eurus at once—locate the Lady Auer and her nephew, Athian—strip them of their benefices and drive them into the Fastnesses!"

"Yes, Surchatain!" The man saluted and spurred off.

Magnus turned back to Ares. "There—I have given my order concerning this woman in your hearing, which is my bond of honor. In case Tancred did not tell you, he has spies that keep him as well informed of events as I am myself—or better! Now fetch him to me!"

Ares conceded, "He will come out to you by nightfall. Wait here, and he will ride to you."

"Not good enough! I want him now!" Magnus ordered.

Ares turned his scar full toward him. "We are allies. You have my word that Tancred will ride out to you by nightfall. If he does not, you may attack. But if you refuse to honor my word and send anyone after him before tonight, I will interpret that as aggression and treaty-breaking, and respond in kind."

Magnus wavered. Once before he had mistaken Ares' restraint for weakness and had been punished for it. He looked uncertainly at Commander Lind by his side, who was trying to intimidate Thom with a steadfast glare. But Thom had long ago perfected a look of languid scorn that was wasted on underlings and messengers, so he was delighted to employ it now. Lind glanced at Magnus, shrugging. "You have until nightfall," Magnus muttered.

"Very well." With a nod, Ares turned his horse and the three of them rode back to Westford. Arriving in the safety of the cobbled courtyard, Carmine slipped from the saddle with a groan. "Thank you, Counselor. You performed admirably," Ares told him, and Thom slapped him on the shoulder, knocking him against the saddle.

"We strive to please," Carmine gasped. "Now, I am most interested to hear how you will incite Tancred to ride out to his nemesis."

Thom looked over in concurrent interest, so Ares invited,

"Come see, then." He handed the reins to the waiting stableboy.

First, Ares gave leave for Fancsali's messenger to return to him with Renée's reply, then he went to the great hall and sat on the throne—something he had done perhaps a handful of times since becoming Surchatain.

He told a sentry, "Summon Tancred and his men." Thom and Carmine stood beside him, one on his right and one on his left.

When word got out that the Surchatain was holding an open audience, palace business came to a standstill and the hall quickly filled. Nicole was one of the first to appear, and Ares gestured her forward to whisper to her. She shook her head, so he nodded for her to stand at the front of the audience.

Bonnie and Sophie came, attaching themselves to either side of her. Melva and Renée quickly arrived, as did Giles, Vogelsong, and the officers of the army. Soon the hall was so crowded that when Tancred and his band were brought, a few people had to be evicted to make room for them.

Tancred looked nervous, understandably so, as he bowed to the Surchatain on the throne. Ares checked to make sure that the amanuensis was at his table near the front, ready to transcribe the proceedings. Then, leaning forward on his elbows on the arms of the throne, Ares said, "Tancred, do you know that we found Chiacos?"

Tancred stiffened. "No, Surchatain."

"And I questioned him about many things, such as your relationship with Magnus and what you wanted with Nicole," Ares said. "Would you care to hear what he told me?"

Tancred swayed on his feet. "Surchatain—he—you would listen to a—a renegade Polonti? The refuse of the earth? He is full of deceit and murder! He is nothing but a murderer!"

Over the surprised murmurings of the audience, Ares replied, "That he has killed, or allowed his companion to kill, is beyond dispute. But Chiacos is not on trial here." He paused to watch Tancred sweat. "I have also learned that you and Magnus have unfinished business, with which I choose not to interfere."

"Surchatain, you gave me sanctuary!" Tancred exclaimed.

Ares held up a hand. "And so I have. I will give you the choice of either staying here or riding out to Magnus, who is waiting for you on the road to Eurus. But if you stay here, I have yet to punish you for taking the Surchataine."

"How shall I be punished?" Tancred asked weakly.

Ares sat back. "I am going to do to you what you planned to do with her."

Tancred cried, "Chiacos lies, Surchatain! The imaginations of those people are warped and twisted beyond belief! He is vileness personified—"

This second outburst against his hand-picked hireling had those in the audience looking wonderstruck, especially Nicole. Had Tancred really been intending to send her back to Ares with a plea for help, now was the perfect moment to affirm that. Instead, his panicky response indicated a different agenda. What did Tancred think Chiacos had told them about his plans for Nicole? What had Tancred told Chiacos that made him weep to take her?

Staring at Tancred, Nicole wondered what kind of snake lay hidden beneath the beleaguered, pitiable exterior. When she remembered that she herself had given him a place at their table, her face flushed in anger. But Ares was speaking, so she concentrated on his words: "If the man you hired is so vile, how could you allow him to touch the Surchataine—someone you claim to care about? To enter her bedchamber and take her by force?"

"There was . . . no other way. . . ." Tancred said haltingly.

"Where were you shot?" Ares asked, looking at his shoulder.

"Where . . . ?"

"Where were you when you were shot trying to get a message to me?" Ares asked.

"I was . . . entering the gates. I had simply tried to enter the gates. . . ." Tancred faltered as Thom was shaking his head emphatically.

"Explain to him why he was not shot entering the gates, Commander," Ares instructed Thom.

"Surchatain, no arrow is expended from the parapet without an accounting. If anyone fires, he must account for it. Therefore, Tancred would have been brought to me at once," Thom said.

"So there is another lie," Ares exhaled. "So many lies that I cannot untangle them all—nor will I try. Chiacos is the only one that I am certain has told the truth, as he understood it. So here is what I offer you: you may stay here and receive your punishment, or ride out to Magnus and make peace with him as best you can."

At this point, the Counselor leaned over to whisper to Ares, who affirmed, "Tell him."

Carmine shook out his full, elegant sleeves, which had gotten bunched up during the impromptu ride. He may also have been exhibiting a little swagger over his new competency. "I was just reminding the Surchatain that Magnus can be deposed if he attempts to dispose of you without a trial, which we will watch closely. If you still have friends in Eurus, they should be able to intervene on your behalf."

"Decide this moment what you will do," Ares ordered.

Tancred glanced toward the companion closest to his right. "What of my men?"

"They will share your fate, one way or another, as they have chosen to do up till now," Ares assured him.

"Then let us leave," the companion hissed to Tancred, and a few others murmured similar wishes. None of them liked the looks of Ares' scar.

"If we have no friends here—" Tancred looked at Nicole,

who straightened coldly. "We will leave," he ended dully.

In Tancred's hearing, Ares told Thom, "See that they are given their horses and that they ride north. I will not have Magnus pursuing them all over Lystra."

"Yes, Surchatain." Turning a satisfied eye toward the fugitives, Thom gestured for his men to escort them out.

"You are dismissed," Ares told the crowd, and they dispersed full of talk.

Nicole met Ares as he came down off the throne, and he took her hand. "Now I feel rather a fool for treating him as a guest," she murmured.

"I would rather be a fool ten times over than ill-treat someone who deserved better," Ares said, then paused. "But I won't suffer lies."

"After all these years. . . ." She began to blink rapidly. "After all this time, why did he decide to come after me now?"

"Because he found the means: Chiacos," Ares reminded her. "Speaking of whom, I wish to talk to him again."

He started to move away, but Nicole gripped his hand. "Let me see him as well, Ares. I want to talk to him, too."

He looked reluctant. "He is not a happy sight."

"I have seen him twice now, unhappily. I want to face him on grounds more favorable to myself," Nicole said.

"As you wish, Lady. I will have him brought up." Ares gave orders, then they retired to the small room off the dais of the great hall.

They sat in the holding room and waited. Nicole looked at the bare stone of the walls, and the mortar crumbling from between the stones, and wondered what measure of hatred Tancred had been nursing these eight years. When she looked at Ares, she saw his brown eyes fixed pensively on her. Was he wondering the same thing—what Tancred had planned for her?

As the minutes attached themselves one to another, Ares leaned forward to take her fingers and press them against his lips. "I am wondering," he said, "why it is taking so long to bring up one man from the upper prison."

The answer came soon enough. A perspiring sentry opened the door and saluted with the word: "Surchatain, Chiacos is missing."

16

Releasing Nicole's fingers, Ares sat back in exasperation. "Who was on guard duty?" That man would find himself in a most disagreeable conversation with the Surchatain.

The sentry deferred to another who came to the doorway: "I was, Surchatain."

"Geurts," Ares said in mild dismay, because he liked the young soldier. "What happened?"

"I put him in the cell as instructed, Surchatain, but an hour ago, the Chataine Melva asked to see him. I gave her leave, and watched from the door as she spoke to him. Then she came out and requested that he be moved to another cell, with more light."

Noting the Surchataine's change of expression, Geurts continued, "I sent a message to Captain Yonge, who came down and looked at the cell that the Chataine asked he be moved to. Chiacos suffered in the damp, she said, and she pleaded with tears that he had suffered enough. Neither of us could see a problem with moving him, so we did, and she left. But not half an hour later when I looked in his cell, it was empty."

Ares rested his mouth pensively on his fist. Grunting, he

got up. "Show me the cell. And summon Melva."

Nicole stood. "Ares—let me go talk to her first." He glanced at her and nodded in mild relief. There were hard questions that needed to be asked the Qarqarian Chataine, which he dreaded. So while Nicole ascended to the second floor, Ares and Geurts descended to the dungeon.

Captain Yonge met them at the foot of the dungeon steps —they were smooth, treacherous stone, slick from centuries of use and constant dampness. No sunlight reached any of these cells, even those in the upper level where Chiacos had been moved to. But Ares could not find it in himself to blame any of the men for acceding to Melva's request when she was so meek, so harmless, and so honored by Ares himself.

The Captain waved a torch down the dark, rough-hewn stone corridor. "I've had some men in his cell, poking around. Come look, Surchatain." Ares, followed stubbornly by Geurts, went down the corridor ten paces to the open cell door. A cluster of men parted to expose a gaping hole in the stone floor.

Coming closer, Ares looked down in the hole to see water about two feet beneath the surface. "What is this?"

"We figure it's a branch of the underground stream that runs by here, Surchatain," Yonge explained. "Somehow, Chiacos knew of it and asked Melva to have him moved to this particular cell. Knowing which stone hid the passage, he could pry it up, drop down the hole, and put the stone back in minutes."

"Where—?" Ares' eyes suddenly glazed over. "Find Thom. Find Deirdre. And come with me quickly," he uttered. Wheeling, he sprang out of the cell and scampered up the slippery stone steps to the lower corridor of the palace. He swung around the corner to hasten down the corridor that housed his old quarters—Thom's present quarters—followed by a score of men.

Arriving at the door of Thom's quarters, Ares thrust it

open and stumbled over a pile of chest armor with the newfangled brassards that Thom had been trying out. Ares regained his balance only to fall on the louvered wooden doors of the garderobe—and there he saw the bolt. Thom had affixed an iron bolt on the doors, which was now drawn across to secure them shut.

Sliding the bolt open, Ares opened the doors and called for a torch. Handed one, he looked down the stream bed as far as he could, and saw nothing.

By the time Ares withdrew from the garderobe, Thom had appeared at the door of his quarters, looking considerably surprised. "Surchatain?" Behind him came Carmine.

"You earned your pay for the day, Thom," Ares said. "When did you install the bolt?" He gestured to the garderobe doors.

Thom glanced at the contraption. "The day you informed me of the risk, Surchatain. Why?"

Ares rebolted the doors closed. "I will show you. Come."

The whole party retreated back down to the dungeon while Ares informed Thom and Carmine of Chiacos' escape. Entering the suspect cell, they all three bent over the hole in the floor. "Where does it go?" Thom murmured, sticking his head down it.

"Geurts will find out," Ares said. He intended it as an honor to Geurts, forgetting about his recent injury.

Geurts came forward and dropped feet first into the hole. He landed with a splash on the floor of the stream bed, in about four feet of flowing water. There, he was able to reach up just high enough to maneuver the stone back in place over the hole, had he needed to. But Ares handed down a torch to him with instructions to look around: "Go as far as you can, but do not get out of sight of this opening. Raise a cry if you find Chiacos."

"Which way, Surchatain?"

Ares hesitated. "Go upstream first."

"Yes, Surchatain."

Geurts splashed off, and Thom leaned down in the hole to watch. Momentarily, the Commander came back up to report, "Lost sight of him. There appears to be a steep incline not ten feet off."

"Which must be, as the garderobe is higher than the dungeon, and the stream flows under both," Ares mused.

Shortly Geurts reappeared under the dungeon hole to pant, "Saw the opening to the Commander's garderobe, Surchatain. Was that far enough?"

"Yes. Go downstream now."

"Surchatain," Geurts acknowledged, gripping the torch.

He was gone for a long time. Carmine went out to speak to a sentry while Ares, Thom and Yonge periodically stuck their heads down to look for Geurts.

Standing, Ares looked around the cell. "The dungeon sits under the northeast corner of the palace. The stream flows away from the palace—east. In walking upstream, Geurts was going deeper under the palace, west. Going east would take him away from the palace."

"Yes, Surchatain," Captain Yonge said.

Then Ares looked back down at the dark hole. He was beginning to worry about losing another man—he didn't even know if Geurts could swim—when they heard faint splashes echoing up from the black stream. Thom leaned far down into the hole and came back up to report, "He's coming."

Minutes later Geurts was back under the opening, soaked, without his torch. They hoisted him up onto the stone floor of the cell, where he had to lie still and catch his breath while Ares stood over him.

"Pardon, sir," Geurts gasped. "The wind doesn't come as easily since the villain knocked it out of me going over the wall."

"Take your time," Ares said with minimal impatience.

Geurts struggled up to sit in a puddle. "Going with the

flow was easy, but coming back upstream was a mighty lot of work. It flows stronger than it looks."

"So do you think Chiacos went east or west?" Ares asked.

Geurts squinted hesitantly. "Depends on where he was aiming to get, Surchatain. But he had to know that there was some other opening to make his way upstream with no light. It's hard going, no place to rest, and nothing to grab onto. It gets narrower, too."

"All right," Ares nodded. "What is the stream like in the other direction, away from the palace?"

"Under here it's, I'd say, twelve feet from edge to edge. But every foot you go, it gets wider. About fifty feet down, the stream branches in two. The left branch goes completely underwater. The right may go farther, but I was swimming by that time—dropped my torch and couldn't see a dear thing. I was mighty glad you had the lights up here over the hole, else I would have been lost down there." His teeth were chattering.

"I see." Ares turned to Thom and Carmine. "What do you think? Where did Chiacos go?"

"If there is no other entry into the palace besides the garderobe, then he must have gone east, downstream," Carmine said without conviction.

Thom agreed. "He was looking to escape, Surchatain. That seems certain."

"Probably," Ares nodded. "But . . . we did not know about this entry. I wish we knew if there were others. . . ."

While they were mulling over this, Counselor Vogelsong could be heard on the fringes of the group of soldiers, politely requesting access. Being so slight of build, he still had not gotten used to exerting the authority of his rank.

"Vogelsong?" Ares called, creating an immediate pathway for him through the men into the cell.

The Counselor appeared with shining eyes and an old scroll. "So it is here! Thank you for informing me, Counselor!" he exclaimed, and Carmine inclined his head.

"What have you there?" Ares asked.

"Surchatain, this is a map of the palace that predates Surchatain Roman," Vogelsong said, delicately unrolling the parchment on the stone floor in front of Ares. After having been rolled up for many years, it opened grudgingly, the fragile parchment cracking. While Ares leaned over it, Thom angled the torch to cast shadowless light on it.

Vogelsong continued, "I could make no sense of it at first. It shows clearly enough the secret passage which my lord had sealed up—but then it seemed to indicate other passages which had no correspondence to any in the palace that I knew of."

Vogelsong pointed out faint lines on the map and Thom murmured, "The blue line definitely follows the secret passage—there is the terminus at the Surchatain's suite and the other two openings in the vegetable garden and fig orchard. But the red line that intersects the blue here...."

The young Counselor chose to be silent and let the Commander figure it out for himself. Ares sat back on his heels as Carmine leaned forward, squinting at the map in the torchlight. "Where did you find this, Vogelsong?" Ares asked.

"Among the old parchments in the lower storage room, Surchatain, when I began cleaning it out several weeks ago."

"The red line is the underground stream!" Thom exclaimed in sudden illumination.

Ares looked at him shrewdly. "You see three circles on the red line within the palace—"

"This cell is one," Thom said at once, jabbing at the map, and Vogelsong reflexively grabbed at his hand lest he damage the old parchment. "The garderobe in my quarters is another. But this third point is the only place on the map where the blue and red lines intersect, and I cannot tell *where*...."

"It is just beyond the cave-in in the ground floor of the secret passage," Ares said, "where Chiacos—or someone—was trying to clear away the rocks."

Dead Man's Token

Breathless, everyone looked at him. Carmine gestured. "All this then—the passage and the stream—was at one point a single escape route which the cave-in disrupted—"

"And which someone was trying to restore," Thom breathed. "But—if this map predates Surchatain Roman, how can it show the stream under the garderobe? I remember when Coyle's men broke out the wall and discovered it."

Ares replied, "How do you think they broke it open so easily? It had been known at one time, before the wall was built over it. The main question is, how did Chiacos learn of it? . . . Vogelsong, who else has seen this map?"

"No one, Surchatain," he said. "When Counselor Carmine informed me just now of the discovery of this passage, and I made the connection to this map, I brought it straightway down here without showing it to a single soul."

"Could anyone have seen it before then?" Ares asked.

"Well, Chataine Melva was assisting me in cataloguing the documents for the new library and had many questions about the map, but, of course, it's ridiculous to think . . ." Vogelsong stammered, but Ares looked at his officers, and they at him.

"We assumed that Chiacos told Melva of the passage," Ares said. "But what if *she* told *him*?"

"Why?" Thom asked in a low voice.

"Clearly, she had sympathy for him," Carmine replied.

"But then, who was clearing out the rocks? And to what purpose?" Thom asked.

"We had better go ask Melva," Ares said, standing.

As they got to their feet, Captain Yonge asked, "What shall we do with this, Surchatain?" He gestured at the hole in the floor.

Ares glanced around. "Leave the stone out, and keep a torch burning in here. Lock the cell door and post a guard outside it at all times. If Chiacos finds his way back, we will welcome him."

While Ares and his men were down in the dungeon, Nicole was up on the second floor asking after Melva. The sentry at the library door told her that Melva was within, at lessons with Henry and Doudney. Nicole paced the corridor outside for a long time, trying to think of what to say to Melva. But nothing came to mind, and she knew that Ares must be coming shortly to speak to her.

So Nicole entered the library unannounced, leaving the door ajar behind her, and observed the typical classroom scene: Doudney lecturing in his tentative way, Henry looking bored and Melva in a far-off trance. All three came to attention at her entrance. At that moment, she had an inspiration.

"Good afternoon, Doudney. Is class going well? It is so gratifying to see the Law being imparted to young minds day after day." Nicole walked behind the table where the students sat.

They turned in their chairs to watch her while Doudney stood frozen at the front of the room. "Knowing the Law gives one such wonderful perspective. It makes so many things clear that, otherwise, seem to make no sense," she continued.

Such as the reason for this little lecture? said the expressions on three faces that looked back at her. Nicole laughed lightly. "Henry," she said, and he straightened in attention. "You know the Law well. Tell me —what is the penalty for kidnapping a member of the royal family?"

"Death," he said.

"Ah. But are there extenuating circumstances that might mitigate the penalty?" Nicole asked, pacing.

Henry frowned. "Only what the Surchatain might allow."

"And what might he allow in such circumstances?" Nicole pressed, still pacing.

"Anything he chose to allow," Henry said with a dry laugh.

"I see. Then, knowing the Law, and knowing Ares, what

do you suppose he would do in regard to Chiacos?" Nicole asked.

Henry's brow furrowed. "Is this a trick question to see if I'm ready to sit for certification?"

"Of course not," Nicole assured him. "I am just asking you to speculate, for argument's sake."

Henry stirred pensively. "I have heard that Chiacos is strange in the head now, so I'd be really surprised if Ares put him to death."

"You mean that Ares would be inclined to show mercy," Nicole said.

"Yes," Henry affirmed.

Nicole glanced at Melva who was watching stonily. "But what if Chiacos escaped? What does the Law allow?" Nicole went on.

"For Ares or anyone?" Henry asked, growing interested in this game.

"For anyone," Nicole said.

"Oh, well, anyone who saw him could turn him in for a bounty, dead or alive," Henry said authoritatively. "And since a dead criminal is safer than a live one, they'd most likely kill him first. He'd be a walking target anywhere in Lystra. He sure would be better off letting Ares decide what to do with him rather than exposing himself to every bounty hunter in the province." As he talked, Henry got the point. "Has Chiacos escaped?"

Without answering that question, Nicole went on to her next point. "What about someone who helped him escape, Henry? What would be the penalty for them?"

"Someone on the inside of the palace or outside?" Henry asked, now fully aware of what she was doing.

"Someone on the inside," Nicole said, careful not to look at Melva.

"That's Treachery by an Intimate, and the penalty is death," Henry said, watching Nicole.

"Would Ares impose such a penalty?" Nicole asked. She had stopped pacing.

Henry weighed this. "That depends on who it was. If it was a guard or somebody like that, yes. But if it was somebody really high up, who he really trusted, like Carmine or Renée . . . no. I can't see Ares executing anybody he was really close to, regardless of what they did. He would banish them, though."

"And what would be the fate of someone he banished?" Nicole asked.

"Oh—worse than Chiacos. Because then you'd have people after you who don't just want to kill you, they want to know everything you know about Ares, so they'd catch you and torture you to find out. Then they wouldn't kill you, but sell you to the slavers for whatever you'd bring in your present condition."

"Thank you, Henry. I believe you have summed up the situation most succinctly," Nicole said. Only then did she turn toward Melva.

But as she did, something caused her to raise her eyes to a point above Melva's head. The other three swiveled to look and saw Ares standing in the doorway.

He was looking at Melva, and the weight of his scar bore down on her. "Come talk with me, Chataine," he said, expressionless. She sat planted in her seat, so he glanced up at his wife. "Will you join us, Lady?"

"Yes, my lord," Nicole said, coming forward. She paused beside Melva's chair, waiting for her to rise. Tossing her head, Melva got up in a show of unconcern while Henry and Doudney looked on in alarm.

With Melva between them, Ares and Nicole walked out to the apple orchard in the descending twilight. The blossoms had been long spent, and small, green fruit graced many hundreds of branches. But since it was neither the season for pruning nor harvesting, there was no one else out here—the servants had even neglected to light the votives in their globes along the path—so the three could walk and talk in relative privacy.

Ambling down the pebbled pathway, Ares reached up to finger a tiny, hard apple. "When I come out here, I get impatient for the fall, and Veola's apple pies. It is easy to lose sight of the pleasures of summer—"

"Say what you came to say, Ares," Melva said.

He stopped on the path and looked at her. "Why did you help Chiacos, Chataine?"

She sighed—a long, deep, troubled sigh. "I felt so sorry for him. He has suffered so much."

"Has he? How do you know what he has suffered?" Ares asked.

She shrugged. "I saw him after he left service here. He would meet me in town the few chances I had to get away. He would tell me about the hardships of his life."

"Hardships that came by his choice," Ares noted. "He left without word to anyone, when he had every invitation to stay."

"And serve you!" Melva snorted. She seemed to grow two inches in her newfound assertiveness. "He loves Druella! He had to leave so that he could go see her, and bring messages to me from her, because you wouldn't allow it!"

"True, I would not allow you to receive messages that I did not also see. But that does not explain why you helped him get into the palace through the secret passage and take the Surchataine," Ares said. Nicole startled and looked at Melva.

The girl was silent, so Ares skipped ahead to more recent events. "You saw the map Counselor Vogelsong found and told Chiacos about the underground stream. Where did he go when he escaped the prison cell? Deeper underneath the palace or east toward Willowring Lake?"

"I don't know," Melva said dully.

"I do not believe you," Ares said. "I believe you showed

Chiacos where the underground stream intersected the secret passage past the cave-in. Were you also helping him dig out the rocks? Did you kill Riever while he stood guard in the passage?"

"No!" she finally protested. "Chiacos—never meant anyone to die. He had hired someone else to help him who was stupid."

"How did you get him onto the palace grounds?" Ares asked.

"He did that himself, hiring on as a festival worker," Melva said. Glancing at Nicole, she added, "I'm so sorry—Chiacos had no choice but to take you. Druella would have been ruined. But Tancred swore to him that you would not be harmed."

Nicole said coldly, "I find little comfort that you place Druella's reputation over my life, especially when we have—"

"I know! I know! Sheltered and protected me! Well, I don't want your protection! I want you to let me go be with Druella!" Melva cried.

Ares began, "Chataine, your life is still in great peril. We fought a war, and lost many lives, to save yours. Druella herself may have—"

"I want to go back to her! I told Chiacos what was on the map so he could get *me* out! It would have been so wonderful to just disappear through the secret passage! But he couldn't get all the rocks cleared away by himself, so he hired an idiot to help him who went to Tancred and told him what Chiacos was doing—so Tancred made him take her instead!" Melva cried. "I'm sick of this place! I'm sick of you!—your Law and your rules and your ugly scar—you're a tyrant and I hate you! I want to go where *I* want to go, and I want to go to Eurus and be with Druella!" she ranted.

Ares gazed at her. "You do not know what you are saying. There are many who still desire your death, to take the throne you are heir to. Druella herself may—"

"Let me go!" Melva shouted. "Let me go, or I may slit your throat one night myself!"

Nicole stared at her in shock, and all she could see was the dress Melva wore, crafted by Lord Preus. Fed at the Surchatain's table, educated by his tutors, clothed by the finest dressmaker in Westford—and what did Melva offer in return? To slit his throat.

When Ares did not react, Melva calmed down, closing her eyes in possible remorse. But no retraction nor apology was forthcoming.

At length, Ares blinked, looking up to the trees. Then he turned his scar back to Melva. "Your request is granted. I will send you with a bodyguard—"

"No more guards," Melva decreed. Intoxicated with the power of finally getting her way, she wanted to drink it to the dregs.

"Shall I send you to Eurus alone? Or will Chiacos come back and get you?" Ares asked dryly.

"I'll just hop a merchant caravan up," Melva said carelessly. Now she appeared to be deliberately provoking him.

Ares swallowed, and Nicole watched his scar throb. "Then you had best go pack whatever you want to take. You will leave tomorrow morning," he said quietly.

Melva clasped her hands in excitement. "Thank you!" she exclaimed, then turned happily back up the pebbled path.

Nicole and Ares watched her go in silence. A moment later he asked in a strained voice, "Am I a tyrant?"

She looked at him with a humorless laugh. "Would a tyrant allow her to call him one?"

He closed his eyes. "She does not know what she is saying. She does not understand the danger."

"She is ungrateful," Nicole countered.

"Should that cost her her life?" he asked, turning toward her.

"If she chooses not to be saved, what can you do?" she said.

Ares stroked his forehead, then raised his eyes to the approaching sentry. "Surchatain, and my lady, dinner waits."

Nicole startled. "Did the bell ring? I did not hear it!"

"You were listening to something else, Lady," Ares said, gesturing toward the palace.

To not keep their guests waiting, they went straight to the great hall and were seated. Ares glanced distractedly at his children, his officers and administrators in their customary places, then waved for the wine steward. As the servant came to make his rounds with the pitcher, Ares looked up again. The table was unusually quiet.

It was Renée who finally spoke, her voice low and smooth. "Where is Melva?"

Ares looked at Melva's empty place. "I doubt that she will be joining us tonight," he said heavily.

There was a short silence before Renée said in a voice lower yet, "I never thought you capable of such cruelty."

He and Nicole looked up, dumbfounded. Renée exclaimed, "How *could* you banish her? She's so young and defenseless! I might survive, but she would not. You're horrible, Ares!"

17

The rest of the table looked stunned at Renée's outburst, especially Bonnie and Sophie. The thought crossed Nicole's mind that Henry must have told Renée about their questioning game in the library. Finding Melva not at table, Renée formed her own conclusions about what Ares had done.

Nicole was gathering herself to correct Renée when Ares, scar purple, said, "Why should I not banish her? She directly enabled Chiacos to kidnap my wife."

"She's just a child!" Renée cried.

Thom retorted, "If she's old enough to conspire in kidnapping and murder, then she's old enough to suffer the consequences. I lost a man because of her treachery."

"But—banishment is likely to mean her death, Surchatain," Vogelsong said, troubled. "I beg you to reconsider."

"Then my man's death, which is a fact, means less than hers, which has yet to happen," Rhode put in quietly. "Does it count for anything that Riever was from a noble family?"

Doctor Savary countered, "As much as I am loath to see anyone die, your man was a soldier, who knew the risks of his service. To banish this girl seems to render null the deaths of those who died fighting the Qarqarian usurper who tried to take her. Would you send her away after such a sacrifice, Surchatain?" he pleaded. Ares clamped his mouth shut while a tiny trickle of blood began to issue from his scar.

Sophie jumped to her feet. "Papa is the Surchatain and you all must do as he says!" she cried.

In the sudden stillness that followed, another voice added brokenly, "But he is good, too. Papa is *not* horrible, Aunt Renée—we should mind him because he is good." The table looked at Bonnie bravely fighting back the tears.

Ares, eyes red, looked across Nicole at Bonnie as the blood trickled down his neck into the white frill of his collar. "Oh, dear," Bonnie fretted, rising from her chair. "You're bleeding again. It does that when he gets all upset." Motherly, Bonnie took her napkin and daubed at the blood on his jaw while the table watched in silence.

At that time, Melva skipped into the hall and plopped into her chair. "Sorry I'm late," she chirped. "I've been so busy packing. I'm going to Eurus to live with Druella!"

Glances were exchanged at the table. "Do you—*want* to go, Chataine?" Vogelsong asked, obviously crushed.

"I *told* Ares I was going," she exulted. "He wasn't going to let me, but I *made* him."

Now everyone looked at Ares, whose expression was unchanged. Deliberately, Renée turned to Melva to utter, "You are such a little fool."

"Why? Because you're an old woman stuck here who nobody wants?" Melva shot back.

"Chataine Melva." It was a quiet voice of authority and compassion which came from the seat across from Renée, and everyone turned to look at Carmine, who had not spoken yet in this debate. "As you evidently have your heart set on going to Eurus, we at Westford will pray for your safekeeping and ask you to remember us with the same affection that we have held for you all these years."

No one could have said anything more devastating to her.

At least that is what it seemed until Ares said, "Chataine, if you ever want to come back, I will come get you."

With her inner heart so fully exposed, Melva decided she wasn't very hungry after all. Taking up her cup and a small loaf of rye bread, she left the table and ascended the stairs to continue packing the little treasures that the Lystrans had bought for her over the years.

The rest of dinner was understandably subdued. Immediately following, Ares accompanied his wife to put their daughters to bed. But tonight, just for a change, he tucked in Bonnie and Nicole tucked in Sophie.

Before sunrise the next morning, Ares sat at the window seat of the receiving room as was his custom. He was unspeakably grateful to have his wife asleep in the next room. He was gratified for the new maturity that Renée, Bonnie and Sophie were showing. (Yes, in some aspects he lumped the three together.) He was glad for the profits from the festival and relieved to leave Magnus and Tancred to settle their differences themselves. But . . . he was heartsick over Melva.

Could he trust Druella's natural affection to preserve her life when she could kill her and take the throne of Qarqar? Could he count on Magnus to protect the Chataine from the numerous assassins that were sure to flock to Eurus upon her arrival? Should Ares make the issue moot by appending Qarqar to Lystra? This option had been urged on him by a number of interested others.

But Ares was most reluctant to take this course. His resources were already spread so thin in managing and protecting the province after the addition of Calle Valley that he could hardly see how he would handle the wildness of far northern Qarqar. The citizens' council of Hornbound, led by a magistrate who was (of all things) elected once every five years, was running smoothly, having grown rich from prudent management of the mining.

As their wealth had grown, so had their power. They had

stopped reporting to Ares at least a year ago, so now they might raise effective resistance to a benevolent takeover. If they objected to Ares' "tyranny," however, so would they also object to anyone else's. For that matter, they probably would not welcome back Melva, should she ever decide to rule—which now appeared unlikely.

In a sudden fit of illumination, Ares realized that he needed to lay out the matter to the council at Hornbound, advising them of Melva's lack of interest in the rulership. Then it occurred to him that to safeguard her life, he must go one step further.

While the sun crept up over the eastern horizon, Ares summoned Carmine and Vogelsong to his receiving room. The younger Counselor, naturally an early riser, was already dressed, but poor Carmine, summoned straight out of bed, required several shots of stout rosemary tea to get his blood flowing. Once he was awake, Ares told them what kind of document he required. And once they had jointly composed this document, Ares summoned Melva.

She came puffy-eyed and wary, already dressed in travel clothes. But her attitude was unaltered from yesterday: "If you tell me that you have changed your mind, I will—I will—"

"No," he said. "You may still leave. But I wish to add one stipulation." With Carmine and Vogelsong standing by, he gestured her to the chair behind the table. She sat, looking considerably smaller in that seat than its usual occupant.

Then Ares laid the document in front of her. "Before I can let you go, I wish you to make a formal announcement of what you have been telling us all along. Signing this will do more to preserve your life than all I ever could."

Melva glanced over the parchment. "A declaration of abdication?" She read it, then looked up at him. "You want me to sign this statement that says I will never rule Qarqar."

"That is correct," Ares said. The counselors watched. Did she understand what she was about to throw away forever?

Dead Man's Token

For the space of ten heartbeats, Melva looked at the statement, though Carmine doubted she was reading it. Then she shrugged. "All right."

Vogelsong handed her a ready quill, and she signed two copies of the declaration of abdication—one which Ares would keep and one which she would take with her. Those two copies were then ratified with the Surchatain's seal.

When Melva's copy was blotted, rolled and tied, Ares handed it to her. "I will no longer command you, Melva, but I would advise that you show this to anyone you meet in Eurus."

"All right," she said. "I'm . . . almost ready to leave."

Ares hesitated. Although she had refused a bodyguard, he could not simply turn her out of the gates. A sentry knocked, and Ares called, "Enter!"

The sentry stepped in to say, "Surchatain, Lord Fancsali has arrived and wishes a word with you."

Ares looked startled, glancing out at the new morning. Then he turned to Melva. "If you will not allow me to provide you an escort, will you allow Lord Fancsali to take you to Eurus?"

"Yes," she said readily. "Yes."

"So be it," he confirmed, and she skipped out of the receiving room.

"She could have said good-bye," Vogelsong murmured.

Businesslike, Ares turned to him. "Have your amanuenses make a hundred copies of this declaration and distribute it in the major cities of Lystra, Scylla, and Qarqar. Also, send a copy to the council at Hornbound."

"Yes, Surchatain," Vogelsong said, depressed.

"Excuse me, Surchatain; I must dress at once, lest I miss anything else," Carmine said, turning out, and Ares looked down at the cotton breeches he himself still wore.

Minutes later Ares, in his dress blacks but unshaven, was downstairs in the foyer receiving Lord Fancsali. "Where have you come from so early, Fancsali?" Ares asked. Behind the lord were two riding companions.

"Eviron, Surchatain," Fancsali said, saluting him in the same manner as Ares' own soldiers did. "I must apologize for the earliness of the hour, but I fancied you were not the type to linger in bed past daylight."

"You are correct." Gesturing to a servant nearby, Ares instructed, "Bring the lord breakfast." To Fancsali, he said, "Come," and led him and his companions into the great hall, where servants began setting up a table to accommodate breakfast for the four of them.

"Again, I am indebted to your hospitality, Surchatain," Fancsali said, sitting. There was a look of wearied determination in his face.

"You were telling me what roused you from your bed in the middle of the night to hasten to Westford," Ares said.

Fancsali laughed as servants brought peach pastries in cream and smoked ham to set before the men. "I am sure you are aware of my proposal of marriage—the genuine one—to your captivating Chataine," he began, and Ares nodded. "Well, I received her reply, and it seemed to me—coy. That is, she seemed not to take my offer seriously. I know that I am thought of as insincere with the ladies, with reason, I admit. It has never troubled me before. But when I found myself pinned by her reply. . . . The more I thought on it, the more I realized that I have never been more serious about anything."

Ares listened in growing amazement. Renée's reply (composed by Carmine) was meant merely to elicit information about Magnus' court, but Fancsali read it as an indictment of his character . . . or a challenge. "I intend to have the Chataine as my wife, Surchatain Ares. I intend to win her affection and her hand." So stating, Fancsali gestured to one of his companions, who unwrapped the pack he had been carrying. From it, he produced a stunning full-length surcoat of red fox.

"This is my gift to the Chataine, as a token of proof—inadequate for her beauty and rank, of course—that my intentions to court her are honorable," Fancsali said, handing the surcoat to Ares.

Whatever else might be said about him, Fancsali knew the forms and requirements for royal courtship. Raising his brows in reluctant approval, Ares handed off the gift to a servant with the instructions that it be taken up to Renée and that she be informed of Fancsali's presence.

Then Ares sat down with the men to encourage them to eat, which they did. He told Fancsali, "I should advise you that the Chataine will ask you, first, what provision you intend to make for your current wife and children."

"They will be amply provided for," Fancsali said hastily.

"Very good," Ares commented. Noting the speed with which Fancsali was consuming breakfast, he added, "You need not rush. It will be a good hour before the Chataine comes down. You will have quite enough time to bathe and shave." This suggestion was made out of grudging sympathy for Fancsali's plight, to help him along in Renée's good graces. Ares knew what she did to men.

"Yes—certainly—" Fancsali glanced around uncertainly, as one unaccustomed to frequent bathing.

"I will have water drawn for you in the lower corridor. You will be summoned when it is ready," Ares said, standing.

Fancsali looked up suddenly. "Surchatain—"

"There is one other matter," Ares said, pausing. "A guest of ours, Melva, is a long-time friend of Surchataine Druella, and wishes to go see her in Eurus. She declines a bodyguard, and I have not sent word to Magnus and Druella of her coming, so I would be beholden to you if you would escort her to Eurus yourself."

"Melva." Fancsali's eyes narrowed in concentration. "Is she the one who spoke of Druella at the table the other night?"

"Yes. Melva was the Chataine of Qarqar whom Druella

and Chiacos brought here eight years ago. But I would have you know, and you must make known to Magnus, that Melva has formally abdicated the throne. She will never rule Qarqar," Ares told him.

"I see," Fancsali said. "Of course I will escort the lady. But—I would beg you, Surchatain, before the Chataine comes down.... Would you be so kind to go press my case to her?"

"Pardon?" Ares asked.

"I fear that she may choose not to receive me, even after receiving my gift. There were matters I was less than forthcoming to her about...."

"True," Ares admitted.

Fancsali winced. "Could I prevail upon your kindness to speak a word on my behalf, to soften her towards me?"

Ares regarded him. "You ask a hard thing of me, to attempt to sway her thinking. But without you, I might have lost my wife forever. So, yes, I will trumpet your virtues to our Chataine."

"Thank you, Surchatain." Fancsali grinned, looking more like his old cocky self.

"Be sure to bathe," Ares murmured, passing a hand over his face as he turned out of the hall.

Ascending the great staircase, he encountered Melva on the way down, followed by servants who were lugging a great trunk. Drawing abreast of her, Ares said, "Lord Fancsali has kindly agreed to escort you to Eurus, Melva. But he will not be leaving right away—he has come to see the Chataine Renée."

"That's fine," she murmured, and there was something inscrutable in her face. With a nod to her, he continued up the staircase, then turned down the corridor toward Renée's quarters.

Upon arriving at her door, Ares sent for a maid to inform the Chataine of his desire to speak with her. He dare not summon Renée when he knew that she was probably not dressed. The maid entered her apartments, then he heard Renée call, "You may come in, Ares." The maid opened the door to him.

Standing in the corridor, he was rendered momentarily blank by the sight of Renée in a sheer silk gown, with her blonde hair cascading around her shoulders. Throwing her hair back, she glanced at him, and he deliberately turned his eyes away to regain some semblance of cognitive ability. "I assume you have received Lord Fancsali's gift, Chataine?"

"Yes, Ares. You may come in," she said lightly. "You may go," she said to the maid. Eleanor had already been dispatched elsewhere.

The maid went out with a slowness which ensured that this episode would be spread all over the palace before the next hour was rung. Ares continued to stand in the corridor, his eyes averted to a point somewhere to his right. "Well, ah, the lord wished me to convey his sincerity in making his proposal to you. It seems that your hedging stirred his interest more than anything else you might have said, except a direct refusal."

"How amusing," Renée said drolly.

"He expressed most forcefully his desire to convince you of his honorable intentions," Ares said, beads of sweat on his forehead.

"Lovely," she noted, rising from the dressing table. "Tell me, Ares—which dress do you think would look best with the fox surcoat?" she posed, opening the wardrobe doors.

"I am not the one to judge," he said, almost falling backward. At that point, he decided that he had fulfilled Fancsali's request to the limits of his own personal safety and reputation. "When you are dressed, come downstairs. He is waiting." And Ares fled.

He arrived downstairs, noting Melva's trunk sitting in the foyer. Neither Fancsali nor his men were to be seen. On the assumption that he had taken to heart the suggestion of a bath,

Ares went to the small room off the great hall to conduct business while awaiting Renée. As her surrogate father, it was Ares' responsibility to see that the courtship went according to form and that Fancsali behaved himself.

The first order of business was Eugenia. In response to Ares' letter, Surchatain Klar had sent his toughest negotiator to drive home his complaints about the trade tariffs. With Klar's representative to deal with, Ares gave not another thought to the lovers until an hour or so later, when Renée appeared at the door of the small room, interrupting the talks in progress.

Looking up at her over a ledger, Ares smiled wryly. She had chosen a relatively simple dress of straight lines and narrow skirt to better set off the fabulous surcoat. "You look beautiful, Chataine—as usual," he noted. Klar's messenger, rising respectfully from his chair, was struck dumb in adoration.

Ares began an introduction, but Renée, never seeing the negotiator, asked impatiently, "Well, where is Fancsali? I thought he would be here with you."

"He had rather a job to do cleaning up. Let us locate him." Directing her into the great hall, he went from there into the foyer, where he instructed a servant, "Summon Lord Fancsali." The servant looked somewhat confused, but bowed and departed. The Eugenian negotiator stood at the door of the great hall to watch curiously.

Long minutes passed without Fancsali's appearance. Renée said severely, "This tardiness does not well support his 'honorable intentions,'" and Ares began to feel uneasy.

Then Tanny appeared and bowed. "Surchatain, Chataine—I regret to make it known to you that Lord Fancsali is no longer on the premises. He and his men departed over an hour ago."

"What?!" exclaimed Renée.

"Where did he go?" Ares asked.

"He did not inform us of his destination, but he carried the Chataine Melva on his horse," Tanny said.

"What?!" cried Renée.

Ares looked again at Melva's trunk sitting in the foyer. Striding over, he opened it. Its contents had been rifled, and a few things removed—apparently what could be carried on horseback. "It seems that the lord has taken his errand to heart," he muttered.

Chest heaving indignantly, Renée uttered in a low voice, "Do you mean to tell me that he left with—that—mouse? After all those assurances of his honorable intentions toward me?"

"It would appear so," Ares said heavily.

"Eyah!" With a strangled cry, Renée ripped off the surcoat and threw it into the fireplace, then she gathered up the narrow skirt and ran up the staircase with amazing speed.

Ares snatched the precious coat out of the fire before it could be much damaged, and handed it to Tanny. "Please see that this, and the contents of the trunk, are placed in the treasury."

Tanny bowed in response. Klar's negotiator tapped Ares on the shoulder. Ares turned to him distractedly, and he noted, "Surchatain Klar would love to have that 'un for a wife."

Ares started to respond curtly, as Klar was an old lecher, then said (to his shame), "Well—tell him about her. She is the Chataine Renée of Westford." Another proposal couldn't hurt. Besides, it may make the tariffs easier for Klar to swallow. On that thought, Ares trotted up the staircase in pursuit of her.

But at the head of the stairs, he paused. It was foolhardy and futile for him to attempt to comfort her. But someone must, or the damage she would do to the treasury in her wrath could cause Giles to harm himself.

So Ares went to his own sleeping chamber and bent over his wife, who was just now waking. "My love, I have a request of you," he murmured, kissing her shoulder.

"Umm?" she said sleepily, raising herself up.

It was but half an hour later that Nicole was enlightened, dressed, and progressing with some apprehension toward Renée's quarters. Nicole could hardly believe the affront—what *was* Fancsali thinking?—and rather doubted her ability to make Renée feel better about anything. But she had promised she would try, so try she would.

She knocked on the Chataine's door and was permitted entrance by Eleanor. Seeing Renée seated at her dressing table, Nicole advanced with words of wounded indignation on her lips. But when she saw the Chataine humming busily as she applied make-up, the words seemed to die for lack of relevance.

Renée glanced at her. "Hello, darling. Hand me that lotion, will you?" Nicole picked up the small mother-of-pearl container and handed it to her. "Thank you." Renée opened it and spread its contents on her cheeks, humming happily all the while.

Nicole stirred. "Darling, Ares told me what happened. . . . He was outraged by Fancsali's behavior."

"How kind of him," Renée said, smirking.

Nicole glanced at Eleanor, who raised her brows in a meaningful way, but said nothing. So Nicole ventured, "I must say, you are taking the offense very well."

Renée glanced up at her in amusement. "Because I have planned my revenge, dear heart. Do you care to know what I am going to do? If I tell you, and Ares interferes in any way, then I shall never speak to you again. Shall I tell you what I plan to do, or do you wish to remain innocent?"

Nicole thought about that for perhaps a heartbeat and a half. "Tell me."

18

Rubbing the lotion into her hands, Renée stood. She evaluated Nicole with that same knowing smirk, then took her hand. "Come. Rather than tell you, I will show you. But I shan't make you assist me, so you can truthfully plead that you could not stop me."

"Whatever are you thinking?" Nicole asked, smiling against her better judgment.

"You shall see." Leading Nicole like a child, Renée took up a small scroll from her dressing table.

"What is that?" Nicole asked.

"This?" Renée held up the scroll teasingly and Nicole nodded. "It is the marriage proposal I received from Lord Fancsali. The real one," Renée said, and Nicole's pulse quickened.

With the Surchataine following, Renée swept out of her apartments and down the great staircase. They descended to the foyer, where the bustle of another day's commerce was in full play. Servants, courtiers, messengers, and merchants went to and fro attending to their separate concerns. Renée observed them all, so Nicole looked around, too.

Thom was contending with the armorer about the weight

of the brassards on the new armor he wanted; Giles was weepily explaining to Klar's negotiator why the tariffs would *not* be rescinded; Georges was firmly propounding to the greengrocer the necessity of delivering *fresh* produce to the palace.

Seeing all this, but not seeing what she required, Renée beckoned to a passing servant. "Please ask Tanny to come to the chapel." The servant bowed, glancing at the Surchataine beside her before hurrying off.

Renée and Nicole then entered the chapel off the great foyer and shut the door against the noise of the world without. The chapel was deserted at this hour; not even Father Birondo was at his duty yet.

Sitting on a rough-hewn bench, worn down from many years of use, Renée sighed, and Nicole studied her. "I do believe that I am understanding something of the power of prayer," Renée admitted, face upturned to the stream of light. "After Fancsali departed so abruptly this morning, I prayed, and then I got the idea of what to do." This revelation was not particularly reassuring to Nicole.

Presently, Tanny appeared in the chapel and bowed to them. Renée said, "Dear Tanny, you have been so patient and faithful, and I have never thanked you."

"The Chataine honors me. How may I serve her today?" Tanny replied, bowing again.

"I need a messenger, Tanny. He must be fast and strong and utterly reliable," Renée said.

"My lady has described every man in my charge, but I will go select the freshest and readiest. Shall I send him here?"

"Yes, Tanny. With my heartfelt thanks." Renée put a loving hand on his arm. As he turned out of the chapel, he met Nicole's eyes. His look was respectful and uncolored, but in their great depth, Nicole saw knowing.

The ladies sat to await the promised messenger, who came within minutes. Renée appraised him, and found him to be everything she desired: strong, intelligent, and eager to serve. He stood at attention, eyes on the wall. "My lady's messenger Rhyan responds to her summons."

"Thank you, Rhyan. I have a most crucial errand for you. Is your horse ready?" Renée asked.

"Saddled in the courtyard, awaiting only myself, Chataine," Rhyan responded.

"Very good. Do you know the way to Lord Fancsali's estate at Eviron?" Renée asked.

"Yes, Chataine."

"Perfect. Then I wish you to ride there immediately and speak directly to Lord Fancsali's wife. You will give her this," Renée said, handing him the scroll, which he put into the leather pouch hanging from his shoulder. "Tell her that Lord Fancsali has proposed marriage to the Chataine Renée of Westford, and that she has accepted. Tell her that the lord requires that his present wife and her children leave the estate by nightfall tomorrow. In compensation for the inconvenience, she may take whatever she requires for the sustenance of her family from the estate, but they must leave by the morrow or they shall be turned out. Have I made myself perfectly clear?"

"Yes, Chataine," he replied, his face a mask.

"Then go at once," Renée ordered.

He bowed and turned out. As he strode through the foyer, Renée followed him, and Nicole followed Renée. The Chataine watched while he mounted his horse and rode out of the courtyard at a gallop. Then she turned and ran back inside the foyer. From there, she mounted the steps that led up to a low-level parapet. Nicole doggedly followed.

Up on the parapet, the guards fell back as the Chataine rushed to a point where she could see the ancient wooden bridge and the turnoff to the east-west road. She leaned on the parapet, her blonde hair a banner in the wind, the sunlight glinting blindingly off the gemstones in her gown. From there, she spotted Rhyan on his horse, spurring to a pace that would guarantee the delivery of the message by early afternoon.

When he was out of sight, Renée sighed in satisfaction and looked back at Nicole. Studying her, Nicole knew that she could never send the Chataine away. Despite all of Renée's insecurities and game-playing, Nicole loved her. How could she not? It was Nicole's nature to love. Besides, Renée certainly made Westford a more interesting place. Nicole murmured, "There is no telling what Lord Fancsali's wife will do when she receives this message."

"Perhaps she should pray about it," Renée said. "Come, dear heart, I've heard that Lord Preus has retained the services of a renowned milliner from Crescent Hollow to design new headpieces for his fall gowns. I'm dying to see them. What say we take a litter to his shop?"

"I would love to," Nicole said, so they ordered a litter and soon set off.

At that time, Tanny was upstairs reporting to Ares the fact that the Chataine Renée had just sent a messenger on an urgent errand east—toward Eviron. "What was his message?" Ares asked in frank, unblushing fear.

"That, I do not know, Surchatain. The Chataine made sure he departed without reporting to anyone," Tanny said.

"Huh. Summon the Surchataine," Ares instructed a sentry. But by that time, she was out of the palace environs. So Ares mulled over the option of sending a second messenger to overtake the first and discover his message.

He let precious minutes elapse while he considered this, then deliberately decided against it. First, Nicole obviously knew what Renée was doing, and had permitted it. Since he could trust his dove to act honorably in any circumstance, why should he go behind her back this time? Actually, now that he thought on it, Nicole might have persuaded Renée to take the course she did, rather than something more odious.

But the primary reason Ares decided against interfering was that Fancsali had, in fact, insulted Renée rather pointedly, and it was her prerogative to respond as she thought best in defense of her own honor and standing. So Ares took a deep breath and turned his attention to other matters.

Shortly thereafter, another sentry requested his ear. Saluting, he told Ares, "Surchatain, Captain Yonge reports that no one has been spotted in the stream that runs under the prison cell. Chiacos has not returned to it, nor made himself known elsewhere. The Captain requests permission to seal up the stone in the cell floor."

Ares gave it some thought. "Tell the Captain to give it another day. Keep the torch burning in the cell, and leave it another day. However . . . tell Thom that I want a rider dispatched to Eurus. He is not to attempt to detain Fancsali. But I wish to know that Melva arrives safely."

"Surchatain." The sentry saluted and left.

The next two days were so full and hectic for Ares that he never remembered to ask Nicole about Renée's message to Eviron, and Nicole did not volunteer the information. His main concern was that the merchant guilds of Westford had united to present Giles with a list of demands for next year's festival, which included a cut in booth rental rates and the exclusion of specified foreign merchants, including any from Eugenia. While Giles handled the uprising with admirable courage and cunning, he still insisted on Ares' ratification of every counter demand.

In addition, Thom's officers had come to him with a sweeping plan for reorganization of the standing army. A disturbing number of civilians in the auxiliary units, which served one month out of every three, resented the disruption of their planting, harvesting, or business to the point of refusing to serve. But without these units, Lystra could not adequately defend her borders. Also, the constant rotation precluded the continuity of training.

So, after lengthy conferences, the Seconds and Captains proposed that any citizen who wished to escape his obligation of service be allowed to pay a substitute to serve in his stead, provided that the substitute was fit and willing to serve. That way, a man could serve any length of time he wished and be paid by a private citizen rather than the palace treasury. The citizen, in turn, could deduct half of his substitute's salary from his taxes. It was an attractive plan in many aspects, but required refinement and testing before being implemented province-wide.

With such concerns as these occupying his mind, Ares gave not another thought to Renée, Melva, or Chiacos until the third day following Renée's message to Eviron.

That morning, Captain Yonge had come to him personally with the request that the stone in the cell floor be sealed closed. "By this time, Chiacos is either long gone or dead, Surchatain. True, it takes little manpower to guard the cell, but all of the prisoners down there are aware of it, and as long as it's open, they'll try to reach it. Two guards were attacked last night alone, and now I hear that word of it has gone beyond the palace."

"Seal it up. With concretus," Ares said, eyes on the duty roster in front of him. From that moment on, Ares believed that Chiacos' body had been washed out to the Sea.

Captain Yonge acknowledged that order with a salute and departed. Ares had the next hour to roughly compute the savings to the treasury after the implementation of substitutionary service. Then a sentry came to his door in restrained excitement, requesting him to come at once to the parapet of the eastern wall.

Ares rose to follow him. "What is it?"

"Surchatain, we received word from several travelers all at once that there is a great fire in the vicinity of Eviron. The smoke of it is visible from the parapet," the sentry reported.

"In Fancsali's woods? What caused it? An invading army? Lightning? What?" Ares asked anxiously as they hastened down the corridor and up the stairs to the palace roof.

"We do not know yet, Surchatain. The Commander has sent scouts to appraise the situation," the sentry reported.

"Good," Ares breathed. They reached the rooftop door and flung it open. The moment Ares was on the parapet, he smelled the smoke. A few more steps brought him within view of the eastern horizon. "Good Lord!" he exclaimed.

Smoke was billowing up from all along the horizon as though from the pit of hell itself. The red and yellow tongues of savage, spreading flames were visible underneath, even at this distance. "There must be hundreds of acres engaged," the sentry murmured in awe. More soldiers and administrators crowded to the parapet to look. Fancsali's wealth was being wholly converted to heat, smoke and ashes before their eyes.

As Carmine drew up beside him, Ares asked tensely, "Where is Fancsali?"

"He was on his way to Eurus, last we heard," the Counselor replied.

A hot gust of wind blew through their clothes and hair. "Last we heard? What happened to the rider we sent after him?" Ares demanded.

"I was coming to tell you that he has just now returned, Surchatain. He could locate neither Fancsali nor Melva. The palace at Eurus would neither confirm nor deny that she had arrived," Carmine said.

"What?" Ares exclaimed.

"Unfortunately, the rider we sent was fast, but not of rank to be acknowledged by Eurus. I will shoulder the blame for that," Carmine said calmly. "I have just now sent an ambassador in livery and carriage to request information as to the whereabouts of our friends and to advise the palace of the fire at Eviron."

Agape, Ares looked back toward the east while more people crowded on the rooftop to look.

Thom joined them. He watched the inferno grimly a moment, then asked, "Are you going to order me to send my men to fight that, Surchatain?" His tone suggested defiance.

Ares exhaled. "No, Thom. Westford is in no danger." One of the advantages of its situation was the firebreak which the Passage afforded. "I would send men out there to die only if they could do something to contain it. But against that monster, I do not see what shovels and buckets would avail."

"Thank you, Surchatain," Thom muttered.

Captain Paramore approached with a spyglass, which he offered to Ares. "Surchatain, we cannot be sure, but—it looks as though the fire started in the heart of Fancsali's estate."

Ares groaned, "Then I fear for his family." He squinted with the glass at one eye to scan the stretch of blazing woodland. Handing the glass back to Paramore, he added, "Keep me apprised." And he turned back down the stairs with heavy steps.

On the way, a sentry met him and saluted. "A messenger has just arrived from Eurus, Surchatain."

The fire transferred itself to Ares' eyes. "I will see him at once."

He trotted all the way down to the small holding room off the great hall, where Magnus' messenger waited. Upon opening the door and seeing him, Ares knew that Magnus was mad at him. Magnus always sent this same blustering, arrogant lackey whenever he was seized with the vain desire to intimidate Ares. "Greetings, Wempe. How are my good friends at Eurus?" Ares asked with curled lip.

The portly man bowed slightly, as if it hurt him. "Surchatain Magnus is quite out of sorts, my lord. Tancred has escaped, and the Surchatain demands that you tell me where he is."

Tancred? Ares had no idea where he was. He shifted, folding his arms. "I will tell you where Tancred is when you tell me where Melva is."

Wempe looked disconcerted. "Melva? Who is this Melva?"

"She is the former Chataine of Qarqar whom Druella served before she became Magnus' wife," Ares answered curtly. "Melva abdicated the rulership and left three days ago for Eurus in the company of Lord Fancsali. I demand to know her state."

"I know nothing of this lady, Surchatain," Wempe huffed.

"Then I know nothing of Tancred. Perhaps he is the one who burned down Eviron, in revenge," Ares said.

"Surchatain?" Wempe queried with a start.

"Perhaps you did not notice it from your carriage. Come look," Ares invited. He led the ambassador to the closest stairway to the roof, that on the west side of the palace. Even here, they had no difficulty seeing the smoke and flames issuing from the heart of the Scyllan wood. "The price of Scyllan oak has just quadrupled," Ares said regretfully, watching Wempe stare goggle-eyed at the devastation.

"Tancred will pay for this!" Wempe cried.

"Before you go hunting down Tancred, I suggest you find Fancsali, to tell him that his estate is in ashes. And when you find him, ask him how Melva fares, then bring word to me of her." Ares' eyes were hard, his scar threatening.

Wempe glanced at him, muttering something that might have been acquiescence. "I must leave straightway."

"Do not forget to return with word," Ares said, watching his bulky back descend the narrow stairs.

By dinnertime that evening, the smell of smoke had pervaded everything in the palace—clothes, hair, food. Fortunately, the area of Scylla that was burning was sparsely settled, being far from the population clusters around the Passage, the Fastnesses, and Eurus. Still, with the blaze drawing ever nearer, and the inexplicable disappearance of Melva, the atmosphere at dinner was somewhat oppressive.

Ares was preoccupied with the various matters he had been dealing with over the past several days, and Nicole was in her own private hell. Having deliberately refrained from telling Ares about Renée's message to Lord Fancsali's wife only to see the inferno erupt in Eviron, Nicole could hardly avoid connecting the two. Of course, she could not know for *certain* that Fancsali's wife set the fire, but—it seemed inescapable. And had she told Ares, as she should have, he could have prevented it.

Burdened with such concerns, both royal parents were singularly distracted when their daughters tried to talk to them at dinner. In a rare, unfortunate lapse, neither Ares nor Nicole was listening attentively enough to apprehend the message behind the girls' complaint. "Papa, I heard the ghost," Sophie said, leaning over to seek comfort at his left side. "It's scaring me. It cries in the wall."

Ares inhaled impatiently. "We talked about that, Sophie. If Doudney continues to read you ghost stories, I will have him turned out of the palace, even if we cannot find another tutor for a year."

"It's not Doudney," Sophie insisted. "It's the ghost."

Bonnie, on her mother's right, seconded, "I heard it, too, Papa! It's really there. We were playing in Mama's sleeping room, and we heard it there."

"Then you should not play in my sleeping room," Nicole chastised her. So the twins said no more about it.

In stark contrast to the rest of the table, Renée was bright and lively. "Terribly unfortunate, about the fire," she said cheerily. "Maybe it will rain."

Nicole looked up in sudden inspiration; her eyes flicked heavenward, and an aura of peace settled around her, though she was not attending to the rest of Renée's happy blather. The lack of response from anyone but Carmine did not seem to deter Renée's witty observations. But her master stroke was to glance down the table at the precise moment that Lord Notham delivered an ill-advised kiss to the cheek of Lady Vivian. Worse (for them)—the lady willingly received it.

"Why, Mother!" Renée cried, and the whole table looked

up, startled. "Why did you not tell me of this wondrous development? To think that the springs of love now gush between you and the worthy Lord Notham!"

Lady Vivian stiffened, but Lord Notham allowed a stupid grin to spread across his jowls. She began a useless defense: "We—"

"The pangs of innocent desire. The agony of seeking a private corner to embrace. The joy of encountering your beloved at an unexpected moment and seeing your own heart reflected in his gaze," Renée effused.

Those at table began smiling and glancing around. Renée's description of young lovers proved to be devastatingly comedic when applied ironically to the aging, self-absorbed pair.

The malicious humor might have been less well-received had Notham or Vivian any true supporters at court, but they had so ruthlessly undercut any friendships that no one objected to laughing at them now. It provided such a welcome change of atmosphere that even Ares reacted with a slight smile.

"To touch the hand of an unapproachable goddess and die for a draft from her lips," Renée sighed, and Thom snickered. Vivian's sexual activities with young, virile soldiers were daily recounted among the palace gossips. "To behold your Adonis, the desire of your heart, and long only to die in his embrace," Renée continued. Someone started laughing out loud at Notham's trying to pull in his stomach and look like the desire of Aphrodite.

Smiling, Ares glanced at Nicole, and his smile faded. She was looking at him, not Notham, and her expression of quiet intensity told him that Renée was speaking only what Nicole was thinking . . . about him.

Ares rushed through the obligations of the evening like a man obsessed, then in no time at all, accomplished his objective of securing his wife, alone and naked, in their bedchamber. He lay across her, burying his face in her loose hair, and she arched her back with a low moan. "I watch you sometimes at council meetings," she whispered.

"Unh," he said, intent on her body.

"I watch you talk to Giles and Carmine; I watch you sign documents and stretch out in your chair, and I like to think about—oh—what you do to me when we are alone—how different you are," she gasped as he pressed her.

He paused, breathing heavily. "Am I hurting you?"

"No," she moaned, gripping him.

"But you . . . never mind." Disconcerted, he closed his eyes and renewed his efforts. Nicole exhaled, reaching down to his iron thighs.

Moments later they both stopped. "What was that?" she gasped. The room was completely dark but for the faint light of a solitary candle.

"Shh!" he panted, turning his head to listen. "It sounds like moaning, or crying."

"Ares, it's coming from the wall! Behind the fireplace!" she cried.

Scrambling out of bed, he stood in front of the dark fireplace to bang on the hearth with the poker. "Hello? Is someone there?"

The respondent cries were quite audible. As Nicole clutched the wavering candle, Ares turned to her and said, "It's Chiacos, trapped in the wall again."

19

Ares jerked on his cotton breeches while Nicole found her robe and a candelabrum to light. He ran his hands over the sealed entrance, but knew it would be impossible to open without assistance.

Throwing open the bedchamber door, he ran through the receiving room and opened the door to the sentry outside. "Summon Oswald, and bring me a long-handled hammer. The ten-pound."

"Surchatain." He saluted as if these late-night demands were routine.

Ares hastened back to the bedchamber where he leaned against the fireplace. He called, "Chiacos! We are going to get you out. Can you hear me?" The only reply was weeping.

"How did he get in there?" Nicole cried. "It was sealed!"

"It has been three days since he escaped through the cell floor. He must have walked up the stream and cleared the rocks away so that he could enter the secret passage. But he did not know we had sealed up all the exits," Ares mused.

While Ares called encouragement to Chiacos through the wall, the hammer was brought. Hefting it, he warned her, "Stand back." Then he swung the head against the concretus seal along the edges of the firebox time and again. Stone chips flew out, striking him in the face or chest, but he continued to pound away at the concrete to no avail.

Oswald arrived, sleepy and bemused. Panting, Ares handed him the hammer. "See if you can open it, Oswald."

Dubious but obedient, the big man hoisted the hammer and landed one shuddering blow after another on the stone. Great chunks of scrollwork fell away, but the entrance remained sealed. Finally, Oswald lowered the hammer to pant, "You told me to seal it, Surchatain, and that I did. It will not be opened."

"Oh, dear. Poor Chiacos," Nicole breathed. "He is trapped in there again," she told Oswald.

Ares glanced around, thinking. "The stone in the cell floor was sealed only today, so the concretus hasn't had long to set. Could it be opened?"

"Probably," Oswald replied.

"Come, then," Ares said, striding out to the receiving room. As Nicole followed, he glanced back at her in her scarlet robe. "Lady, you will distract all of us," he said reprovingly. She flew back to the bedchamber, slamming the door behind her.

In his breeches, followed by a growing number of soldiers, Ares hurried down to the cell that housed the escape passage. A score of torches were brought, as well as tools and prybars.

Taking one, Ares applied it to the edge of the concealing stone. Two other men did likewise, and the stone came up reluctantly, gummy concretus falling away from its edges. Thom arrived to assess the situation, and Oswald enlightened him.

As Ares looked down into the inky blackness of the hole, the men in the cell parted, and Nicole came forward. She had taken the time to gather her hair back and put on one of her gardening dresses, so as to be decent. He glanced back at her, and she said, "I told Chiacos that we were sending help another way."

He nodded. "Give me a torch."

Several voices answered him, saying much the same thing. Thom, being closest to Ares' ear, prevailed to repeat, "Why should you go after him, Surchatain?"

"Chiacos knows what happened the night Magnus' parents were murdered. I intend that he shall tell me," Ares said grimly.

"My lord, I do not believe that was the Commander's question. He was desiring to know why *you* should go after him," Nicole said, pale.

"I want to see what's down there," Ares replied. "Hand me that torch."

Amid the strained silence of so many who disagreed with this course, he was given a torch. Holding it in his left hand, he sat at the edge of the hole and scooted in, swinging himself down from the edge with his right.

Landing in the black water, he was mildly surprised at its warmth. When he was standing upright on the bottom, the water came to his lowest rib. The stream bed was smooth rock under his feet, with only a few inches of silt on the floor. The current flowed smoothly against him, to guide him; he knew he had to walk upstream.

Glancing up at the circle of faces peering anxiously down at him, Ares began walking underneath the floor of the cell, which, at the start, was about three feet over his head. He swung the torch from side to side, seeing the stream bed exactly as Geurts had described it. At one point Ares noticed the water marks on the limestone walls. Apparently, the depth of the stream varied in concert with the tides of the Sea.

He pushed against the oncoming water step by step. In his first dozen steps, the stream bed inclined up sharply and he had to strain against the flow. With the head of the torch sputtering against the damp stone above him, Ares was forced to lower it even as the water crept up to his third-lowest rib. The sides of the channel also narrowed from ten feet apart (under the cell) to six (where he was now). He trudged up the incline, gripping the slippery rock on his right. At least there was no question of getting lost, as there were no branches to wander down . . . yet.

Keeping an eye on the roof, he spotted a dark opening ahead. In relief, he splashed forward rather carelessly until he was under it. When he raised the torch, however, he was disconcerted to see the inside of wooden louvered doors and a water wheel. After a moment, he recognized this as the garderobe in his former quarters. Thom had saved himself some aggravation, and possibly his life, by bolting it closed.

Now oriented as to where he was, Ares continued upstream even as the ceiling dropped and the water rose further. Soon, the water was at his nipples, the torch level with his head. He knew that he could make it to the secret passage because Chiacos had made it, but he hated to lose the torch in the process. Knowing that Chiacos did it blind both impelled and irritated him.

Suddenly Ares lost his footing on the slippery bottom. Half the torch head was momentarily immersed, extinguishing half his light, but he grabbed the wall with his free hand and righted himself before the torch could go out entirely.

Thereafter, with the water lapping over his shoulders, he pulled himself along by means of irregularities in the wall. At last, he caught sight of another dark opening in the roof. Extending the torch upwards through it, he saw portions of a rough-hewn rock wall six feet away. This was it.

Laying the torch on the edge of the opening, Ares hoisted himself up, grimacing with the effort. He kicked until he was able to prop his elbows on the side of hole and drag himself out. Then he sat up, panting, and looked around.

The terminus of the tunnel was just as depicted on the map. He was looking at unrelieved stone in front of him and on either hand. Apparently, the passage had never extended to the outer wall, and anyone who relied on it to do that would have found himself trapped.

Turning, Ares lifted the torch to throw shadowy red light on a pile of rock and rubble, with a black crawl space cleared out at the top. What they surmised appeared to be exactly what happened: Chiacos had come up through this opening and spent the next several days clearing a path to the rest of the passage.

Throwing water out of his eyes, Ares gripped the torch in one hand and crawled up the rubble to the small opening at the top. He tossed the torch onto the rubble on the other side, then pulled himself through the narrow opening, wincing as the rock scraped his bare skin. Chiacos had made it wide enough for himself, but he was thinner than Ares.

At length, he succeeded in wriggling his way through two feet of rubble to the other side, where he retrieved the torch. Here, the passage became familiar: he followed the curve to the door that led into fig and plum orchard, now sealed. Ares could see no sign that Chiacos had tried to open it.

He then passed the second door, leading out to the vegetable garden, and again noted the concretus undisturbed. Of course, remembering his efforts with the ten-pound hammer, he knew that Chiacos couldn't have opened any of these doors had he tried.

Progressing to the upper level, Ares began to call, "Chiacos? Chiacos!" He should be able to hear him from here. Ares passed the chained and sealed door to the Surchataine's quarters, then paused and retraced his steps to look at it closer. The peephole had been gouged out and the rusty chains broken away. Moreover, there were scratch marks in the concretus around the edge of the door. Apparently Chiacos tried to get out here.

Somewhat disturbed, Ares resumed his search toward the end of the passage, now but seventy feet off. "Chiacos!" Why had he chosen to go back into the palace instead of downstream to a more probable escape? "Chiacos!" Why had he attempted to exit the passage at the Surchataine's quarters, and not before? "Chiacos?" What had he used to gouge out the peephole and scratch the concretus?

There was sudden movement in front of him—glimpsing the flash of metal, Ares instinctively leapt back as a blade raked his chest inches below his throat. The knife went through skin into muscle, causing Ares to recoil in blind pain. Grasping his chest, he felt warm blood cascading over his fingers. "Chiacos! I've come to get you out—!"

The blade flashed again, and Ares raised the torch defensively, so that the skin on his knuckles was sliced open and he dropped the torch. "Are you mad? What are you doing?" he cried, holding his left hand.

In response came Chiacos' anguished weeping: "I do as I have been commanded—it is but death . . . blood and death—" The rest of it was gibberish.

Ares stepped back, watching in disbelief as Chiacos, face distorted in the flickering red torchlight, wielded the bloody knife yet again. In advancing, he stepped on the head of the torch—barefoot—snuffing it. The passage was immediately cast into dense darkness.

Ares had an instant to consider defending himself, wounded, in the dark, against an armed madman—then he turned and ran down the passage as hard as he could, guiding himself in the blackness by raking his right hand along the wall as he went.

With the pounding of his heart in his ears, he could hardly listen for footfalls behind him or the whiz of a blade flying through the air toward his back. So he did not try; he only ran, dizzy with pain. He stumbled down the passage to the lower level, then followed the curve to the cave-in. There, he scrambled up the rocks, knowing how vulnerable he would be in squeezing through to the other side.

Sure enough, as he was working his shoulders through the opening, he heard rocks shift behind him. Swiftly backing out again, he grabbed a rock and heaved it blindly in the direction of the noise. A thump and a groan told him he had hit his target, but, weakened as he was, he knew better than to try to fight. Ares dove for the crawlspace again, pulling himself through in one brutal motion, gasping as dirt was ground into open wounds.

He blindly slid down the rocks on the other side head first, feeling for the hole in the floor while listening to the scrabbling of Chiacos' coming through the crawlspace above and behind him.

When Ares' arm plunged into empty space, he lost his balance and toppled into the stream with a splash. A cascade of rock attended his entry, but he was not concerned about getting hit—only getting drowned. The current carried him twenty feet before he was able to get his face clear of the water and take a breath.

But his strength was ebbing in the rushing water, his sight failing in the darkness; as hard as he tried to get his feet underneath him, he felt himself being swept along. He tumbled down the steep incline, then glimpsed the light from the cell opening ahead, but he knew he could not stop to climb up into it. "Thom—" he gurgled, and went under again.

There were muted shouts—he felt hands grab at him, but with nothing but wet skin to grasp, they could not hold onto him and he passed them by. He choked on a mouthful of water, coughed it up, and then felt himself go under again.

Suddenly someone grabbed his arm, wrenching his shoulder. With his downstream progress halted, he was able to get his feet under him and stagger back toward the opening alongside his human anchor. Ares couldn't see a thing but the hazy shaft of torchlight that played on the dark water ahead, turning it into a pool of blood. He made for that light with all his strength even as it faded dangerously.

"Tide's rising!" Thom's voice called from the blackness beside him. "Get him up. There, now!" The opening yawned above him; he raised his arms and numerous hands pulled him up through the hole. He braced wet, bloody hands on the edge of the hole and hoisted himself out.

The cold stone floor brought him to momentary alertness. Nicole was bending over him, weeping violently. "Why are you crying? I am not hurt," he insisted, then blacked out.

For hours—how long, he did not know—Ares drifted in and out of feverish sleep. He suffered incoherent nightmares of dead men in streams of blood while he unconsciously knocked away cups of water that were persistently placed at his parched lips. Through the mists, he heard Doctor Savary's voice explain to someone about the noxious miasma of the stream—then he was unconscious again.

He woke, at last, when his fever broke, and spoke the thought uppermost in his mind: "He didn't pursue me."

He blinked. Strong afternoon sunshine filtered through the shutters of the infirmary. He was weak, sore and hungry, but his mind was clear. *Chiacos didn't pursue me. Why not?*

Shifting, he saw Nicole, asleep, with her head on his right shoulder. He became aware of a disagreeable, throbbing pain, and looked down to see bandages covering his upper chest.

Tentatively feeling under the bandages, he detected the catgut stitches. Raising his left hand, Ares regarded the bandages swathing his knuckles, as well. *Chiacos is expert with knives*, he thought. *If he wanted to kill me, he would have. But it is almost as if. . . he wanted to drive me away.*

At his movement, Nicole started up. She breathed, "Oh, Ares!" Then she turned her head to call, "He is awake!"

"Understood, Lady," an unseen sentry responded.

She sat up on the bed, and Ares noted that she had taken the time to change into a proper daytime dress, though it was rumpled. In fact, she looked rather groggy as she took up a bowl and spoon that had been on the bedside table.

"Doctor Savary says that you must have the broth as soon as you are able, my lord," she murmured, dipping the spoon into the bowl with shaking hand.

"Umph," he grunted, pushing himself up to a sit. "I *am* hungry," he said in surprise, while the mystery of Chiacos' actions nagged at him. Why did Chiacos attack but not kill?

He leaned back into the pillows and let her feed him gruel by the spoonful. "I suddenly thought. . . . I realized that, as I came through the rocks, Chiacos did not pursue me. He let me leave. What happened to him?" he mumbled.

"I do not know, my lord," she said lightly. Her tone indicated that her ignorance was deliberate. "But the Commander requested to be summoned when you awoke, so he may tell you. Another," she instructed, raising the spoon.

By the time Thom appeared, closely followed by Carmine, Ares had finished the whole bowl. He felt so much stronger that he acknowledged Thom's salute by asking, "Did I waste the whole day lounging in bed?" He glanced at the late afternoon outside.

Carmine replied, "You went down into the underground stream early yesterday morning, Ares. We feared we had lost you . . . several times. Word has already spread of your death."

"Nonsense," Ares said, and Nicole closed her eyes. "What happened to Chiacos?"

"I do not know, Surchatain," Carmine said, resuming a formal tone.

So Ares looked expectantly at Thom, who replied, "I do not know either, Surchatain."

Exasperated, Ares demanded, "You know nothing of the whereabouts of the man I risked my life to go after?"

"Oh, you are asking his whereabouts?" Thom asked, brows raised. "I thought you had asked what happened to him, which I do not know. If you are asking his whereabouts, I could venture a likely guess."

Ares stared at them, then glanced at Nicole, who purposefully held a goblet of wine to his lips. He took a drink to ease the throbbing pain, leaned his head back, and said, "A straight answer, Thom. What do you know?"

"When we pulled you out of the stream and determined that you had been the target of an attack, we immediately put the stone back in place and resealed it with concretus. It is quite set by now," Thom replied blandly.

"There was no sign of Chiacos behind me?" Ares asked.

"No," Thom said.

Carmine asked, "Why did he set upon you, Ares?"

Ares lowered his head to think. "He said something about a command. He was weeping and moaning incoherently about something he had been commanded to do."

"As he was weeping when he took me," Nicole observed.

"But he allowed me to escape," Ares insisted. The others studied him. Ares reiterated, "He fulfilled what he had been commanded to do, but let me leave."

"That makes no sense, Surchatain," Thom said.

"There is something more we do not know. Chiacos must be found if we are to discover it," Ares said.

"How shall we find him?" Nicole asked.

Casting about, Ares replied, "He could have ridden the current past the cell out to freedom. That was the original escape route, after all."

Thom and Carmine glanced at each other, then Thom confessed, "No, Surchatain. While you went west, I sent Claye, an excellent swimmer, east in the stream. He barely made it back. The water blocked both underground branches—and that before the tide came in. Whatever escape that stream afforded in the past is no longer there. The water is too high."

"Poor Chiacos. His derangement killed him at last," Nicole murmured.

"He was not deranged. Someone compelled him to act as he did," Ares said in illumination.

"Yes, he was protecting Druella," Thom reminded him.

"She is too powerful to be deposed on an old tale," he scoffed, hand on his throbbing chest. "It is something more immediate. I wish to heaven that I knew what would drive a Polonti to such treachery."

"We will never know now, Ares," Carmine observed.

That much seemed indisputable, so Ares reluctantly put it from his mind. "What of the fire?" he asked, turning to the window.

Thom gestured. "It is still burning, though much of it was put out by the rain we had last night. If it rains again tonight, that should douse it for good."

Nicole blurted, "I prayed for the rain."

Ares looked at her, but a sentry requested entrance, which Thom granted him. "Surchatain. Commander. Counselor." The sentry saluted them all before handing a small folded parchment to Ares. "A messenger brought this from hands unknown, Surchatain."

"It has been opened," Ares said in disapproval.

"Yes, Surchatain—it arrived unsealed. Half the palace has already seen it, and the Chataine Renée says that she is throwing the biggest fest Westford has ever seen to celebrate," the sentry replied.

"Poor Giles!" Nicole said.

"Celebrate what?" Ares said, but answered his own question by reading the message out loud. "'Greetings from a friend of Westford who has heard that you are searching for the Qarqarian Chataine Melva. Let it be known to you that she has eloped with the Lord Fancsali of Scylla, and both were seen two days ago in Crescent Hollow.' That is all it says."

"Who is it from?" Thom asked.

"It is unsigned," Nicole observed, leaning over Ares' shoulder to look at the note.

"It is from Tancred," Ares said, handing it to her.

"How do you know?" she exclaimed, turning it over.

"I recognize his handwriting, from the letter he sent you after we got you out of the tower and burned down half of his palace," Ares told her.

"But—that was years ago!" she protested, handing Thom the note.

"Some things you never forget," Ares murmured, leaning his head back again. He watched Thom examine the short letter, then lay it on the table beside the candle, now burned down low. Why did it strike him odd that so much of the parchment was blank? Ares murmured, "So . . . Tancred considers himself a friend of Westford."

Carmine observed, "He must have known he would escape when he agreed to ride out to meet his brother rather than accept your punishment. Tancred has friends yet at Magnus' court."

"But I do not, still," Ares said, peeved. "Thom, when will you get me spies into Eurus?"

Thom looked thoughtful. "If we could locate Tancred, he seems to know a great deal . . . he certainly escapes a great deal. Eurus must have secret passages, too."

Ares eyed him. "He was in Crescent Hollow three days ago."

"I will send Alphonso and Derrick—"

"Moeck and Buford, as well," Ares said.

"Very good, Surchatain." Thom saluted upon turning out.

"Pardon me, also, Surchatain," Carmine said with a bow. "I must go reassure Giles that the fest our dear Chataine is planning is to celebrate your recovery, so that it does not matter what it costs."

"Thank you, Carmine," Ares said, relieved.

As the Counselor left, Ares squeezed his wife's waist, looking up at her in gratification. "Your daughters have been waiting outside since early morning," she noted.

"Then let them in," he said.

In moments two petticoated whirlwinds blew in to cover

him with kisses. "Papa!" "You're awake!" "We've been waiting for days!" "I got my dress all wet crying."

In their tumultuous advance, Ares was not sure which twin was squealing what. Somehow, Bonnie wound up kissing his scar and Sophie his clean cheek, and no one thought anything was amiss. But the swirling skirts dislodged the letter from its place beside the candle stub to rest atop it instead.

Sophie saw the tendril of smoke first, and snatched the partly burned parchment from the flame. Snuffing the glowing edges with her fingers, she chided, "Bonnie! You are so. . . . Papa, there's writing on this."

"Yes, I know," he began, then apprehended her meaning when she held the letter under his nose.

The rest of it was not blank, for the heat of the flame had revealed the invisible writing. In apparently the same hand, the writing disclosed, "The child has been released, and Druella has arranged for his transport to Eledith."

Ares read the sentence over and over while his family watched. "Eledith? That is the capital of Polontis," Nicole observed. "Who would go there but Polonti?"

At that, his face lit up in comprehension. "A child!" he whispered. "Chiacos and Druella had *a son* that someone was holding against my death. Chiacos fulfilled the conditions for his release at what may be the cost of his own life."

"Who would do such a thing?" Nicole cried. "Tancred?"

"No," Ares exhaled, "not if he's going to tell us about it. But . . . we must ask him, when the opportunity arises."

(The story continues in *Games of God and Men*.)

Glossary

Agnes, Sister—nun in charge of the abbey south of Westford
Alphonso (al FONZ oh)—a lieutenant in the Lystran army
amanuensis (a man you EN sis)—a secretary
Ares (AIR eez)—Surchatain of Lystra
Aron, Lord—jeweler of Westford
Athian (A the an)—challenger for the throne of Lystra; son of Lord Backvold of Westford
Auer (OW er), **Lady**—sister of Lord Backvold
Backvold, Lord—a nobleman of Westford whose son Athian challenged Ares for the throne
Bagur (BAY ger)—the Polonti potter in Westford
Ben—Ares' former page, now a soldier in Lystra's Red Regiment
Birondo (beer ON do), **Father**—the priest following Father Haward in the palace at Westford
Bondurant (BON du rahnt)—son of Druella and Magnus of Scylla, a few months older than Bonnie and Sophie
Bonnie, Chataine—seven-year-old daughter of Ares and Nicole, twin sister of Sophie
bothy—a hut for farm servants
bozah—an illegal sleeping potion that can be fatal when overused

brassard—armor for the upper arm, from the elbow to the shoulder

Buford (BYOU ford)—a lieutenant in the Lystran army

calk—a protrusion on a horseshoe to increase traction or adjust stance

Calle (kail) **Valley**—province west of Lystra, famous for its vineyards and fairs, which Ares annexed after defeating its Surchatain in battle

Carmine (CAR men)—Counselor at Westford, ex-husband of Renée

cassock—a long, black, close-fitting garment worn by clergy

Chatain (sha TAN)—son of the ruler of a province; the feminine is **Chataine** (sha TANE)

Chau (cho)—a Polonti renegade

Chiacos (CHEE a cose)—a Polonti guide who served Ares briefly before disappearing

Claye—a Lystran soldier, an excellent swimmer

concretus—Latin for "concrete," which the ancient Romans used extensively in building. While knowledge of it was lost to the rest of the world until the 1700s, Ares' engineers rediscovered it.

Corona—capital of Seleca

Coyle—an engineer at Westford

Crager (KRAY ger)—a Captain in the Lystran army

Cratch—occasional companion of Lord Fancsali

Crescent Hollow—capital of Calle Valley before that province was annexed to Lystra

crux—a gold coin minted in Scylla

Danae (dan AY)—the late Surchataine of Scylla, wife of Ossian and mother of Magnus and Tancred

Dansington—small hamlet in desolate northern Lystra

Davignon (da VEEN yon) **Lord**—a nobleman of Westford

Deirdre (DEE dra)—(1) wife of Roman the Great; (2) Commander Thom's wife

Derrick—a lieutenant in the Lystran army

dirk—a short, straight dagger
Dorn—a notorious slave trader
Doudney—the tutor at the palace of Westford
drawn and quartered—to have a person's arms and legs each tied to a different horse, which were then driven in different directions
Druella (dru EL ah)—formerly maid to Chataine Melva, now Magnus' wife and Surchataine of Scylla
Eleanor—Renée's maid
Eledith—capital of Polontis
escarole (ESS ca role)—a kind of endive, used in salads
Eugenia (you JEN ee ah)—the province west of Lystra, ruled by Klar
Eurus (YUR is)—capital of Scylla
Eviron (ee VIRE on)—the town attached to Lord Fancsali's estate in Scylla
Faguy (FAH gwee), **Lord**—a rich shipping merchant operating out of Prie Mer
Fancsali (FANK sah lee), **Lord**—a rich adventurer from Scylla
Fasoro (fa SO roh), **Father**—the previous priest at the palace of Westford, now deceased
Fassnacht (FASS not)—a Scyllan potter
Fastnesses—mountain range forming the partial border between Lystra/Qarqar and Scylla/Seleca
Fawler (FOLL er)—a scout with the Lystran army
frumenty—a custard
garderobe (GAR de robe)—a water closet, indoor commode
Gargus (GAR gus)—a slave trader who operated in Scylla
Genevieve (JEN e veeve)—Steward Giles' wife
Georges (JEOR jes)—dinner master at Westford
Geurts—a Lystran soldier
Giles (hard *g*, long *i*)—the Steward at the palace of Westford
Godbold—an engineer at Westford
Hauffe—Carmine's personal attendant

Haward, Father—the priest following Father Fasoro at the palace of Westford

Henry—former Chatain of Lystra, Renée's half-brother

Hevlik—a soldier at Westford

Hoose—a soldier, a friend of Henry

Hornbound—capital of Qarqar

Juscen (JOOS en)—a nobleman of Eurus, friend of Magnus

Klar—Surchatain of Eugenia

Kleven—a soldier at Westford

Lieterstad (LEE ter stad), **Lord**—a rich nobleman, originally of Calle Valley

Lind—the Commander of the Scyllan army under Magnus

livery—dress uniform worn by servants

Lute—second son of Talus, brother of Cedric (the previous ruler of Lystra)

Lystra (LIS tra)—province once ruled by Roman the Great, now ruled by his descendant Ares

Magnus (MAG nus)—Surchatain of Scylla; his first marriage to Renée ended with his rejection and humiliation of her

Melva—Chataine of Qarqar, now under Ares' protection

Merle (murl)—head laundress at Westford

Moeck (moke)—a lieutenant in the Lystran army

Nicole (ne COLE)—Ares' wife, Surchatainc of Lystra

Notham (NOTH am), **Lord**—a nobleman of Westford, father of Lady Rhea

Ossian (AH shun)—Magnus' father and Surchatain of Scylla before him

Oswald—Second in Command of the Lystran army under Commander Thom

Paramore (PAIR ah mor)—Captain of the Blue Regiment of the Lystran army

parapet—the top portion of the palace wall, behind which runs a walkway

pence, copper—the smallest monetary unit traded in the southern Continent; 20 pences equal a silver piece

Poison Greens—the mountain range dividing Lystra and serving as a boundary between western Lystra and Qarqar

Polontis (po LAWN tis)—mountainous province far northeast of Lystra, home of the hardy, courageous, but unsophisticated **Polonti** (po LAWN tee)

potage—soup or broth

Preus (proose), **Lord**—the premier dressmaker in Westford

Prie Mer (pree MARE)—small coastal town, Nicole's birthplace

Puck—a herding dog that Ares brought back from Hornbound

Purdy—childhood friend of Nicole's, now overseer of livestock at Westford

Qarqar (KAR kar)—mining-rich province to the northwest of Lystra

ramekin—hash made of bread crumbs, cheese and eggs baked in individual dishes

Renée (ren AY)—ex-wife of Carmine, half-sister of Henry

Rhea (ray), **Lady**—Lord Notham's daughter, who had been stringing Ares along before he met Nicole

Rhode (road)—Second in Command of the Lystran army under Commander Thom

Rhyan—a Lystran messenger

Riever (REE ver)—a Lystran soldier

Robert—Nicole's late father, a tailor in Prie Mer

Roerich (ROE rick)—the administrator of the palace at Crescent Hollow

Roman—the first great Surchatain of Lystra; author of Roman's Law; great-great-grandfather of Ares

royal—the basic monetary unit traded on the southern coast; the value of one gold royal equals fifty silver pieces

Ryle—Thom and Deirdre's three-year-old son

Sagar (SAY gar)—a subordinate of Surchatain Magnus

Savary (SAV a rie)—the physician at Westford

Scylla (SILL ah)—the province to the east of Lystra, ruled by Magnus

Seleca (SEL e kah)—once-great province to the northeast of Lystra, now impoverished and riddled with slave markets

smelts—small, troutlike fish

Sophie, Chataine—seven-year-old daughter of Ares and Nicole, twin sister of Bonnie

Soucie (SOO see)—wife of the Second Rhode

Surchatain (SUR cha tan)—the ruler of a province; the feminine is **Surchataine** (SUR cha tane)

Talus (TAL us)—the Commander who murdered Surchatain Bobadil (Ares' grandfather) and seized the throne of Lystra; Renée and Henry's grandfather

Tancred—younger brother of Magnus, ruler of Scylla

Tanny—veteran messenger of Westford

Thom—Commander of the army of Lystra

toilet—the process of dressing and grooming, especially one's hair

Ulm—Qarqarian usurper who had killed Melva's father and attacked Westford

Ursula—Nicole's maid

Veola (vee OH la)—the kitchen mistress at the palace of Westford

vielle—a stringed instrument, precursor to the violin

Vivian, Lady—Renée's mother

Vogelsong (VO gel song)—a Counselor at Westford

Wempe (wemp)—a high-ranking messenger in Magnus' service

Westford—capital of the province of Lystra

Yonge (yung)—a Captain of the Lystran army

Books by Robin Hardy

The Streiker Saga
Streiker's Bride
Streiker: The Killdeer
Streiker's Morning Sun

The Annals of Lystra
Chataine's Guardian
Stone of Help
Liberation of Lystra
(first published as *High Lord of Lystra*)

The Latter Annals of Lystra
Nicole of Prie Mer
Ares of Westford
Prisoners of Hope
Road of Vanishing
Dead Man's Token
Games of God and Men
In Extremis
All Mirrors and All Suns
The Laughing Side of the World

The Sammy Series
Sammy: Dallas Detective
Sammy: Women Troubles
Sammy: Working for a Living
Sammy: On Vacation
Sammy: Little Misunderstandings
Sammy: Ghosts
Sammy: Arenamania
Sammy: In Principle
Sammy: Grave Agreement
Sammy: Love Shouldn't Hurt
Sammy: The Consolation of Bucephalus
(continued on next page)

The Idecis
Unknown Name, Unknown Number: A Wimsey Reade Mystery
Padre and its sequel *His Strange Ways*

Edited by Robin Hardy

Sifted But Saved: Classic Devotions by W.W. Melton

Made in the USA
Las Vegas, NV
04 May 2024

89545253R00166